# Praise

"*Dream Kids* is a beguiling exploration of the perils of high school, the commodification of youth, and the dangers of cyberbullying. Reminiscent of Helen Schulman's *This Beautiful Life*, Michael Wayne Hampton's searing novel is a deeply unsettling portrait of privilege and proof that the kids are not all right."

DAVID JAMES POISSANT, AUTHOR OF
*LAKE LIFE* AND *THE HEAVEN OF ANIMALS*

"How anyone survives their teen years is a mystery, but Michael Wayne Hampton has come close to solving it in his singular novel, *Dream Kids*. Hampton fastens a remarkable and rich cast of characters to a plot from the headlines, capturing the wallop of punk rock and the yearning of a text sent at midnight. Uncompromising, unrelenting, and understanding, Michael Wayne Hampton has reached that stunning artistic achievement of opening our eyes and not letting us look away."

TOM WILLIAMS, AUTHOR OF
*AMONG THE WILD MULATTOS AND OTHER TALES*

# About the Author

Michael Wayne Hampton is the author of five books of fiction. His criticism, essays, fiction, and poetry have appeared in numerous publications such as *Atticus Review*, *The Southeast Review*, *3AM Magazine*, and *Fiction Southeast*.

In 2013 he won The Deerbird Novella Prize, and in 2012 his work was nominated for Best American Short Stories. In the past he has been a semi-finalist for the Iowa Short Fiction Prize, and a two-time finalist for the World's Best Short Short Story Contest. In 2014, he was awarded an Ohio Arts Council Individual Excellence Award.

Learn more at
*www.michaelwaynehampton.com*

# Dream Kids

## A NOVEL

MICHAEL
WAYNE
HAMPTON

A catalogue record for this
book is available from the
National Library of Australia

*This book is dedicated to all the '80s teen movies
and punk rock that informed my youth.
They remain ever-present flames.*

# Chapter 1
## The Kid on the Floor

AT OUR SCHOOL, my crew was the bad kids, but the kids from Cherokee Hills wouldn't stop calling us "Dream Kids." They got that from all the noise the press made over our school. They pretended they were joking even though they weren't. Normally we wouldn't have put up with their shit-talking, but we were at a party on their side of town, so we played it off. Jenna had promised they had Molly so we came for a chance to roll and so she'd stop begging us to join her. She'd been depressed lately, aching for love drugs to lift her up. The summer was almost over, but we were still burning, trying to stay awake and use up every minute of freedom we had left before school started again. We'd decided it was worth the drive if her CH friends had the new science, even if she was the only one of us who was tight with them. She was desperate to get on their level, but we mostly went along to see how bent the night got.

Tyler took on three kids from Cherokee Hills in beer pong in the dining room while I sat wedged between Paige and Jaycee on the couch. I watched him toss ping pong balls and drink fast to get gone. I was dying to talk honestly with Paige one more time, but she was too busy texting to notice me. I wished Tyler would've gotten into a fight to make the night more exciting, but there was no way he'd take on those CH kids when he was that outnumbered. Hanna would probably catch him before he went too far, anyway. Every guy needs a girl to save him from going over the edge. That's why I picked Jaycee up at the bus stop and brought her along. Someone had to stop me from going too hard and make sure the night rolled smooth.

I screwed the top off this plastic bottle of vodka I'd brought and passed it to Paige to remind her that I existed. She put down her phone, took a drink, and joked about how the CH kids all wore their school gear like billboards. Even though it was summer they still had on their ridiculous football jackets with this snaggle-toothed bulldog on the back. That's where they got their nickname. We were Dream Kids, and they were the CH Bulldogs, although they called themselves the CH Bullies. Maybe going by another word for assholes made them feel like gangsters, but wearing those jackets only made them look like sheep to me. See, if you wear someone else's logo you're their property. Paige passed the bottle my way and turned back to her phone. I didn't bother to start with her again since I had taken half of a next-gen Adavant before I picked Jaycee up and it was kicking my buzz off-center. You have to pace yourself when you party or else things turn dark, fast.

Jaycee rubbed my shoulder to make sure I was steady. I was glad she had come to say goodbye to good times. Regardless of what the rest of my friends said behind her back, she belonged with us. The way she mothered me was kind of sweet. Sure, by then I was tilting a little, but I could hang. I wasn't like the kid on the floor.

\*\*\*

See, the kid on the floor couldn't handle it. The rookies always fell apart first when a party got raging. When first-timer kids got staggered they either ran out the door to disappear into the sweaty night away from the drunk chaos, or felt apart where they stood. He should've got the scene was for professionals before he turned casualty. I mean, I didn't even know whose house we were at by that point. I yelled, "Whose kid is this?" but no one claimed him. Paige put down her phone, took a bowl out from her purse, and packed it while I hyper-focused on that kid lying face down on the carpet. I was glad he wasn't a girl. Girls who passed out got stolen away quick, but he was safe since he was only this dumb kid who couldn't hang. I took his picture with my phone to share later.

My friends and I could hang. Like even if we had pre-gamed until we were seeing ghosts only, or had smoked until we walked like zombies, we knew how to handle ourselves. We'd talked ourselves through it. It was simple. See, you tune out the world and tell your body what to do step by step. If you need to go to the bathroom, you tell your legs to stand up, then look at your feet and say "walk" until they do. Everyone knows you're way gone, but they won't screw with you if you keep moving like you got this. You lift the seat and tell yourself to pee. Then you talk yourself back to wherever, grab another drink, listen to the music, and if you concentrate really hard then when you speak what you say almost makes sense. You can hang.

The kid on the floor must have been a party virgin. They were the worst because they are so stoked to be out of their own house for once that they'll do whatever it takes to prove they belong. Party virgins will take anything you hand them to show what a badass they are and don't have the balls to argue or ask questions because they're so desperate to belong.

There's this game, right? If someone knows there's a party virgin trying to rage hardcore they tell everyone on the sly so no one stops them. Instead, everybody acts like they're that kid's best friend and pushes them to get crazy since the point is to destroy their little fantasies. Destroyed like waking up piss-soaked in a park, or with their moms crying over them in some hospital. That way, when it's over they understand that they can't hang and that it was stupid for them to try in the first place. We've put in years learning how to hang, and no party virgin is going to make it through a night with us. We give them everything they could ever want, and they blow themselves up in no time. The game was supposed to be funny, but when I saw the kid dropped like dirty laundry I couldn't manage to laugh

\*\*\*

I learned about being a party virgin the hard way. On my first day at The Dream Academy I showed up with a brand-new backpack filled with these notebooks and pencils I would never use. I wore this outfit my mom bought at Kohl's to match the one this mannequin wore, and it looked like I'd stepped out of a catalog. Back then I was so nervous no one would like me. I used to think I had to dress the right way and say the right things to get people to want me around, until I realized that the only way to score real love was to not care about what anyone else thought. I mean, I guess you can have a connection that the other kids don't, and they'll pretend to be your friend, but that's fake. You can't care if you want kids to love you since being above all that stress convinces them that you have a secret that stops all those *love me* feelings. If you walk in innocent and hopeful the way I did when I was a freshman, then the bad kids will find you fast.

On my first day at The Dream Academy, I walked around in my catalog clothes with my schedule out like a total nerd, when this senior girl named Chelle came up to me and gave me a kiss on the cheek out of nowhere. I didn't know about the game. I was this skinny kid with zits trying to figure out where his classes were when all of a sudden this hot girl kissed me and handed me a note. She left before I said a word. After that, my nerves kicked off. The note she gave me had her name and number on it and said to text her. There was no doubt I was in.

That night I waited for it to get dark before I texted her "Hey ;)". She texted me back and asked where I lived. I sent her my address, and she told me to be outside my house at midnight since she wanted to party with me. The idea of kicking it with the older kids after one day of high school sent me spinning right, but a second later I started shaking since I'd never snuck out before. Regardless I wasn't about to flake on my shot. I laid in bed in my new clothes and waited for my phone to signal that it was time to make my move. Maybe I just wanted to see where I'd end up.

I left my house like a ninja and waited on the sidewalk for Chelle. Before long she pulled up with her friends and we were off. It was a fantasy. In one day I'd gone from this nervous kid jerking tags off his jeans to the pimp of the school, without even trying. I shot a picture of her friends and me hugged up in her car with my phone, and still have it. I wanted proof to show what a player I was, but after what happened I saved it to remind myself not to trust any girl who loved me for no reason. Chelle taught me that.

Things went wrong from the start, but I was so eager to belong that I didn't get that the older kids had me marked. As soon as I hit the door I had kids passing me drinks two at a time and cheering for me to down them like a beast.

What happened next wasn't because they drugged me or anything. They didn't have the science back then like we do now. It was because I was dumb. The rules about pacing and mixing were a mystery, so I chased beers with jungle juice, vodka with straight whiskey, and mixed all the things that never go together in a rush to be the man. That's why it happened. Afterward, the older kids called me Mouse my entire freshman year even though my name is Bryce.

I didn't see the picture that went around school until the next Monday when a girl in my history class showed it to me on her phone. If I'd found out sooner maybe I could've stopped it, but the morning after the party my mom found me passed out in her flowerbed. She started screaming for my dad to call 911 since I was naked and had trouble making words. Chelle had painted my face with this purple lipstick that made it look like I wasn't breathing. When I got better, my mom wanted the details about how I got caught, but I was too ashamed to admit anything. I wished I'd died when I found out the girls took a picture of my junk and sent it to everyone. They joked that it looked like a mouse, but whose junk looks good when they're drunk and freezing? I never told on those kids. I didn't talk to my therapist about it either because who wants to tell that story? I spent the rest of that year cringing whenever I saw a kid on their cell phone, but I was never a party virgin again. I studied hard to hang.

\*\*\*

The kid on the floor was in for it when Tyler got bored with beer pong and turned on him. Jaycee told him to relax, but he wasn't about to let a scholarship girl like her order him around. I'd heard before she got her scholarship and transferred to our school that she was one of those girls who ended up getting carried off by three psychos at some party when she couldn't hang, but I didn't believe it. She was the only one of our crew who played it straight edge, and her damage was all money. The only time she went off was when someone pressed her about being a charity case. Then she'd fight, and not like girls do when they call each other names and yank hair, but for real. While other girls snapped their heads back like puppets when they fought, Jaycee dove in like she wanted the pain. One time she got into a fight with this girl at a party who kept on about her Goodwill clothes and it took three of us to pull her off. When we sat her down she started to bawl like she was the one who'd gotten beat down. That was the last time I ever saw her get violent. Maybe she decided there was no way to fight against what kids had already decided about her.

Hanna saw what was about to happen and got between Tyler and the kid on the floor. She tried to flirt him down all sex, but he shoved her away. I wanted to stand up for her, but I was there and I wasn't.

One of the CH Bullies sat next to Paige while Jaycee asked me what I thought Tyler was up to. I said I had no clue, but when I saw him go through this desk in the corner I knew the washout was in serious trouble if he needed tools. I told her not to worry about the kid on the floor. There was no way to save him now.

The music bumped louder as I turned back to Paige and heard every word she said. If I had been straight I would've tried to take her away, if she'd let me, but I was sinking. The rest of the room shrunk as I listened to her snickering at the CH Bully's game. It gets that way sometimes. Everything else is rubbed out, but one thing comes through super clear. Your mind goes where it wants to, and the rest of the scene goes hazy like everything is happening behind this wall of curtains. Then in a blink, you're back.

"I heard all your teachers are headcases and like half of your classes are about magic tricks and sushi and stuff," the CH Bully said. Paige passed him a bowl to shut him up, but it didn't work. She was tired of answering the questions the other prep school kids had. We all were so fucking tired of explaining where we landed. "My friends said your school is all Silicon Valley so like you don't even have books or anything. That cannot be true, right?"

"Our school is different," Paige passed the bowl my way. The end of it was wet, and I hoped it was from her lips. I missed them. "It's more about making us think for ourselves."

"It's just a school," I said. "It's out there, but we get by. We're not in love with our school like you guys."

He turned around to model his Cherokee Hills football jacket and popped its collar. "State champs." The bulldog on the back looked like it jumped out at me.

"Tyler!" I shouted. "State champs, right?" I pointed at the CH Bully and played super impressed.

"Shut up Mouse," Tyler said. "At least they have a football team." He only said it because he was drunk, but I wanted to kill him anyway. Then he yelled for somebody to turn off the music, but when no one did he cut it off himself. The rest of the kids got quiet, not because he'd told them to, but because the atmosphere had shifted on them, and for a second they couldn't figure out how. Jenna snorted bumps of Molly off the beer pong table with her CH friends and ignored the action, while Paige and Tyler cheered since it felt right to celebrate. I lifted my plastic bottle to toast as Tyler moved on the kid on the floor. The washout must've been a freshman since the worst things always happen to you when you're too young to see what's coming.

"We're starting a new year, right?" Tyler said. "So let's sacrifice a virgin!" He pulled a marker out of his back pocket and dropped it next to the kid on the floor. I tried to tell if the kid was breathing or had puked, but he was still flat and blank. Jaycee put her head on my shoulder and whispered that I should stop him, but it was hopeless, since the kid wasn't one of ours.

"I'm going first." Tyler pulled the cap off the marker with his teeth and drew a hipster mustache on the kid's face. The music blared back to life as he checked his work, but it must've felt too grade school so he gave him a devil beard to go with it. Finally, he jerked down the kid's pants and wrote LOSER on his tighty-whities in big block letters. "So he knows his name," he said.

Tyler's dad was a big-time judge and his stepmom was a prosecutor so he could get away with anything. The worst he'd ever gotten was therapy. Our parents believed therapy solved everything, but it was only the easiest way for them to avoid talking to us themselves. They liked who they said we were better than the truth. Never having to pay for anything made Tyler coldblooded though. It was like nothing could touch him.

I shot a picture of the kid all marked up which made Jaycee scoot away from me and asked me to take her home. It was the kid's fault he was laid out all comatose, but she scowled as if I was the one torturing him. I put my phone away and told her that we should hang out in case things got wicked. Mostly though, I wanted to stay in case Paige got off her phone. Our junior year was only a few days away, and I was thirsty to get her back. The night was long. Anything felt possible.

Tyler got bored with coloring on the kid and tossed the marker as he went to grab another drink. The kid's face was streaked with black and purple, but he didn't reach up to wipe it off. His eyes weren't focusing. You'd think that marker smell would've made him come to. Party virgins are all the same. Paige went off with the football hero while I finished my bottle. The point was that there was no point. Jaycee left to find a washcloth, and I promised myself the next time I'd stay straight and stop the game. It felt old.

***

I didn't want another drink. Alone on the couch, I got this creeping feeling that I'd reached the edge and was sure if I pushed it then I'd wash out too. When you're on the edge you basically have two choices unless you have Adderall or Ritalin to rev you up again.

The first choice is to chill. Your buzz will wear off, and you can start over. This is the best way to go since usually wherever you are, sunk into a couch or crashed on a bed or whatever, you're safe. If you want to hang, you have to recognize when you're on the edge.

The second choice is to switch up. This takes practice since you have to keep track of how much you've done and watch how it's hitting you. This isn't an option for freshmen. Everyone is different, and if you take the wrong thing, like a handful of Vicodin when you're already wasted, you're not going to wake up. No one will call 911 for you either. They'd be too freaked out.

Paige came back after the CH Bully went to Molly with Jenna and his friends. I'd lost interest in trying it by then. Next to me she sparked a bowl and held it up to my face since she saw how crippled I was, but I turned it down and tried to kiss her. That only made her laugh. I'd made the biggest party foul you can. I got honest at the wrong time instead of hiding what was inside. See, hiding what's going on inside yourself is a big part of being able to hang.

"When are you going to talk to me?" I asked.

"What do you mean?" she said. "I'm here. We're talking."

"You know what I mean," I said, but she just sighed and went to the kid on the floor. She stroked his hair like a doll, whispered in his ear, then waved me over to play doctor. I made my way to him and lifted his head up. It fell like a dumbbell. The CH Bullies saw us nursing on him, and one of them said our school made us soft. It wasn't like they were public school kids, but their prep school must've bred pricks.

"Take a hit babe," Paige said. "It's too good to waste." She stuck the bowl in the kid's mouth, but he was iced. Whoever got him went too far. See, the game is only supposed to teach rookies a lesson. That's all.

"He's totally out," Jaycee said, mopping his face with a rag. The more she wiped him the more his face turned purple, and I had to get away. "It's not coming off."

"It won't for days," I said. "Soap won't take that stain off him."

*** 

Kids came, and kids left. Jenna sat on one of the football heroes' lap in a recliner, rolling against him like a kitten flopped onto a warm blanket as Paige went to try the new science at last. As she held the back of her wrist to her nose I prayed that what I'd heard about Molly was true, that after it hit her brain she'd crash into me full of love like we were back in seventh grade. Maybe the only times that make sense are in the past.

"Hey." Jaycee jerked on my arm. "Hanna needs to chill Tyler out." In the dining room, Tyler was racing through beers, desperate to impress the crowd cheering him.

"She can try," I said, "but he'll blow her off. It's like their foreplay, or something." Tyler was the richest kid at our rich-kid school, and Hanna was by far the most popular girl. Maybe they had to date like there was this script for high school romance they were stuck with. They'd been together since middle school, but I'd only seen them happy like half the time. Maybe that was enough. Regardless, she was the only chance we had to keep him from going completely off.

I shot Hanna the sign to rein him in, but when she tried to take him by the arm he jerked it away like she was playing party police. She let it slide and stumbled to hug him which only made him trip over the kid on the floor and spill his drink down his shirt. His eyes changed when the CH Bullies started to howl at the sight of him drunk and drenched. I told Jaycee to get ready to bounce.

Tyler lifted the kid off the floor up by his shirt with one hand and got ready to lay into him, but Hanna shoved him hard enough to break his grip.

"You can't hit a kid that's out. That's not cool!"

"His name is Loser," Tyler said. It's like that. Someone calls you a name and it sticks, especially if there's a story attached to it and you hate it. It took my entire freshman year before most of the kids stopped calling me Mouse. Tyler was the only one who still did, but only when he was blitzed and evil, not that it made it any better. He was way stronger than me, so I had to pretend that it didn't bother me. In high school there are things you can change, and things you can't. If you stay obsessed with the things you can't change you'll go crazy. The best you can do is survive what you can.

"How did they get that way?" Jaycee asked, more to herself than to me.

Tyler went through the kid's pants where they bunched around his ankles. "Loser has got to learn."

I wanted to stop him, but when everyone's watching it's hard to stand up for a kid you don't know. It's safer to stay quiet and be glad that it's not you.

"What time is it?" I asked Jaycee, but she wouldn't talk to me. I asked if she'd gotten her box from the school yet, even though I was sure she had, but she played deaf. It felt like she blamed me for the scene going down, even though I was totally innocent. I'd only shot a pic of the kid. That was it.

Paige joined Tyler in treasure hunting through the kid's pockets, and then they crashed beside us. Tyler searched the kid's phone while Paige flipped through his wallet. They were so wicked happy that I got what Jaycee meant when she asked how they turned out like that. It was only a game. We were just kids, and someday we'd be better. I believed that.

Paige took a five-dollar bill out, stuffed it into her jeans, and then slung the kid's wallet over her shoulder. "No license so he didn't drive here," she said. "What a waste of life."

Tyler scrolled through the pictures on the kid's phone since he didn't have the logic to lock it, but there wasn't anything worthwhile. Most of his pics were of his dog so he must not have had many friends. With nothing good to share, Tyler got bored and texted a bunch of the kid's contacts that he was gay and hoped they'd still love him. That made him laugh until he could barely breathe. He always went straight to the gay shit as if that was the worst thing you could call a person other than the N-word, but I guess he got that from the country club. I bet the only gay or Black people he ever saw growing up were ones he could get fired. When texting got dull he handed the phone to Paige.

"It's weird," she said. "Like one of those phones you have to buy minutes for ahead of time."

"Poor kids are stupid," Tyler said, which made Jaycee shade red.

"Money doesn't make you smart," I said, but Jaycee stomped off anyway. I wanted to follow her, but my chances of getting Paige alone were running out.

"Take another pic of him," Paige said. "No one will believe how bad he got it." I took out my phone and shot him again. The kid was smeared and motionless on my screen, and I guessed that it was human nature to walk over people who couldn't stop you.

"So are we going or what?" Jaycee asked. The second she came back, Paige left, which made me sorry I'd brought her. She would've sulked about being left out if I hadn't, and I did like her, but she was forever blocking me when it came to Paige. Plus, the kid on the floor had turned her mood shitty. It's hard to watch somebody you can't save when you have a heart.

"We can't leave that kid here," I said as I tried to make out where Paige had gone.

"I can't watch this. Can we at least grab some air?" Jaycee said.

***

Outside, kids smoked in a circle and ignored us. Above us, the stars were high and bright, but the moon was missing. I eased into a deckchair and wondered what the world would be like if the sun never came up again.

"How much longer do you plan on staying?" Jaycee asked. "I can't miss the last bus."

"Look, as soon as things turn back kind inside we'll bounce. It's always like this." I pulled off my hoodie and wrapped it around her so she'd stop shivering. "You'd be warmer if you'd have a drink for once."

"Oh, and end up like that kid? No thanks," she tugged my hoodie over her t-shirt. "This party is the worst. We're not at a celebration. We're at an execution."

"Don't be a drama queen. We're celebrating the end of summer, right? Two days from now we'll be back in school dealing with all the shit I don't want to think about now. You can't let what happens to that kid get to you."

"I shouldn't have come," she said. "This is the first time you've paid attention to me all night. It's like you're afraid to talk to me in case Paige notices or something."

"She's my friend. We've got history. You're my friend too."

"Yeah," Jaycee said as she tucked her arms into my hoodie. "We're real close."

"Is that bad?" She acted like she wanted to pick a fight, but I was too fogged up to understand what else had her sour. Then the noise inside got crazy loud. The worst wasn't over yet.

In the middle of the living room, Tyler was over the kid on the floor admiring what he'd done to him. He pounded beers two at a time while Hanna begged him to calm down. My friends and I were drifting easy, but Tyler's switch had flipped and there was no way to bring him back. Maybe it was genetic or something, but he was like an X-Man when it came to partying. When that switch flipped inside his head it was the same as if he'd just started, and major trouble was bound to follow. Jaycee and I moved inside and saw how he'd buried the kid with garbage and beer cans.

"Stay here," I said. "If he gets worse, grab Jenna and make her kick him out."

"Find Hanna fast!" Jaycee said.

Hanna was in one of the bedrooms going through a dresser when I found her. She was putting something into her pocket but stopped when I yelled that she had to get a handle on her man before he set the place on fire.

"He is only playing monster for attention," she said. "I'll take care of him if you take care of me."

"Fine," I passed her three Adderall. "Sharing is caring, but you seriously have to get him out of here."

"You got it. If he's over the edge I'll need these to keep up." She popped two in her mouth and chased them with a swig of Diet Coke before marching off to take out Tyler. I'd never seen her happier. She lived for drama.

Hanna tried to talk Tyler down, but he repeated everything she said like a bratty kindergartener. She gave up and went to kiss him, but he stopped her and said she was boring. That set off a screaming match, but I had no doubt they'd bang it out before the morning came. They had that kind of love.

Hanna shoved him away to pick back up on her scavenger hunt of the house. After she disappeared, Tyler cracked a fresh beer, then froze like his hand was waiting for instructions on how to drink. Jaycee and Paige sat on either side of me on the couch. It was like someone had hit a big reset button, and the last two hours hadn't changed anything at all except for the kid on the floor. They laid where he had been buried under trash.

See, that night was supposed to be a good time, but it got twisted, thanks to Jenna. If we had gone to our regular party house where we belonged it would've been kind. Nothing could hurt us there. Instead, we were in another town, in a stranger's house with kids we didn't know. It's okay if you don't know where you are, but you better know who you are with. Otherwise, you're dead.

\*\*\*

"I haven't seen you in weeks," I said, but Paige just sped up her texting. "When can we hang again?"

Jaycee said she had to go to the bathroom and left.

"Oh yes!" Paige squealed. "I've got to go!"

"Is everything alright?"

"Don't be a child," she said. "Do I look worried?"

"I was only asking. Where are you off to?"

"I'm going to a college party! It's pretty exclusive." She hurried out the door without taking her eyes off her phone.

"Why can't girls ever stay still?" I asked Tyler as he slumped next to me.

"They love leaving," he said with a shrug. "They're all the same you know? It's like they want you to chase them and ignore them at the same time, but either way, they're never satisfied. They want to live out this messy love story that is magic and doomed all at once like a movie."

"I don't watch those kinds of movies," I said, "but I feel you."

Tyler asked me if I wanted to shave the kid on the floor's head, but I didn't feel like searching the bathrooms for a razor. I only wanted to get home and hoped that what I'd heard was true; that it doesn't matter who you were in high school because once you get out you can be whoever you want. No one remembers who you were, and even your school pictures are of somebody else.

Jaycee came back after Tyler got up. I figured he was going to find Hanna until I saw him sneak out the back door.

"Where'd Paige run off to?" she asked in this fake concerned voice.

"Some college party, I guess. She was all wrapped on her phone. I don't know why she even came."

"What did you expect? She's dating a college guy now."

"Where'd you hear that?" I asked, but she couldn't remember since she didn't think it mattered.

"We should get out of here," she said. "Nothing good can happen now."

"Are you sure about the college guy? I mean, where'd she meet him? Who is he?"

"I don't know, okay? I'm not into rumors."

An engine started up outside, but it didn't sound like a car. I looked out the sliding glass doors that led to the backyard, but there was no way to see through it with the lights on inside.

"It's a fact," Hanna popped up behind us. "Everybody knows about her college boy unless they're totally stupid." That made her giggle, and she kissed Jaycee on the mouth for real. The kiss ended in a second, but there was no doubt, everyone at school would say they hooked up. If a story is better than the truth that's what goes around. I never heard the official version of the Mouse story when I was a freshman, and I'm glad I didn't. If I had I might've gone psycho killer.

"Why'd you do that?" Jaycee asked. Her face had turned pink as sugar-free gum.

Hanna looked at me, and said, "Someone had to."

***

The engine outside revved louder, and all of a sudden I got clear. It happened that way sometimes. I would be faded to the verge of going out, and then in a blink I would be straight like I hadn't touched a thing. I was in a single-level house where the floor was covered with smashed Solo cups and trash. The dining room table had been dragged into the living room and was soaked with beer. Jenna was in a recliner surrounded by CH Bullies. My friends laughed, and fought, and kissed, and there was this kid on the floor laid out like a doll that somebody had dropped and forgotten.

I brushed the trash off the kid on the floor's head and told Jaycee we had to leave. The kid on the floor was watching me and nothing. He was there and he wasn't.

Before we made it for the front door I asked Hanna what happened to the kid's phone so I could call his mom or whoever, but she said she saw it floating in the toilet. No one was going to fish it out. I mean, kids were still peeing in there. A phone wasn't going to stop them. There was only one bathroom so some kids were going in the sink. At the end of a true rager, everyone turns into an animal.

One of the CH Bullies cut the music as the rumble of the engine popped and sputtered, then it fell into this slashing helicopter rhythm. That got everyone's attention and we all rushed to the backyard to see what monster was coming at us.

Under the security lights, Tyler raced around on a riding mower shooting smoke and grass into the air as he leaned it into a turn, then cut the wheel straight and raced out of the light toward the edge of the dark and past it. Hanna screamed for him to stop, but her voice was eaten up by the chopping growl of its engine. When a couple of the CH Bullies started to chase him he wheeled the mower onto the street. Its blades sprayed sparks as they spun into the curb before he drove away.

"He's just an attention freak," Hanna told the football hero holding Jenna's hand. "I swear he'll bring it back."

"Whatever," he said. "It's not like anyone cares."

The crowd rambled back inside as Jaycee and I waited for Tyler to return until there was no reason to expect he would.

"That was a fancy lawnmower," Jaycee said as if he'd stolen a Porsche.

"It's just a mower. Whoever it belonged to will buy another one. It's no big deal."

"I guess things don't mean much for rich people no matter how nice they are." She was baiting me to fight, but I let it go.

\*\*\*

Hanna left to track down Tyler before he got busted mowing the street out of his head, and then the CH Bullies bolted in case the police traced him back to the house. In under a minute the place was empty except for me and Jaycee, and the kid on the floor.

Jaycee said the kid looked cold and went to find something to put over him while I checked out the medicine cabinets in case there was anything worth taking for later. By the time I got back she had cleared from his head and draped a blanket over him. Neither of us spoke. We were in this one-story house we had never seen before on the other side of town. The air was still and cool. Jaycee dialed 911 from the phone in the kitchen, then dropped it when the operator picked up. That was it. I put my hand on her back, gave the mad scene one last look, and slammed the door behind us. We had to go.

\*\*\*

It was hard to find my way back to the main road since my phone's GPS wasn't connecting, but I figured it out before any flashing lights lit up behind us. I drove the speed limit and kept an eye out for ambulances, police cruisers, or Tyler swerving down the sidewalk, but all I saw were nice homes filled with families who would never appreciate how lucky they were to sleep through their last night of summer in peace.

"Why'd you ask me to come?" Jaycee asked. We were closer to our side of town, and she had relaxed for the first time that night.

"I like having you around because you would never do this." I scrolled through the pictures on my phone with my free hand until I found the shots of the kid on the floor. "You saved that kid."

"You saved him too," she said. "What's next? Are you going to send those pictures to everyone so they can joke about what a loser he is and feel superior?" I told her I'd delete them if she wanted me to, but she said to do whatever I wanted. After she passed my phone back she directed me to her bus stop and pouted. Tyler was right. Girls were always expecting magic and got pissed when it didn't come.

When we got to the bus stop I offered to drive her home, but she said that I was too gone to make it that far without blindsiding a tree and killing us both. "Besides," she said. "I don't want you to see where I live. You wouldn't understand."

"You don't give me enough credit," I said, "but it's your call. Look." I held out my phone for her to watch as I deleted every picture of the kid on the floor. "I was just bored. I would've helped him if I could have."

"Erasing those shots is the best kind of help," she said. "Can I keep your hoodie? It's cold."

"You can have it forever," I said and shot her wearing it even though she tried to dodge away from my phone. I loved the way her hair curled out like brushstrokes and all but covered her sad green eyes.

As she huddled up on the bench to wait for the last bus I got this feeling like there was something I was supposed to say, but no matter how hard I tried nothing clever came into my head. Before long it felt silly to wait in my car staring at her, so I honked, waved, and drove off.

***

On the way home I tried to make sense of everything that'd gone down, not just at the bus stop, but the whole night. It was supposed to be a party. I should've been happy, but instead I felt as if I'd failed a giant test. The closer I got to my house the more I wondered what Paige was doing with her college boyfriend, what it was like for Jaycee to wait for a bus alone, and if an ambulance got to that kid on the floor before it was too late.

I parked in my driveway as the sky changed from black to purple. The stars were gone. I checked my phone and was sad I'd erased those pics of the kid on the floor. I still wonder what happened to him. What if the family who lived at that house was on vacation, or had moved away a long time ago? What if no ambulance ever came? I wanted to see him again, to get what I must have looked like when my mom found me dropped for dead on her roses. Jaycee covered him up to be nice but half-covered by that garbage pile he would be easy to miss. See, if you only looked at that pile of trash from the door, quick like I had, you would never know anyone was there. Never.

# Chapter 2
## Kids with Gifts

**THE SATURDAY** afternoon after that lame party with Jenna's friends from Cherokee Hills, after we'd all gotten back to good, we met up at the country club to open our presents. Normally we had to break into the country club late at night when it was empty. Even though Tyler had every security code to the place, we were too smart to hang out there in the middle of the night. That was begging to get busted. So most of the time we ran in, lifted whatever, and then bolted before anyone noticed we were there. None of us had spent much time there during the day before, but Tyler promised he'd gotten permission from his parents for us to use this conference room in a building the club rented out for weddings rehearsals and corporate parties.

We'd parked our cars where the maids and waiters left theirs and followed him with our boxes under our arms like we were going camping. Tyler led us down a trail paved with pebbles to this building surrounded by pine trees. I knew the country club was massive but had no clue there was this decked-out mansion hidden in the woods next to the golf course. I didn't ask about his lawnmower ride, or what happened later. The day was too perfect to ruin with questions like that. While he punched in the code I felt the sun break through the trees and wash over me. It felt like starting over.

We followed Tyler across the hardwood floor of this dance hall, then down a corridor toward a conference room. The whole time we scoped the place for adults and kept quiet like burglars. After we had all filed inside he closed the doors to the conference room while we settled into these plush leather chairs around a long wooden table that was polished like a mirror. Then we dropped our boxes from The Dream Academy in front of us and pushed back our chairs like big shots. I was happy no one had opened theirs yet. It was way more fun to play Christmas morning and share the fresh weirdness together.

***

Hanna guessed the school had sent us temporary tattoos. Paige thought they might've mailed jigsaw puzzles. I hoped they'd sent us movies, but I doubted it. It wasn't The Dream Academy's style to send anything useful.

Tyler promised that we'd be able to blast our boxes with shotguns later. He swore he'd gotten the okay for that too. Paige made rat-a-tat noises and pretended to mow down her box with an invisible machine gun, but Jaycee hugged hers to her chest and didn't seem into the whole idea of blowing it away. It was like she never got real presents.

I asked who wanted to go first while Tyler left to find party favors, and Jaycee raised her hand all excited as if we were in class. She was so excited to rip hers open that nobody argued about it. Maybe being a scholarship kid made getting anything seem like an award. She curled her fingers under the top flap, took a deep breath, and was seconds away from tearing it open when Tyler returned with this metal cart set up with an ice bucket, liquor bottles, and glasses. We were high rollers.

Jaycee let go of her box and moved to set us up with drinks like a waitress, while Tyler flopped into the chair at the head of the table, all mob boss. After we had our drinks and toasted, he gave Jaycee the sign to get on with it.

\*\*\*

The first thing you have to understand about The Dream Academy is that it wasn't a normal school. It was an experiment. If a kid was lucky enough to get in, and nobody heard how they picked who did or didn't, they had to wonder what they were in for once they got their first box. At least all my friends did when our first ones arrived at the end of middle school. The boxes scared us back then, but our parents told us not to worry, since The Dream Academy was reimagining what high school should be, whatever that meant. Since our parents had seen the school played up on the news, they were too crazy proud that we'd been accepted to listen to what we thought or wanted. Before we got picked we were sure we'd end up at a normal private school like Cherokee Hills, The Christopher School, or Saint Mary's, but once we got chosen to be Dream Kids our parents had something to brag about, and then there was no way out. The first boxes we got, the ones filled with movie scripts and Play-Doh, didn't bother them at all.

\*\*\*

Jaycee faked taking a drink, then ripped the tape off her box.

"What did we get this time?" Hanna asked.

"See for yourself," Jaycee said. It must've felt good for her to have something over us, if only for a second.

The first thing in my box was a comic book called *Kids of the Future*. It was sure to be the first thing I blasted when I had the chance. I was too old for comic books. The Dream Academy should've known that.

Underneath the comic book was a new copy of *Keys to Success* which was this inspirational book written by our principal whose last name was Keys. He must've thought that title was smart or something since he made sure every student got a copy of his book at the start of each year. No one I asked had ever read it, or would admit it if they had. Most of my crew had heard enough inspirational talks to write a book like that themselves. I couldn't wait to go gangster on his wonderful advice.

"Who's got bags?" Paige asked. She held up a pink one with her name printed on it before taking a pic of it to post and hate on later.

"I do," I said. I watched her tear her bag open with her teeth and wished it wasn't so hard to steal her away and talk for real. There was nothing to do but wait for her to get bored with whatever trip she was on. You can't speak to a girl when they're wound up in being someone else.

The first bag in my box was blue and had my name written on it as if it was made just for me, but that was impossible. I'd wondered before if the school had some secretaries trolling our Twitter or hacking off Snapchat for data or whatever, but if they did it was useless. No one is who they are online in real life.

"Let the oddball parade begin." I shook the pile of junk out of my bag onto the table. Most of what we got belonged in a claw machine, or at the bottom of a Happy Meal.

My bag had a cheap disposable camera in it, a Rubik's cube, and a set of watercolors. I lined them up in front of me for the others to see while they did the same. Tyler got a plastic bank that was shaped like a dollar sign, Hanna got a deck of cards with yoga poses on them, and Jenna got some toy monsters. None of it made sense because that wasn't the point. The Dream Academy expected us to find our own meaning in life. We got out our phones and snapped on them to broadcast what a waste of time they were.

Paige tossed out this bracelet kit she got on the table and frowned. "Like I've got time for crafts," she said as if the kit was an insult.

"I'll take it if you don't want it," Jaycee said, faster than she meant to, which made her come off eager as a freshman.

"Whatever," Paige said. "You're not even drinking. You're such a grandma you'll probably love it. I bet you have like a hundred friendship bracelets at home."

"Relax," I said, "She's not an old lady because she keeps it straight edge. We came here to have fun, right?"

"I don't trust anyone who keeps it straight edge." She pulled out her phone and spun her chair sideways. "They're one step away from being achiever kids."

"What's wrong with being good?" Jaycee asked.

"Good girls are fine for high school, if you want to be high school, but believe me they always end up getting it the worst in the end," Paige said with this snotty voice. "Forget it. My boyfriend's text bombing me again. He's so thirsty."

"Yeah," I said, "I'm sure he can't wait to hear from you." She ignored me and thumbed her phone all super interested to show how her college hook-up was way more important than me. It would've been easy to hate her if I hadn't loved her before and didn't burn to feel that way again.

"No one at Cherokee Hills has to put up with this nonsense," Jenna said. She forever talked up Cherokee Hills like it was high school Heaven. "If my friends there heard we got mailed toys they'd never let me live it down."

"What did they send you?" I asked Jaycee, to wipe the shade off her.

"A toy piano and junk like everyone else got," she said, "but this is nice." She picked up a metal four-leaf clover from her pile and held it up.

"Lucky you," Hanna said. "The best things I got are these chocolates wrapped up like Olympic medals."

"Don't eat those," Tyler said. "They're probably old, and the last thing you need is chocolate."

"I got them because I'm on the gymnastics team, dick," she said, throwing her candy at his face.

"No one pays attention to your bouncing little clique," Tyler said. "It's not like you girls are cheerleaders."

You have to understand that The Dream Academy only had a gymnastics team since it was an Olympic sport, co-ed, and completely non-violent. They said they offered it to inspire a spirit of international camaraderie and healthy competition, but that kind of talk was standard for them. The school rented out a Y since it didn't have a gym, and you'd never think Hanna and her team competed for a school if their uniforms didn't have The Dream Academy logo on them. No parents ever came to watch them compete. Most adults were like that. They'd pay if they didn't have to be there, as long as we were in these posters and team pictures to show their friends later.

At the bottom of my first bag was a note from Principal Keys. I pulled it out and read it in my best politician voice. "You are the leaders of tomorrow. Take these objects and give them a purpose. Plant a seed, paint a portrait, or take them apart to see how they work. The future is yours!" We all broke down.

"Time for bag number two?" Hanna asked.

Paige put her phone away long enough to take out her second bag. She didn't apologize to Jaycee. It was like nothing happened at all. When we dated in middle school I loved the way she smelled like suntan lotion all the time, and I wondered if she still did sometimes. It's weird what you hold on to.

"Hold up," Tyler said, then he took off while we shoved our objects waiting for purpose back into their bags.

"They have to know I'm on their gymnastics team, right?" Hanna asked as if it bothered her that the school might not have been drooling over the medals she'd won.

"Sure. I bet they track every post you make," I said. "You think?"

"No way." Hanna giggled. "If they read my posts there's no way I'd still be on the team."

***

Tyler came back with an ashtray and a box of cigars. His parents had been on the board of the country club his entire life so it was a second home for him. He'd spent his whole life opening drawers and finding out where they kept the keys. "You're up Paige," he said, scooting the ashtray her way.

Paige pulled a Ziploc bag out of her purse that had two fat nuggets in it and made a big deal about how she got them from her boyfriend. Maybe dating a college guy made her feel the way Jaycee did for scoring a music scholarship like she'd been given this great award that proved she was special. While she picked apart the buds Jaycee refilled our drinks without anyone asking her to, and it frustrated me that she was still trying to fit in.

Jaycee was solid with us, but she acted like we'd abandon her if she didn't go out of her way to prove how much she cared. Maybe that's why she was always flirty with me, or maybe she was one of those girls who had to have a guy love her to love herself. It was like she couldn't see how cute she was, or if she did, she didn't trust it.

In no time, Paige had hollowed out the cigars, packed them, and sealed them into blunts before passing them around. We could've passed for a real board meeting with our cigars, and big drinks. We were operating on high.

Hanna put her feet on the table and puffed. "Our parents would be proud of us if they could see us now."

"They should be," Tyler said. "We're living their dream."

I stuck my blunt in my mouth but didn't light it. I didn't want Jaycee to be the only one not smoking, or for Paige to have the pleasure of watching me enjoying her boyfriend's score. The others puffed away though, and I kind of wished our parents did walk in and catch us blazing. That way they would've seen what all their stress made us do to survive.

"Your parents are going to be royally pissed when they smell this place," I told Tyler. "You shouldn't have told them we were coming here."

"I didn't." He broke down like he'd heard the funniest thing ever. "Don't worry. They'll blame the Mexicans if they even notice." I told him that was so wrong, but he said that was life.

***

Jaycee pulled the second bag out of her box and opened it before anyone called her a good girl again for not smoking, and I followed so she didn't go alone.

Our second bags were stuffed with dozens of college brochures. All those schools waited for kids like us. We'd been repped as the most-forward thinking students in America in a couple of magazines, and Principal Keys probably had staff working overtime to get us into top-tier universities so he could brag about our acceptance rates and raise the tuition again. His mind was on the money no matter how much progress he talked. One time he was on *60 Minutes* and spent his entire interview preaching about how teaching young minds was like this fierce video game battle like in Street Fighter II. Later on, the school made us spend a day playing the game, then we had to watch his interview and write an essay over it. Mine was about how Blanka was an unfair portrayal of native peoples. I got an A.

"Do this." Paige fanned out her brochures. "It'll blow your mind." She'd ripped the tops off her brochures so there was no way to tell which school they belonged to. An old stone building that could've been a cathedral. A happy multiracial group of students studying together underneath a tree. A young, dressed-down professor standing in front of a PowerPoint presentation. Modern art murals and computer labs went on forever. They were all the same.

"I want to go to old church behind hot girls walking with books for sure," Tyler said.

"Why waste your time there?" Hanna asked. "You should go to winning basketball team and huge library. It's way more fun."

"I only want to get this year over with," Jenna said. "Maybe they'll send me to Spain or Japan for my senior year. Any place is better than here."

\*\*\*

You have to get that The Dream Academy constantly changed the rules since it never made up its mind about what it wanted it to be. We never knew what to expect. For the last two years all the seniors had been sent off to spend their senior years away for what the school called

"Evolutions Abroad." That made juniors like us the same as seniors since we were the oldest kids around. I hoped the school would ditch the program before we moved up since I hated the idea of being somewhere foreign and friendless, but everyone except me and Jaycee considered it the pay-off for putting up with three years of weirdness. Paige said that by next year she'd be chilling on a beach in Greece and might never come back.

I pulled a folder from the bottom of my box. "We've got one last thing to do before we get gangster." Our boxes always had a folder with our core class schedule inside them along with a list of electives that was over ten pages long. The first half of my schedule was pretty standard with classes like English, chemistry, and computer science, but the rest was up to me since The Dream Academy wanted us to be "self-directed learners." I scanned down the list of electives, but the only one that looked decent was this digital film-making class. If I got shipped off I figured I'd make a movie about it, an orphan in the world kind of thing.

"Who wants to think about school when we have shot-guns?" Tyler pushed his chair back. Hanna and Jenna cheered, then strutted out the door with their boxes. "You coming?" he asked, but left before I answered.

Jaycee started to pack up my box for me until Paige called her my assistant.

"I'm being nice," she said. "I like to help."

"You need to quit being so nice. It's not normal." Paige laughed, but it was at whatever her boyfriend had texted her. When she was on her phone, nothing else existed.

"What's normal then?" Jaycee asked.

"Are you ready to blow up your box or what?" I asked Paige, loud so she had to answer.

"Grow up," she said with this pity face. "I have to pick up my boyfriend." Her eyes stayed on her phone as she got her things and left. The last time we'd officially dated was seventh grade, and she only came back to me when another guy dumped her. I was this safe place she could heal up, then leave when she felt better. I put my head down between my arms and closed my eyes so I didn't have to watch her go.

\*\*\*

At first the humming and whispered words were part of a dream, a gentle wave that moved over the ocean, across the sand, and then lifted into the air and bled into the clouds. The song floated softly, outside my dream world and real, until I lifted my head up and saw Jaycee singing low to herself next to me. I listened to her sing until she saw me and stopped.

"What were you singing?"

"This old song from my Pop Vocals class last year," she said, embarrassed that I'd caught her in that private moment. "It's called 'How Will I Know.' You were really out huh?"

"I suck at sleep. I try to go out at night, but it never works so I end up spent when I should be fresh you know? You should've left me. I would've left you."

"Would you?" she asked, and I nodded. "No, you wouldn't. Can you do something for me?"

"We should go. I'm bad company right now." I had four or five next-gen Vicodin and half a prescription of Adderall in my car, but if she wanted anything else she'd have to wait.

"You're not bad company. I want to ask you something important."

"What?"

41

"Do you think I have talent?" She braced herself as if she was ready to take a punch. The worst thing a kid can do is care that much what anyone else thinks.

"Sure you do. You're hot."

"That's not the same thing." Her shoulders slumped as she turned her four-leaf clover over in her hands. "Forget it."

"You know what I mean." She kept her head down, so I kicked her chair to get her attention before framing her up with my disposable camera. "Say cheese!"

"You're a dork," she said. "I look awful, and I *despise* having my picture taken!"

I clicked the camera, and it flashed as she put her hands over her face. "Pictures are all that matter. See, that's the point. Think about this okay? The way you look at seventeen is probably the best you'll ever look in your entire life. After this you, me, and everyone we know falls apart in slow motion."

"Nice philosophy," she said, as I shot her again. "You really know how to cheer a girl up."

"I'm going to make you a star."

"I'm taking this." She pulled the camera away from me and tossed it in her box.

"Come on. We've got shotguns waiting to give our lives a purpose."

"You go. I have to clean up before someone gets fired because Tyler's an asshole."

"No one expects you to do that, you know. You don't have to play waitress."

"Is that a bad thing to be?" She pushed my chair away. "My mom is a waitress."

"I mean you don't have to try so hard. You're one of us."

"Does that mean too good to clean up?" Whatever joy my photoshoot had laid on her was gone, and I didn't feel like fighting. Maybe if I'd been a better person I would've stayed to help her cover our tracks, but instead I took my box and left her to rinse glasses and empty the ashtray. My box flapped open in the breeze like a doped bird between my hands as I paced back through the woods. The urge to blow it away was strong.

***

Cracks from the shotgun blasts pointed the direction to the target range as I followed them across the putting greens, where old men in golf outfits gave me these "What are you doing here?" frowns. I pretended not to notice and nodded their way to play like I belonged. My stomach went acid from their stares, and I wondered if Jaycee felt that way around us sometimes.

The smell of gunpowder was thick in the air as Tyler fired another shot to show Hanna how it was done. My ears rang, but it was nice to be distracted from thinking.

"I'm going to make this fly," Tyler said as he loaded his copy of *Keys to the Success* onto a metal arm attached to springs. Then he told Hanna to get ready. She gave a thumbs-up, and lifted a shotgun that was way too big for her to her shoulder. "One. Two. Three!"

Hanna fired the gun and her butt hit the ground as soon as it went off. She whined a little as she rubbed her shoulder, then Tyler snatched her gun away.

"I told you to hold it tight," he said in this disappointed dad voice. "You never listen to me."

"I've never shot a gun before! I tried my best."

Tyler helped her to her feet, then kissed her cheek. "Okay, then just pull the chord for me. Don't sulk. It takes practice." Hanna held his hand and together they walked off to find the book. Once they did Tyler loaded it back onto the machine and told her to give him a countdown.

He aimed his shotgun at the sky while Hanna waited to pull the rope. I stood next to him to stay out of the line of fire. "I'm not a prick," he whispered. I hadn't called him one, but maybe he'd read it on me. "You have to be rough with girls." He stood statue still. "Then act sweet so they melt you know?"

"That only works for you," I said, as Hanna counted one, then two.

"It works for everyone. You have to break them up. That way when you make them feel better you're their hero." Hanna counted three and sent the book across the sky. Tyler leaned in, and when he fired his guide for success exploded like a pillow rigged with dynamite.

"Awesome!" Hanna raced to hug him.

He pointed his smoking barrel toward the sky. "I am deadly!" he shouted, but who wouldn't be if they grew up with a gun range?

Jenna dropped her box down and motioned for Hanna and me to make an execution line. "Let's get this over with."

Hanna sulked until Tyler went drill sergeant and barked for her to fire. The blast knocked her back on her heels, but she managed to stay upright that time.

"That was better," Tyler said into her puppy dog eyes. Then he elbowed me and told her she was a born killer. That made her smile.

Jenna and I blasted holes through our tomorrows at the same time. When we pulled our triggers it sounded like a car bomb had gone off, and after the smoke cleared the range was a manicured green field covered with a blanket of plastic, scraps of paper, and mutilated cardboard. It looked like a town leveled by a tornado. I was sure whoever had to clean it up later would hate us, and never imagine that they were picking up after certified leaders of tomorrow.

\*\*\*

Tyler lit the fireplace in the dance hall as I laid on the floor, not wanting to stay or go. Most of my life was spent that way, waiting for something to happen to break the boredom of having time without any real purpose.

Jaycee's curly brown hair was matted to her face with sweat as she joined us with her box intact. On top of it she had the newly polished ashtray with what was left of our blunts. "I thought you might want to finish these," she said. I pulled out my phone and shot a pic of her standing there. "Don't," she said. "You have to delete that. I don't want pictures of me floating around for kids to hate on."

"But you're so choice," I said and meant it whether she believed me or not. I could've loved her if I wasn't so afraid that getting close to her would destroy any chance I had to get Paige back.

"Yeah," Tyler said. "I'll ask my parents to hire you."

"Stop it," I said. "She's trying to cover for us."

"That's good of her," he said. "She's a real *good* girl."

Jaycee pushed open one of the bay windows to let in the fresh air. It smelled like perfume from the bushes outside and calmed the gunslinger mood that hung on us. "It's nice here." She stretched her arms into the sunlight flooding through the branches.

Tyler hit what was left of a blunt and passed it to Hanna. "I guess for you," he said. "For me it's nothing. If you see anything long enough it doesn't register, no matter how pretty it is."

"Do you think that goes for people too?" Jaycee asked as she sat by me and offered this stub of a blunt. I tossed it into the fire to watch it burn. The gas flames stripped it to ash and sent it up the chimney and away.

"Can I have this?" I held up Jaycee's bag of toys.

"For what?" She put her head on my shoulder.

"I want to burn them so I can see how they turn out. You know, after the fire's gone and they're cool again."

"If that makes you happy." She rubbed my back as I shook all her presents onto the hardwood floor. Maybe she hung on me because I stood up for her. I tossed her toy piano into the fire and watched it turn into a slick of goo.

"What will your parents say when they see how we trashed the shooting range?" Jenna asked. It's no fun when kids smoke out and go paranoid. You have to respect the balance and settle into that hazy split so that the part of you who's high listens to the part of you who's steady.

"The grounds crew will take care of it. That's their job, right?" Tyler never got nervous when he was stoned, but it would've been better if he had. The paranoid kids shut up sooner or later out of fear of saying the wrong thing. When Tyler got high though, he wanted to talk big ideas which was forever annoying. He'd start making speeches to no one until it felt like you were in a room with this TV you didn't want to listen to but couldn't turn off. "Let me ask you all a question?" And he was off.

"What?" Hanna asked.

"This is for everyone. We're all Dream Kids, right? That's what they sell us as at least. But whose dream are we living? I mean, like, right now."

"Who said we were?" I threw Jaycee's four-leaf clover into the fire. The flames arched over it until it glowed red as a Valentine.

"My mom's," Jenna said. "She loves our school since they let her teach whatever she wants to and give her props for being a freak." The rest of us didn't answer because Tyler was already on Jenna's lead.

"That's what I'm talking about," he said. "They give us all these choices, but never explain what they're supposed to add up to."

"It's not so bad," I said. "Most kids don't get to fake their way through high school, right?"

You have to understand that, if anyone wanted to know what the students at The Dream Academy truly thought about it, my crew would be the worst kids to ask. They'd be better off asking the achiever kids who loved the place. Those kids forever talked about going Ivy League and couldn't imagine a life without constant praise and bonuses. I stretched out on the floor and pictured them all at home desperately trying to give meaning to their toys and comic books. They believed what they were told. It was probably nice to imagine a world of colleges with hip teachers and gorgeous co-eds dying to be their friends. The achiever kids were sure that one day they'd all be super-rich, even if they already were, but having money didn't solve anything. It only meant our parents could afford to pawn us off on dream schools they could brag about and send us to therapists when they didn't want to know what was going down in our heads.

Jaycee was my only friend who took The Dream Academy seriously. She felt lucky to be rescued from whatever public school she'd been at before, and constantly worried that the school might switch up and drop her music scholarships since it changed so much. She told me once that she'd never go back to public school if they cut her scholarship, but dropping out sounded like a dream to me. It meant you were free for real.

Tyler told us it was time to go since the cleaning crew was about to show, and lifted Hanna to her feet before tossing the rest of the evidence left into the fireplace. I wanted him to thank Jaycee for helping him out but was sure that would never cross his mind. I closed my eyes and smelled the ash and flowers in the air until Jaycee and I were alone.

"Can you drive me home?" she asked like she doubted I'd bother.

"You said you didn't want me to see where you lived before. Why now?"

"You're usually too bent to drive, and besides I don't have a choice. You have to swear though that you won't tell anyone what my place is like."

"I'm not always bent," I said. "Maybe you could keep me straight."

"I doubt it." She laughed, but not like she thought it was funny or anything. "Come on."

We hooked pinkies to seal the deal as her four-leaf clover shined white-hot in the middle of the fire.

\*\*\*

Jaycee didn't talk about our photoshoot or what I'd done to her good luck charm while I drove down into the city, then along the river. Instead, she made me promise over and over again not to mention where she lived to the others while my phone's GPS called out the directions. I guess she figured if they heard that she lived in the projects they'd torture her over it. I wanted to say they were better than that, but they weren't.

"What kind of music are you into?" she asked once we made it to a street lined with storage units and factories with smutty brick towers coughing smoke.

"Whatever's on the radio." I was pissed that I'd have to use the GPS on my phone to find my way home. I'd lived in Cincinnati my whole life but had never been to her part of the city. I mean, I'd heard about the projects and all, but it was like how I heard about third-world countries. They existed, but I didn't have a reason to care.

"Real music is never on the radio," she said. "You should fix that."

Men in oversized basketball jerseys waited on the corners with their hands in their pockets while they scoped out the street. I didn't want to stop, but Jaycee said I was acting like a total rich kid. I parked by a chain-link fence outside her apartment tower, and she kissed me goodbye.

"You didn't have to do that," I said.

"There's nothing wrong with being sweet."

She walked to her building with her box in her arms. Shirtless grade school kids ran across the parking lot, yelling crazy while they tossed this ratty Nerf football back and forth. She was lucky to have a future, to be living her mom's dream.

\*\*\*

When I got home I crashed in bed and sent Jaycee the picture I took of her on my phone when she was shining with sweat. I texted that Cinderella would be jealous, and hoped she'd forgive me for not deleting it. She looked too perfect to erase.

# Chapter 3
# Kids with Choices

**I WASN'T** lying when I told Jaycee I sucked at sleeping. Every night I tried to go out and catch eight solid hours, but my mind wouldn't let me. It'd race from one thing to the next until I ended up wasting time watching weird short films online or staring at the walls begging to blackout. See, sleep is like love. You can worry about it, pray for it, or do whatever you think will make it appear, but it only takes you away when it wants to. The more you beg for it the more it stays away.

The night before the first day of my junior year I didn't sleep at all. It wasn't that I was new school nervous with a head full of "Will they like me?" or "Are my clothes cool enough?" or anything. It wasn't because of my Adderall either since I hadn't used it in weeks since there was no reason to speed to get stuff done. See, instead I was obsessed with listing all the things I had to change about myself. A fresh year gave me the chance to hit the reset button and choose to be better for once. It's easy to imagine you can be brand new when it's late and you're alone. In the middle of the night anything is possible.

Beside my bed I found this shopping bag my mom had left for me. Before every new school year she bought me a stack of notebooks and ink pens like I was still in middle school even after I explained to her that most of our work was done online. She never listened to anything I said though.

I took out one of the notebooks and considered the things I had to do differently to survive my junior year, then wrote them out. After I read them though, I got depressed since they reminded me of the lists I had to write out when I was in therapy. My therapists were forever trying to get me to plan out my future instead of listening to what was bothering me, but what teenager has a master plan for the rest of their life? Most of us only want to be left alone.

I laid back on my bed and read my survival guide out loud, hoping that I'd wake up my mom or dad. It was pathetic, but the worst part about not sleeping is that you're totally isolated. I cleared my throat and read:

## *My List of Fantastic Promises*

1. Find out what makes me happy.
2. Save the party virgins when I can.
3. Make Paige love me again.
4. Figure out things with Jaycee.
5. Listen to music that's not on the radio.
6. Lay low in school.
7. Don't get caught up in other kids' drama.
8. Spend more time with my family.
9. Learn to make movies.

I wanted to believe I could do the things on my survival guide, but they only made me feel dumb after I read them to the walls. I tore out the list and tossed it on my nightstand. It hurt to know that I'd never be the kind of person I wanted to be.

After hours of lying like a corpse, the sun started to inch through my blinds. I pulled myself up to get ready. It was the beginning of my last year before getting shipped off, and all I wanted to do was sleep.

***

When I got to school everyone had to go to the auditorium for the opening assembly before our first class. The freshmen walked in like it was picture day and were directed to the front rows. I hoped that no one had told them about The Freak Show but was sure somebody had. Kids can't keep secrets in high school. They text whatever they hear whether it's true or not, and the bigger the disaster the faster it spreads. That's why I only shared stories that weren't about me or didn't matter. You can't share real secrets anyway because there aren't words for them.

The freshmen guys were young enough that their parents could've walked them to class but acted tough, which was stupid since there was no way they weren't scared shitless. Guys can't let out what's inside us though without getting called for it, but acting cold turns you that way sooner or later.

The new girls played with their hair and tried to get noticed. Some must've thought they were hot by the way they posed and turned back our way, but what passes for hot in middle school comes off desperate in high school. The ones who were truly Gucci would get picked off fast anyway, especially if they were down. Girls who were down scored quick love but were also the first ones cut loose. No guy would ever date a girl who got banged out the first week of school, at least not until the story was so old no one cared.

I sat with the rest of my bad kid crew in the last row. Jaycee and Paige were on either side of me when the principal took

52

the stage. Paige was completely spaced, and I hoped that Jaycee wasn't role modeling her because she'd decided to dress all slouchy too. Paige was wasted since she knew the drug dogs never sniffed around the first day of school. The Dream Academy did teach us how to work a system, and maybe that's what life is about.

"What do you think they'll do this time?" Paige asked. The scent lifting off her was oily and true. She'd bragged before that her college boyfriend's herb was Cannabis Cup level, and I secretly wished I had that kind of green so she'd want me again now that she was sold on being a total hippie.

Jaycee put her head against me. She smelled like bar soap. It was a relief that she hadn't flipped into a stoner cliché like Paige. She wasn't built for it. No matter what you're into it takes practice. Start off hardcore and you're bound to crash. I wanted to tell her she was perfect, that she didn't have to be anything, but it was too early to say anything heavy.

"I don't know." Paige leaned across me. "But I saw Mrs. Lovins and her friends carrying their costumes so for sure belly dancing. If her boob pops out again I'll puke."

"Shut up," Jenna said, and hate-faced Paige for bringing that up.

"When did her boob pop out?" I asked. Mrs. Lovins was Jenna's mom, and the main reason she was constantly aching to transfer to another school. She taught some of the art and English classes at our school, and even though she was at least forty she was a total pixie. The only time she ever got pissed off was when we didn't call her Carol since we were supposed to be on a first-name basis with our teachers. My crew played formal though so our teachers got the message that they were on their own side.

"She was performing at this fair our Movement and Dance class had to go to," Paige said to Jenna more than to me. "She got all into the beat, and when she shook her hips fast and put her arms over her head her top fell down. I mean, it didn't come completely off, but I totally saw her boob."

"How'd it look?" I asked.

"You're sick!" Jenna slapped at me, but I was out of reach. "I don't want to think about my mom's boobs. It's bad enough that I have to be in her class."

"So other than belly dancing what's your bet?" I asked. "Mariachi band? Chinese acrobats? Bagpipes?"

"They did Mexican stuff last semester," Tyler said, putting his feet up on the seat in front of him. "They've had all summer to plan though, so who knows what they've got cooked up? Maybe it's all Jenna's mom."

"I'll die if it is," Jenna said, using her fingers to fork her hair over her eyes.

"She loves the spotlight." Paige let her head fall onto my other shoulder, and I had to stop myself from touching her messy blonde hair.

***

The lights dimmed as the music started. "Here we go," Jaycee said. "The flags are coming out." I leaned forward to take my mind off Paige and watched the parade of flags from around the world get carried across the stage by our teachers. Jaycee gave me this cheesy grin. Her hair was as messy as Paige's as if not brushing your hair was the new thing. The teachers marched in a circle as the principal took the mic.

See, you have to understand that The Dream Academy wasn't our school's whole name. Its full name was The Dream Academy Experimental High School. Every student was part of one giant test. We were lab rats.

Maybe if it'd been a circus 24/7 it wouldn't have been so bad, but half our classes were standard, like chemistry, Spanish, and Algebra. The teachers told us getting into our school was like finding a diamond on the beach, whatever that meant, and said that we should appreciate how way ahead of other schools it was.

The other half of our classes were dedicated to "finding our path," and ranged from electives like yoga flow to hip-hop poetics and abstract art studio. It was like the school was sure that sun salutations and slam poetry would guarantee our spot at a big-name college but spending that much time with pixies and burn-outs had to read as a waste of time to any serious college.

The Dream Academy advertised itself as this amazing step forward, but inside the classrooms had more board games than books. When they changed the rules on us there was no doubt that whoever was in charge hadn't figured out what it was supposed to be or were trying to see how much they could get away with to prove a point. Maybe it was all a game, or maybe the school hadn't grown up yet either.

\*\*\*

"Welcome back students," Principal Keys said after the last flag went off stage. "Can you hear me? Can you hear me in the back?" No one answered.

Every year started with The Freak Show. It was supposed to expose us to other cultures, but it made them look like cartoons. Any school that started off with a "World Friendship Celebration" probably read too eager to the Ivy League.

"Students give a hand to our faculty," Principal Keys said as he motioned them to come back on stage and bow. My crew tried to sleep while the other kids clapped like they'd been ordered to. He hadn't bothered to introduce himself but owned the stage. I guess all his fundraising taught him how to work a crowd, but it only made me sure his guru speeches were a total act.

"I bet he starts with that old visualize your future sermon again," Tyler rummaged through Hanna's purse for gum without asking. "At least he knows how to bank."

"Again, welcome students. Thanks to your wonderful work, and my humble efforts, we were able to raise over five hundred thousand dollars in private donations last year alone. Now that's something to be proud of!" He clapped his hands together as 500,000 flashed on a screen behind him like we were a business instead of a school.

***

The screen went black. "Before we start our journey this year, let's bow our heads for a moment of silent reflection. This is not a religious service, nor am I personally religious, but let's join together in the spirit of kindness and acceptance. Close your eyes and concentrate on the universal peace and friendship." His voice fell as he offered us a prayer that wasn't. The other kids bowed their heads along with him while my crew waited for the madness to start.

"He hasn't said his name yet," Paige whispered. "Those freshmen probably have no idea who he is."

"They do if he's the one in the spotlight." Jaycee got stiff as if something was eating her. "Whoever gets the most attention calls the shots." The phony prayer service ended as Jenna's mom walked on stage and took the mic from Principal Keys.

Jenna's mom was Mrs. Lovins to us, but the achiever kids called her Carol which made her issue worse. Her issue was that she thought she understood us. For example, she played whatever songs were "most downloaded" before class as if we weren't already sick of them. The worst problem a teacher can have is not realizing that they're old and out of touch.

"I hope she drops the mic like Kanye," Paige said to jab at Jenna.

"She won't. She did the whole Kanye thing last year," I said. "She's in her belly dancing gear so she's bound to dance. She's an artist like that."

"Don't call her that," Jenna hissed. "She'd *love* it."

"She paints and writes poetry, right? That makes her an artist?" I asked.

"She's not an artist. She's a teacher who thinks she's one. Our house is covered with her ugly paintings and awful love poems in frames. I swear she's got a split personality or something. An artist has to at least know what they love." Jenna was ready to scream, and it was gorgeous.

"An artist can't love two things?" I asked since stoking her was more fun than any dance recital.

"She's right," Jaycee said to shut me up, or take the heat off Jenna. "No one can love two things completely."

"We're going to celebrate World Friendship together! Are you with me?" Jenna's mom shouted as she cupped a hand behind her ear and leaned toward the audience. The kids up front cheered. "Let's get this party started!"

Jenna sank into her seat.

A group of guys dressed all National Geographic with African shirts and boxy hats circled around the back of the stage. Then they beat their palms against these wooden drums and danced while they sang in some African language at the top of their lungs all Lion King. They were all white.

Jenna's mom ran to the corner of the stage, then swayed her way back into the spotlight with the rest of her belly dancing troupe. They had on veils and sparkly bras, and we could see through their dresses, thanks to the floor lights.

"What are the odds she pops one out again?" Tyler asked, snapping a pic to post later. Jenna said she'd stab him if he kept on.

"Jenna's mom wears Spanx you guys?" Paige giggled. As she rolled her face against my neck, I nuzzled her, but stopped when I saw Jaycee clenching her fists.

"Hey Jayce, do you think they're going to twerk?" I asked, but she didn't answer. I meant to cheer her up, but Paige acting flirty had her twisted. She had on a candy neck-lace like she used to wear in middle school, and part of me wanted to bite through it to taste sugar and go back to when things weren't so complicated.

The Freak Show ended when the drummers gave out, then Jenna's mom led her ladies off stage as the house lights came up.

"What a waste of time," Jaycee said.

"No way," I said. "I'm ready to hug the world now. We should talk, okay?"

"About what?" She wouldn't look me in the eyes. Maybe she was afraid I was going to lecture her about dressing like a Paige wannabe, but there was no use in that. Nobody wants advice, and no one stops anything until they're scarred from it.

"Just walk with me," I said.

***

Outside Jaycee rested on a bench while we watched the men from The Freak Show load their drums and costumes back into their minivan. They were dads again.

"We'll be late for English." She pulled a dandelion out of the grass and twisted its stem into a knot.

"No, we won't. Jenna's mom has to change first. We're cool."

"Are we?" she asked. I said sure, but that didn't lift whatever had her pinned down inside.

"It's a new year, and after this we're gone unless they change the rules again. You ever think about what you want to do?"

"I have to take guitar this year and a music composition course for my electives. Maybe that will make me an artist. Who knows?"

"I don't mean school, like with your life," I said. "This is going to be over soon. What do you want to do?"

"I don't have a plan like that. I just want to be happy," she said, "but that's a lot to ask."

"No one's happy unless they're doing what they want. Happy isn't something you can decide to be. It's like wishing for world friendship you know?"

"What do you want to do?" She blew on the dandelion's head and sent white fluff onto the breeze.

"I was thinking about maybe learning to make movies so when I get shipped off, if I do, maybe I can do that."

"Would that make you happy?" she asked. "Going away? Making movies?"

I stood up and motioned toward the doors as the tribe of dads drove away. "Something has to. I mean, we're lucky just to be here, right?"

"That's what they say." She wound her hair into a ponytail. "We have more chances to figure out what we want than normal kids, and we've got time."

\*\*\*

Jenna's mom hadn't come in yet when Jaycee and I made it to our first-period English class. Six achiever kids had taken the desks in the very front as usual so my crew was posted up on the love seat and bean bags that made up the rest of the furniture. The Dream Academy said that even the classrooms were designed to let us find our own space as if that was vital for learning. With her mom out, Tyler went back to torturing Jenna to pass the time. "I bet your dad loves the way your mom shakes it," he said. "He probably has her dance for him every night."

"Shut up, Tyler. My dad can't stand her either. He wants me out of this place as much as I do." Jenna said. "I bet she only volunteers with special needs kids so there's no way to completely hate her."

"What special needs kids?" I asked.

"Oh, my mom does these art classes for mentally handicapped kids over the summer," Jenna said. "I'm sure it's for her ego, to feel like she's changing lives or whatever."

"Don't be mean," Hanna said. "That's sweet."

"It probably takes slow kids to deal with her," Tyler said. "Hey Jenna, you ever wonder if you're a little *special*? Like, if your mom is the reason you got picked?"

"Leave her alone." Hanna struggled to get comfortable in her bean bag chair. "She's smart. She can't help it if her mom works here."

"I'm trying to have fun. You don't have to act like my mother you know?" Tyler pushed the side of Hanna's bean bag until she almost fell off it before he caught her. I couldn't stand the way he picked on her, then saved her at the last minute, but it got results.

When Jenna's mom came in I was glad she'd changed into her usual droopy shirt and wavy skirt combo instead of staying dressed up like she belonged in a harem. It was the least she could do. "I hope you like our opening show," she said. "Now I'm sure you all know my name by now, but if you don't it's Carol. Let's get started." She handed out envelopes with our interest evaluation tests along with an ink pen and a board to write on. The tests were useless since there was no way a test could point out our path in life, especially at eight in the morning when we were half-dead.

***

The Dream Academy made a huge deal out of the interest evaluation tests on their website and ads. They swore that letting us find our own way would make "Every dream kid their own singular star in the sky." But if everyone was a star, then no one was, right?

"You have ten minutes to do your best, but don't think. Just be open and honest," Jenna's mom sat on the top of her desk all cool-teacher, while I opened my test and tried to ignore Paige draped across the futon across from me. She chewed her candy necklace and watching her mouth work it was too much to take.

The interest evaluations were supposed to be personality tests I guess, but they weren't like the ones I'd taken for my therapists before. Those were no sweat. All I had to do was figure out what wouldn't make me come off crazy. Sometimes I had to rate how happy or sad I felt that day or circle feelings off a list, but that was it. See, therapists and psychiatrists only knew what I let out, and they hinted what I shouldn't admit to, like thinking about suicide and stuff. The interest evaluations were so insane there was no way to know what they were supposed to judge.

The others started their tests, and even though it felt good to have my crew together for most of my classes the achiever kids bothered me. I only recognized one of them, this girl Heather, who was bent on being President of the World someday, and the other achiever kids were exactly like her. Some of them probably believed the rumor that I was a dealer, even though I'd never sold in my life. I didn't trust them. That's why I kept my circle small, to avoid ending up in a story I couldn't control. My nerves sparked at the thought of those achiever kids judging me, of the test scoring my insides, and as soon as Jenna's mom turned away I popped a Xanax to chill out.

The test was opened in my lap, but I couldn't focus enough to read it. The sound of Jenna's mom's bare feet smacking against the floor made my anxiety worse. When she made her way to me she put her hand on my arm, and that cranked the voltage in my brain higher until my hands trembled. I wanted to tell her to step off but was afraid to say anything in case I started to do that dumb stutter-mumble thing I did when my nerves took over. When she took her hand off me she smiled to play friendly. That was another one of her issues: she smiled too much. Maybe people like you better if you smile, whether it's fake or not. Jaycee started to sing to herself, and if I'd slept the night before the sound of it would've helped.

"No need for first-day jitters," Jenna's mom said. "Just put down the first thing that comes to mind." Then she went to her desk and eyed us hopefully.

The first page of my interest evaluation asked if I liked Thai food, what color my favorite socks were, and which holiday I loved most. There were over fifty questions, so I had to answer in a hurry to finish. I didn't have time to think about what I was letting out, but that was probably the point. I used my worst handwriting so nobody could read what I wrote and get the wrong idea.

"Time's up," Jenna's mom said after I got the first fifteen questions done. "Put your tests back into their envelopes, seal them tight, and bring them to me." She patted her hand on her desk, and we stacked our envelopes into a pile while she hung a corkboard on the wall.

"What's that for?" Jaycee asked. The board was covered with pink note cards with the names of electives written on them.

"You got me." I searched for a card marked "Digital Film-making" but didn't see one. Maybe she ran out of cards or forgot it.

"I hope you didn't think those tests were important," Jenna's mom said, then sat a trash can by her desk. "This semester you will let go of who you think you are and concentrate on the *you* that hasn't been discovered." She took the first envelope from the stack, tore it in half, and dropped it into the trashcan. She kept on that way until they were all garbage. She must've assumed that production would inspire us to open our minds, but the sight of the achiever kids hate-facing her brought her back to reality.

"She can't help herself," Jenna said through her teeth. "She always has to prove how smart and different she is, and that just proves that she doesn't know anything."

"This semester is about diving into the unknown," Jenna's mom said super positive to win us back. Then she took a bag from her desk and held it up. "Let's see where fate takes you." She reached into the bag and pulled out a fistful of darts. "Don't be afraid of risk. Get in line, and we'll jump together!" Jenna left as the rest of us lined up to throw our darts.

One of the achiever girls went first, and her darts landed into cards marked "Asian Horticulture," and "Sitcom Philosophy." After Jenna's mom handed her the cards she moped back to her seat.

Paige threw her darts without aiming. I missed what she got, but she was on her phone again before I had a chance to ask. My darts stuck in "Abstract Art" and "History of Punk Rock." Jenna's mom handed them to me, totally thrilled that I'd landed in her Abstract Art class, but I sulked back to the loveseat. I was supposed to have a choice, but she'd flipped the rules. Maybe that was supposed to teach us that making plans is useless.

"Life is about random encounters, about finding the love you never expected. Now write your names on your cards and leave them for me. I'll make sure you're enrolled by tonight. And don't forget your first homework assignment for this class is due tonight," she said as the bell rang.

\*\*\*

In the hallway after English class, I heard the girl who'd thrown the first dart bitching to that achiever kid Heather that she didn't want to spend four months studying reruns and bonsai trees instead of real subjects, but Heather stuck out her chin reminded her that Carol meant for us to appreciate that learning was its own reward. One class in, and Heather was a true believer.

"What'd you get?" Jaycee asked, while I searched to find where Paige had run off to.

"Not filmmaking which is all I wanted. You're lucky that your music scholarship sets your electives. At least you get to do what you're into."

"It sucks that you didn't get what you wanted, but you don't need a class to make movies, right?" Jaycee said, "Maybe Jenna's mom is right though. What if you don't know what will make you happy?"

"Jaycee, if I don't know what'll make me happy then nobody does," I said. "You need to stop buying into everything you're told. It's pathetic." She dropped her head and turned away. If I'd been a better person then I would have taken it back, but it felt better to see her hurting too.

***

My mother was still in her yoga outfit on the couch, hypnotized by this show where guys dressed like doctors talked about juice cleanses when I got home. My little brother Johnny was stripped to his Batman underwear, and busy hacking on the throw pillows with a foam sword. I thought about going upstairs before either of them noticed me, but remembered my list from the night before. That made me hang around for a while as the TV doctors held up kiwis and pointed to a blowup of what skin looks like as it ages.

"Where are his clothes?" I asked my mom as Johnny swung his sword like a berserker.

"What? Oh, he got muddy so I made him strip. How was school?" She turned off the TV with a frown as if I'd robbed her from discovering the secret to staying young forever.

"It was the usual sideshow, but it's only the first day."

"You might not understand why they do what they do, but it's for a reason. If they didn't have a plan then they wouldn't have the reputation they do."

"You can buy a reputation," I said. "It's called advertising."

"Don't be smart."

"I'm not. I'm completely dumb."

Johnny hacked at my legs with his sword and kept his chin buried into his chest like a boxer as he let out a growl. I put a knee up to fend him off, but he was too wired to stop his attack.

"Relax," I said. "I don't want to play war with you."

My mom took his sword away, and he asked for yogurt. "Your father said it's time to get him on some medicine. I'm sure he's got ADHD."

"He's five," I said. "He's just being five."

She led him to the dining room, and I followed. Once he had his yogurt he calmed down and slurped the goo, beaming.

"See," I said. "He doesn't need pills."

"Your father says they have low-dose patches now," she said. "And give school a chance for once. You're fortunate to have so many options."

"What you say?" Johnny asked with strawberry goop smeared across his cheeks.

"She said you need a patch."

"Like a pirate?" He slapped one hand over his eye, then plunged his plastic spoon into his yogurt cup.

"Kind of," I said. "Where is dad?"

"He's gone again," she said. There was something she wasn't saying, and it showed. "He'll be back soon."

"Whatever. He hides in his office when he's home, anyway."

"He's working hard so he can pay for your school, Bryce. Be glad you don't have to worry about that yet."

"Whatever," I said. "He just needs a reason to feel good about disappearing all the time." While she washed off Johnny's skinny chest with a dish towel I escaped upstairs to forget about the choices I had lost to chance.

*** 

My body was still static in my room that night. When I don't sleep my anxiety is hopeless to manage. It swells up in me, makes me feel like I've got to fight and cry at the same time. Like I can't breathe. Like being crushed, holding in a scream that's trying to claw its way out of my throat. It wasn't fair that I had to throw darts for my electives. I got played. The school forever talked about our finding our own path, but Jenna's mom proved that was a joke.

I logged into my school account and read about the electives I was stuck with until Christmas. Jenna's mom taught the Abstract Art class, which meant that I had to deal with her sappy lessons twice a day for the next four months since I had her in English too. I doubted I'd last that long.

My History of Punk Rock class was online, which was a plus, even if it was taught by this burnout named Kenny Klimax. There was an email from him waiting for me that read, "Details for class coming. Mostly have to listen to tracks until they leave teeth marks on your brain. Playlist soon. Listen to this for now— Rise Above, Kenny." His email had an attachment for this song called "Parents" by a band called Descendents. The song wasn't about getting money or shouting how swag you are like normal music but I liked the words. I wasn't a toy, and one day I might explode.

The song got me juiced to take on Jenna's mom, so I went to the web page for our class to do my English homework. She'd posted her prompt, and it was my turn to set her straight for once.

Bryce Hughes Advanced English Composition Personal Inventory

1. Tell me about yourself? Who *are* you?

My name is Bryce. I'm seventeen. I have a father, a mother, and a brother who's bound to get patched with meds soon because that's what kids get now. He doesn't understand what a patch is, and my mom probably won't tell him.

2. How do you feel about your personal writing history, or literature in general?

Writing is easy. Like if your grandmother died or you're anorexic you write about that and get an A. No teacher can fail you if you write about something tragic. They're not allowed to.

3. Is there any area of writing that you feel personally drawn to?

No. I wanted to learn to make movies, but you forced me to throw darts instead of giving me a choice. You can't tell the truth when you write because no one cares about your problems. They're too busy with their own.

4. Tell me your biggest fear when it comes to writing.

I'm afraid you'll bore us with pep talks. I'm scared we'll have to write about why drugs or racism are bad. It's like our teachers want to make sure that we're good kids. We know who we are.

5. What are three things about yourself that I wouldn't guess?

1. My mom has a tattoo on her back that's supposed to be a butterfly, but it looks like a blue waffle. She's way too proud of it. I don't like to go to the pool with her because of it.

2. I have a lot of drugs, but they're from doctors so it's all good. Some are mine, and some are from my dad.

3. I searched you online. I read your blog. You wanted to be an artist or a poet before you turned teacher, but now you're stuck. You probably gave up. I saw those pics of your painting and read some of your poems so now I know more about you than you'll ever know about me.

After my homework was done I reached inside my dresser, pulled out My List of Fantastic Promises, and drew a line through the number eight.

1. Find out what makes me happy.
2. Save the party virgins when I can.
3. Make Paige love me again.
4. Figure out things with Jaycee.
5. Listen to music that's not on the radio.
6. Lay low in school.
7. Don't get caught up in other kids' drama.
8. ~~Spend more time with my family~~.
9. Learn to make movies.

I shouldn't have counted the ten minutes I spent with my mom and Johnny as a success, but I had to feel like I was making progress. Then I crashed on my blanket and waited for the sun to go away.

I texted Paige to see what she'd gotten for electives but doubted she'd get back to me if she was off with her new boyfriend. Even if she wasn't smoked out and brain dead she'd delete my text just to stay in control. She'd never wanted me if I wanted her.

All I wanted to do was sleep, but it was useless since the middle of the night was when my stress hit hardest, worries about what I didn't do and should've. I pictured Jaycee's sad face in the hall when I left her and decided to make up for that if only to feel better about myself.

"I like when u sing," I wrote and hit send. Tyler was able to smooth over worse with less. Maybe all anybody needs is a reason to feel proud.

I turned my phone off and drank Nyquil to drift away. The first day was over. There were months left to find what I needed to be happy, even if I didn't get to choose what it was.

# Chapter 4
## Kids in Commercials

PAIGE WAS so close to being a commercial kid. I mean, they all kind of looked like she did, before she went stoner, at least. In beginning, you saw pictures of them kicking a soccer ball, dressed for graduation, or hugging a kitten. At the start, those kids were totally safe and had no clue what's about to happen. Paige was that way too.

The commercial kids were popular like Paige. Kids looked up to her since she acted so mature and was dating a college guy. Maybe that's why it happened. Whenever you think you're bulletproof, you're not.

Paige's family was rich like one of those perfect families on a TV show so that may have helped her odds. The commercial kids had TV families too.

***

Outside the auditorium, I tried to change Tyler's mind about putting Jaycee to the test, but he wanted to be sure she wouldn't turn on us since as she was all straight edge. The way he saw it if she didn't break out of her good girl phase soon there'd be nothing to stop her from going informant if we ever caught major heat. She'd hung around and stayed on the edge for too long, and it was time to find out if she was down for us.

"She's solid," I said. "You're going to get her bent."

"She's up for it," Tyler said. "I told her she has to get wild for once you know?"

"I don't care what you told her," I said, as a teacher opened the doors to the auditorium. "If she's coming so am I."

"Of course." He smirked. "I promised her you would."

The Dream Academy made us watch the commercial kids every year, unless our parents signed a permission slip to excuse us. Jaycee was the only one of our crew who'd ever gotten hers signed. In three years, she'd never heard the speeches or seen the gory pictures the cops shared. Their pictures were worse than any horror movie I'd ever seen, and the first time I saw them they shook me bad.

***

After the first month of classes, we had to go to a program every Friday. The commercial kids always came first. The school put off the programs until we had our classes down before they scared us with real life, but our school was screwed up enough without thinking about dying.

The auditorium lights dimmed as we filed in. Funeral music played softly, but it didn't bother me because I knew what to expect. No matter how horrible something is, if you see it enough times you get used to it. I bet the first time the cops had to mop up a dead guy it tore them up, but after a while, it was probably the same as mopping the floor. My crew was as cold as the cops. We'd seen it all and more.

I slumped in the back row and tried to sleep, but Tyler and Hanna were whispering in front of me so there was no chance to pass out, since when kids whispered I worried that they're talking about me. Jaycee sat next to me, and

I kicked the back of Tyler's seat since her showing up had to be his work. It was wrong to pressure her into sitting through the commercial kids when she didn't have to.

"Hey!" Tyler said. "She has to see this so she can learn to forget it, right?" He had a point. The more things you can forget, the better off you are. If I'd been able to erase Paige and took our random hook-ups for the nothing they were, my life would've been one big birthday party.

The auditorium went black, and the only lights came from kids playing with their phones in the dark. When the principal took the mic, all the phone screens went out, and the room got quiet. I hoped the new mom was hot.

"I want to thank you for coming today," Principal Keys said as if we had much of a choice. "These programs are never easy, but they're important. What you're about to see is disturbing, but it might save your life. It's easy to feel invincible when you're young, but you'll soon find out that's not the case." He started to say something else but lost his nerve and left the stage.

"How long do you think this will take?" Tyler asked Hanna, but she was playing Candy Crush on her phone inside her purse and only shrugged.

Once Principal Keys left the stage, the new mom took his place. It was always a mom. Dads can't talk about what they've been through. The new mom didn't dress down like the others who'd come to speak. Instead, she had on skinny jeans, a fluffy white top, and red high heels. I guess being on stage made her feel like she was a star, like *The Real Housewives of Dead Kids*. Every program had to have a new mom since after a mom gave her speech she probably couldn't tear up anymore. I mean, how long can someone cry?

Maybe Paige survived because she didn't believe in God like her parents, or maybe it was because our city was too big for people to notice. The commercial kids all went to church and lived in these little towns where their death was a total tragedy. They got a moment of silence at the football game, and their friends lit candles outside their schools to show how much they missed them. Maybe that's why Paige made it. Maybe God only lets you die if you believe in him, and you're dying makes everyone stop talking for a minute.

The mom started by saying how difficult it was for her to have a baby in the first place. She gave these embarrassing details about her husband's sperm count and their in-vitro sessions. Some of the kids laughed, not because they thought it was funny, but because they'd never heard an adult talk that way. She ignored them, and her story sounded like science class until the slideshow started. A baby picture of her kid came on the screen behind her, and she called him her miracle. Next to me, Jaycee seemed crazy worried since she didn't know what to expect.

"Think of it as a bad movie," I said, but she was frozen stiff. Maybe the commercial kid reminded her of somebody she knew. "Tyler is right. Ignore all this, and you'll be gold." She held my hand, and I let her. Her fingers felt like popsicles as the commercial kid's pictures from little league, from family vacations and trick-or-treating, played across the screen. I put my other hand on top of hers so it didn't feel like holding hands with a snowman.

The weird part was that the commercial kid's mom watched the pictures. That never happened. Usually, they talked about how much they loved their kid and said they'd never be the same without taking their eyes off us. Then they left before their kid's commercial came on.

"She's got guts," Tyler said.

"I bet she only wants to see if it still hurts," I said.

The mom lasted until her kids' prom pictures started, then she lost it and rushed off stage. No mom could make it to the commercial, guts or not.

Jaycee started to cry but tried to hide it. I didn't blame her for making the mistake of imagining the kid as an actual person. If I hadn't spent so much time daydreaming about what it'd be like if I didn't exist I would've cried too. It's not that I didn't want to cry. I just couldn't.

The commercial played the kid's pictures again over the dates when he was born and died. In the end, his prom picture came on to show where he'd spent his last night on Earth. He was preppy and smiling. Then the words DON'T TEXT AND DRIVE took up the entire screen in giant white letters. The auditorium stayed dark to let us think about what that kid could've been if he hadn't texted while driving. In the dark white squares from kids on their phones lit up. The commercial kid had vanished.

The lights came up as a cop pulled two storage tubs on stage. He started to flop out these long plastic bags that smacked when they hit the floor. The stage was covered with them by the time he finished.

"You might not recognize these," he said without offering his name, "but they're body bags. Each one of these represents a young man or woman your age who lost their life due to texting while operating a motor vehicle last year."

I held Jaycee to keep her steady. Her mouth moving, but no words came out. She was counting the bags. I told Tyler we should go, but he blew me off.

"This past month alone I've knocked on the doors of three mothers like the one who spoke today and told them their children were dead. I'm not only here to show you the danger of distracted driving but also to save myself the trouble of ever knocking on another." The cop looked down at the carpet of body bags and bowed his head.

I told Tyler we had to leave, that Jaycee had had enough already. "The cop is about to show more crash shots. You want her to have that hanging on her?"

Tyler got that a horror show wasn't going to help him get Jaycee in the right mind to test her so he gave in. We all walked out together. None of the teachers stopped us. They were used to kids leaving before the gore parade continued. You can take a story no matter how depressing it is. Everyone has a story that'll make you miserable, but a story is different than witnessing the bloody truth. When we made it through the doors I felt proud to have rescued her from those pictures.

\*\*\*

The four of us chilled out back and waited for the program to end. The sky was blue and clear as if nothing was wrong anywhere in the world. The other kids who'd checked out early stood around talking or smoking cigarettes since the only adult outside was a janitor who was there to make sure we didn't bounce. The janitors didn't care what we did as long as they didn't have to clean it up. I dug the way they hated being at school as much as we did.

Hanna opened her purse and handed Tyler a cigarette. He took a draw from it and passed it to Jaycee, but she pushed it away. I hoped she would change her mind and stay home. She didn't need to prove anything to me.

"Don't stress about those kids," Hanna said, scooting closer to Jaycee. She liked to play mom sometimes to balance the bitch shit she pulled. "That's only the first program, you know? We still have the razor kids, and the skeleton kids to look forward to. Maybe even the naked kids, too."

"I can't get used to it," Jaycee said. She took the cigarette from Hanna and tried to drag off it, but totally failed.

Hanna took it back before she coughed herself to death. "Life is sad enough without showing everything that can go wrong."

"Who are your favorite kids they throw on us?" Tyler asked, talking to forget.

"They're so many to choose from," Hanna said. "The commercial kids who text and die so they get to be on TV. The razor kids who cut themselves up to show how awful their life is. The skeleton kids who never eat or throw up when they do. I guess my favorite ones are the naked kids who sext the wrong guy and end up going viral. They're the worst."

"You think it's their fault?" Jaycee asked.

Hanna dropped her cigarette and crushed it. "Who cares? It's funny."

"Why do they show us that?" Jaycee asked. Her legs trembled until she had to hold them still.

"Because they think it'll save us," Tyler said. "They're wrong."

"Have you seen Paige today?" I asked Hanna to change the subject. She hadn't answered my texts for days and had skipped out again to hang with her college boyfriend.

"I haven't seen her since she hugged me last week," Hanna said. "She's totally fake."

"She's just off again," I said. "If she shows tonight have her text me."

"Tonight is for the new recruits only," Hanna said. "I have to get them trained."

The crowd from the program let out and made car crash noises in the hall as the janitor motioned us inside. I grabbed Jaycee's hand again and squeezed it. "Ignore that kid. He's only a picture now."

"Right," Jaycee said. "But the pictures are the worst part."

"So let them go." I put my hand on her leg and imagined where we'd be when night came. She was determined to shut Tyler up for good, and if she wanted to be bad I had to let her. There's no point in being good if you don't understand that it saves you.

*** 

Hanna lived in this subdivision between two huge parks. Every house was surrounded by trees even though the nearest Starbucks was less than a mile away. Tyler and I stalked up the trail that snaked between the trees and houses until we got to her backyard. He'd brought a butcher knife to scare the new gymnast girls, but I'd made him leave it in his SUV. Hanna promised that her parents were gone, but if they weren't her Police Chief dad would definitely shoot a kid with a knife before asking questions. That'd be too lame a way to die to score a commercial.

We climbed over the split-rail fence behind her house then snuck across her lawn. Tyler got all Seal Team Six and threw me hand signals to stop or move. The night was warm and clear, and it felt good to play army again the way we did when we were little.

Tyler eased up the stairs of Hanna's back deck to check out the living room while I waited for him to give me the sign to move. After a second, he slid open a door and I followed him inside. Hanna had played by the script.

We left the lights off as we made our way from the living room to the kitchen. Tyler took slow ninja steps until he reached the fridge, then stuck two beers into the pouch of his hoodie before closing it and going down the basement stairs. I stayed ninja too so none of the girls heard us. At the bottom of the stairs, he busted through the door with this maniacal yell. The new girls screamed too and jumped onto each other, while Hanna broke down.

"You girls ready to get crazy?!" Tyler cracked both beers, then poured them into his mouth at the same time. There must be some playbook for spoiled rich bros when it comes to partying because they all acted like cavemen. They had to show off how drunk they were, and by the end of the night ended up headbutting a wall or fighting with their girlfriends to prove what alpha males they were.

"You aren't supposed to be here," Hanna said as if she wasn't in on it, then threw her arms around Tyler's soaked shirt. She was the only girl in the basement I recognized which made me nervous. The worst thing you can do is go wild with kids you don't know since there's no way to know how they'll twist what went down.

I crashed on this sofa with Tyler and checked out the recruits who were on the floor around a coffee table. Each of them had a paper plate in front of them covered with pills or mints, and cans of Monster to drink.

The alarm on Hanna's pink phone went off, and the girls swallowed one of the pills or mints off their plates then chased it with their energy drink like they were programmed or something. After she made sure they downed their dose she sat on Tyler's lap and held up six fingers. That made him lose it, and he said before too long those girls would be tweaking like meth heads. When I asked why, Hanna pointed at their plates.

"They have to pop a diet pill every half hour," she said, but when I didn't laugh she said it was for their own good because they had to make the weight to compete.

"You need to lose weight too." Tyler patted Hanna's butt, and she went sour before stomping back to her recruits. "Think about it," he said.

I texted Paige to see why she'd skipped out, while Hanna disappeared into the bathroom. The new girls stared at their plates to avoid looking at us. They were already on the wrong side of the story.

Hanna came back and dumped the girls' plates into a garbage bag. She glared at Tyler, but instead of apologizing or playing what he said off like a joke he let it hang between them. She'd never admit it, but I bet that's what made her a secret skeleton kid.

When the plates and Monsters were gone, Hanna had the girls stand shoulder to shoulder in a row, but they were too jittery to keep a straight line. "Watching your weight is only the start. You need cardio too!" She did jumping jacks and told the girls to step up. Their faces were red and slick.

"Should I take a picture of this?" Tyler asked.

"Get real," Hanna sat on the arm of the sofa. "This never happened."

"Not even one picture for you?" he asked.

"You think I want this on the record?" she said. "And I'm skinnier than those bitches."

"Yeah, but they're brand new. What's your excuse?"

"We should go. It's getting late," I said. Paige wasn't answering my texts, and the scene was too wicked to hang around.

"This is nothing," Hanna said. "You have no idea what the seniors did to me when I started."

"They probably only wanted to be sure you were one of them," Tyler said. "That you were down to go through whatever, you know?"

Hanna told the girls to speed up as we made our way to the stairs, but before we left, Tyler told her to get her workout on. He laughed when he said it, but it made her slam the door shut with a bang.

We made it across the yard and over the fence into the woods. The moon was yellow, and the ground was wet with dew. "I'll build her back up," Tyler said, more to himself than to me. I kept quiet. What was done was done.

\*\*\*

Tyler moved his gym bag out of his passenger seat then got into the backseat so I had to drive to pick up Jaycee at a bus stop. It was past midnight, and he doubted that she'd show. The only reason he thought she might was that he said she was thirsty for me. I told him she knew better, and that only freshman girls imagined they were in these high school fairytales.

When we got to the bus stop, Jaycee had on the hoodie I'd given her. That made me wonder if Tyler saw something I didn't. As I drove his Escalade he texted Hanna to make up. Jaycee sang to herself, and part of me wished that she'd flaked. There was no way to rescue her then. She was glowing as if she was about to have the best night of her life. I probably acted that way when Chelle picked me up back when I was a party virgin. Nothing good comes from dreaming. Hanna was a sweetheart before she started gymnastics. Maybe our entire generation turned cold because of nights that were meant to be magic but turned into nightmares.

Tyler texted as Jaycee sang a song I'd never heard before. By the time we reached the country club, it was as if I hadn't been driving at all. We rolled up the drive with the moon lighting our way and parked in the employee lot. Jaycee got out and scanned the grounds to make sure we were in the clear, then Tyler punched in the code to the servants' entrance. It worried me that she was so excited to get stolen away like a princess.

The main mansion at the country club was massive and smelled like cigars and pine trees. I used the light from my phone to see where I was going, but Tyler ran ahead of us blind and never hit a single chair. Jaycee held my hand the way kids do in haunted houses as we followed him up one staircase then another until we reached a room I'd never seen before. It was some kind of gym.

"No lights," he said, then left. Jaycee sat on a weight bench while I walked around this indoor pool and tried to hide that I was checking my texts. The glass wall facing the golf course looked like shower glass from the steam rising off the water.

"What's this?" I asked Jaycee. Paige had sent out a group text, and on the screen was a blurry picture that looked like a brick with peach smudges on it. She wrinkled her face and said she didn't care.

"Tell me the truth. Why are you here?"

"Didn't you want me to come?"

"I want you to be you. Breaking in to get wild isn't your style. What does it prove?"

"Nothing," she said, "but it'll make the others stop treating me like a party virgin."

"You need to stop apologizing for being yourself. I wish I was steady like you."

"The others only call me straight edge because they don't have the balls to call me poor to my face. After this, there won't be anything they can say about me out loud."

"I'm not going to let you go too far. This is stupid you know?"

"Yeah, but sometimes I wonder how far I can go," Jaycee said. "Like, what I'm capable of."

"Tonight's the wrong time to figure that out. We shouldn't stay here long. The rule is we grab and go. It's always been that way."

"Maybe tonight is special?"

The sound of glass hitting glass brought back that haunted house vibe as Tyler came in with his arms full of bottles. He unscrewed one, then passed the other to Jaycee before stuffing the rest in his gym bag. The room was blue and wavy from the lights under the water.

***

At first Jaycee struggled to manage more than a sip, but Tyler kept on her to act like a pro, so she sped up until she slipped away inside.

"Partying at our level is for lettermen, not for freshmen. You're a junior. It's about time you earned your letter," he said. "There aren't many girls who can hang with Bryce and me, but we believe in you. We believe!" He pumped his fist like a cheerleader. "So what are you going to do?"

"She is above the game," I said. "We should take her home."

"No games tonight," he said. "This is only a test."

Jaycee wobbled to her feet. Her mouth hung open as she lifted her bottle into the air. "I have no idea what you're saying," she slurred.

"I'm saying let's go swimming!" Tyler cannonballed into the pool with his clothes on and splashed us. Jaycee and I broke up while he acted like a dolphin and motioned for us to join him.

"Areyagonna?" she asked.

"No," I said. "I'm your bodyguard tonight. This is what you wanted."

For a second, she stopped as if the pool and the bottle in her hand were pieces that didn't fit together. Tyler pressed her to dive in until she had no way to say no. He'd convinced her that she had to fit in, and I'd let him do it. She fell awkwardly into the water and bobbed up wide-eyed and gasping until he swam to her. Then he bearhugged her and spun her around. She never took her eyes off me. Each turn made her shrink away until she broke free and doggie-paddled to the ladder. After she pulled herself out she gagged water onto the floor.

"Bad enough now?" she asked me when she could speak.

"Let's just leave already," I said. The later you stay where you don't belong, the worse it gets.

"Not yet." Tyler muscled himself out of the pool and wrapped his arms around her from behind. He whispered in her ear, then moved in to kiss her. Her arms flexed as she bowed back, but he kept on until he was inches from her lips.

"I'm not going to do it. I've got expensive taste." Tyler laughed, then let her go. She fell to the floor like a wet towel.

"We're done here! She passed your test already."

"Sure," he said. "See, she's not so good after all."

Tyler had his story and went back to playing nice. He stole a tennis outfit from the gift shop for her to change into, and after she did we loaded his score of stolen liquor bottles and drove off. She cradled the plastic bag with her drenched clothes to her chest and shivered the entire way back. Her fairytale didn't turn out the way she'd imagined, and it was obvious that she was already trying to forget it.

***

It was past three in the morning when we dropped Jaycee off at the bus stop. I asked her to come back with us to my car so I could take her home, but she wouldn't listen and didn't want me to touch her as I walked her to the bus stop. I hated to leave her by herself alone in the middle of the night, but without my own ride I was afraid of getting stranded too.

"Are you sure you'll be okay?" I asked.

"I can take care of myself. I don't need you feeling sorry now."

"I want you to be cool though," I said, as Tyler honked his horn.

"Are you cool?" she asked. "Do you have expensive tastes?"

"Tyler's an asshole, but he can't help it." I went to hug her, but she stepped off.

"It doesn't matter. Forget it, right?"

"Right," I said wishing I could get an Uber for her without coming off as a rich kid trying to pay his way out of hurting her feelings.

"You're a *great* bodyguard," she said. Her eyes were red and watery. "Am I bad enough now?"

"No. You're beautiful. I'll text you." She collapsed onto a bench under the ugly orange glow of a streetlamp to wait for her bus as I got into Tyler's Escalade. I asked him to wait until it came, but he drove away. I stared off at the stars and wondered if I'd ever be able to save someone for real and cross number two off My List of Fantastic Promises:

2. Save the party virgins when I can.

\*\*\*

On Monday this is how Hanna told the story. Paige was on her way home from her college boyfriend's house, and only half-high so that had nothing to do with what happened to since she smoked more than any of us. It wasn't because she was texting and driving either. That's what all the commercial kids did. They sent a text, one of their friends answered it, and when they looked down at their phone, in that one second when their eyes were off the road they died. It only took a second, a few feet left or right, and they were dead forever. Maybe that's why Paige didn't get to be a commercial kid. She wasn't texting. She could do that with one thumb without watching the screen like a pro. See, she was sending out the pic of what she'd stolen.

Paige isn't a thief, but sometimes you need proof if you want kids to believe you. She took the picture and hit send, but when she looked up she was off the road. She freaked and jerked the wheel and lost control. Her Lexus sideswiped all these parked cars before it stopped, and when it finally did the windshield caved in on her. See, real commercial kids go head-on and die. Paige said the cop from the program was the one who found her all messed up and crying, and that he didn't say a word to her.

All the kids had heard the story by the time I found her. She had hidden out in one of the study rooms above the library so no one would ask her about her face. Every kid with a cast gets tired of going over the same story, but I had to see her damage for real.

I sat next to her, and she ignored me until she got that I wasn't going to leave. She had her messy blonde hair over her face, but it didn't hide the stitches that wound up the side of her head. I tried not to stare at them when I asked why she crashed. She didn't explain and just slid me her phone. On the screen was that picture she'd sent, the one I'd shown Jaycee at the county club.

"I found it in my boyfriend's closet, and was not about to let that go," she said with a giggle that sounded like it was mostly from the memory of something funny.

"Why were you in his closet?"

Paige tore a sheet of paper into strips to keep her hands busy and her eyes off me. "I was checking to see if he kept his stash in there, like a whole brick I could gank, but instead I found that!" She pointed at her phone.

"What is it?"

She touched the stitches on her cheek like she had to feel the threads to make sure they were there, then raked her hair to cover her bandaged ear. Her eyes got big as she held her phone to my face. "A sex book!"

"A sex book?"

"Yes! Like a how-to book about doing it. Isn't that hilarious?"

"You almost died over a sex book? What happened to it?"

"I don't know," she said. "Probably still in my Lexus. They towed it off after the wreck."

"When your mom finds it in your car she's going to freak." I wanted to tell her what a moron she'd become but seeing her stitched together and bruised made it impossible to do anything but hold her.

"Yeah." She slid away from me, "but she needs to laugh, right? She spent the whole weekend crying every time she saw my face."

"Dumb," I said.

"Right?"

# Chapter 5
## Kids Who Sweat

**EVERY FALL** semester The Dream Academy required juniors to get a job for six weeks. It sucked, but a lot of kids had it worse than we did. We couldn't touch the girls at Saint Mary's when it came to suffering. Paige's sister Kelsey went there because her mom figured it'd help her be her own person or something. Kelsey said she had to volunteer for three hours every week or else she couldn't graduate with her class. She knew girls who had to get in a van after school to feed homeless people. She said they didn't even go to a shelter, but were driven around for hours by their chaperones until they had found enough homeless people to give apples and sandwiches to.

Kelsey was lucky since she only had to sort through the donations for the school's thrift store. It only sucked when she had to go through bags of gross clothes. One time she showed us this picture on her phone of these clothes that looked like they'd been fished out of the sewer.

"Who'd drop that off?" I'd asked.

"The devil," Kelsey said and meant it. Saint Mary's told kids the devil was everywhere, and she was sure he had his claws in Paige deep.

Dream Kids like us didn't have to deal with homeless people or nasty clothes, but we still had to work more than we wanted to as if it wasn't enough to take our regular classes and weird electives. In our junior year, we had to do this "Evolution through Labor" project for two months to learn the value of hard work and all, but most kids were slick enough to land cushy internships through their parents' connections.

***

The first week of October all the junior kids got called into the auditorium for this program about how we could be anything we wanted to be. Tyler came in late because he had to finish making a water filter out of sand and a milk jug for his wilderness survival elective, and I prayed whoever taught that class didn't teach him how to build a fire. If they did he'd burn down the country club for sure.

I searched for Paige before the program started, but was sorry when I found her. She was texting again and smirking all sunshine at whatever her boyfriend sent her. I tried not to care, but the fact that he studied books on sex made me afraid that he'd done things with her I'd never heard of, and that she'd never leave that kind of talent.

Jaycee dropped beside me as Principal Keys started the program. He didn't tell us what jobs to get, if we'd get paid real money, or anything useful. Instead, he walked in circles and rambled on about finding our calling, that thing deep inside ourselves we were meant to do. "I'm not talking about what you love now," he said, "because that will change. Most of you will see that what you love now won't matter in six months."

"That's depressing," Jaycee said. "If he loved computers so much why did he get shipped to us?" I shrugged and spied on Paige until it felt pathetic. Then I gave up.

Jenna's mom came on after the principal finished. In our Abstract Art class, she acted like she was from a different planet, and went barefoot most days. "I'm sure you know me from class or through my daughter, but I'm here today to talk candidly about my journey."

Jenna groaned as her mom sat yoga-style on the stage to show how different she was as if being different was her true calling. She hadn't stopped correcting me when I used her last name. "Call me Carol," she'd say, all miffed, "not Mrs. Lovins. You know better. That makes me sound so old." Jenna said her mom didn't shave her pits, which was hard to believe, but I figured she'd know.

"By the time I was twenty-five I'd dropped out of four different colleges. I had no direction," Jenna's mom talked the way kids do in group therapy sessions where they have to open up and decide what to leave out at the same time. "I had demons then. I was lost."

Jenna put on a serious shade since her mom had cursed her by not saying what her demons were. Kids were bound to press her for details for the rest of the day, and if she didn't have any it'd be a disaster. When kids don't have details they imagine the worst.

"But no matter how lost I was, I always had my art." Jenna huffed as her mom perked up. "I wrote poems on paper bags. I painted soda cans. I didn't see it then, but I loved creating with all my heart. Art was my true passion." She told us how she went to art school, did some crazy shows in Los Angeles, won all these awards, and eventually came to our school to share her calling with us. By the end, she talked fast about her gallery shows, about the poems she had published in magazines, and all the artists she knew who weren't much older than us. "They're doing it," she said. "You can do it too if you surrender everything else besides that one burning need. How many of you want to do it?!" The whole audience broke down and cheered.

"Your mom sure made a lot of kids want to do it," I said.

"She's an idiot," Jenna put her hands over her face. "Art doesn't pay. That's why she teaches. Art is a total waste of time."

"Don't say that," Jaycee said. "Music is art, right? Music matters."

"Is she any good?"

"She sucks," Jenna barked as if I was on her mom's side. "You should see our house. You can't even tell what her paintings are supposed to be. They look like a bunch of colors smeared together, and her poems don't even rhyme!"

"She does love art though," I said, but Jenna ignored me. If her dart game hadn't stuck me with Abstract Art I would've dropped it, but I blamed Jenna for not setting her mom straight from the start. If she had, maybe I would be making movies instead of waiting to get my homework from a burnout like Mr. Klimax who'd disappeared after the first day of school.

"If you hate your home so much, move to the party house," Jaycee said. "That way you won't have to deal with her."

"I'm going to. Things are screwed at home, and I can't deal with it anymore," Jenna said. We had to line up for our job forms before I found out what she meant, so I pictured her mom shooting up then passing out next to the toilet. Anything was possible if she had demons. A librarian passed me my forms for Evolution through Labor, but I crossed out its title on my way to class. We had our own name for it, "Sweat Time."

***

When I got home from school I found a note from my mom that said she was with Johnny at a play date and would be back later on. My dad was off on the drug business again. He'd missed Johnny's last two doctor appointments, and my mom was acid over it since it was his idea to get him patched in the first place. I didn't understand why she cared though. He worked so much that he was never around, and when he was home he stayed in his office. She had been a single parent for my entire life. She just hadn't realized it.

I liked the quiet of the empty house. For a while, I laid in bed listening to all that nothing. Before long though I had to move or else I'd pass out, so I checked my email. After two months of school, Mr. Klimax had finally sent the rundown for my History of Punk Rock class. I thought he'd blown it off, which was fine with me since we'd all get an A if it was on him, but he said he'd been touring and didn't have the internet. It was a weak excuse, but the class read like it'd be a breeze. All we had to do was download this massive play-list he'd put together, and listen to the songs over and over again until we got our final project. I downloaded it onto my phone, folded up my Sweat Timesheets, and left for the party house to game plan. On the drive to pick up Jaycee I played the first song, "Work-Rest-Play-Die" by Subhumans. It was this sped-up Irish drinking song and had some kind of political message that was lost on me. There was no need to stress though. If he was down to fake teaching, I was down to fake learning.

*** 

Jaycee waited outside her building reading her Sweat Timesheet when I rolled up. The wind blew leaves around the cracked parking lot and tousled her hair, and for a minute I wished that I could forget Paige and love her. She deserved someone who cared about her, who saw how choice she was, the way I did. She hadn't mentioned the night Tyler tested her after it went down, and I hadn't brought it up. Nothing said meant nothing happened.

"I finally got my work for History of Punk Rock," I said as she got in. "Do you ever have to listen to music for your classes? I've got this giant playlist to get through."

"We listen to music all the time," she said. "That's what music scholars do. Have you played it yet?"

"A little. The songs aren't normal. They're not about making dollars or sex you know? They're about being broke rejects, or fighting. It's all noise. I'm just listening to them until I figure out a way to pass."

"Music isn't about passing or failing. Let me hear one."

I thumbed my phone at the first stoplight and put on Black Flag's "Rise Above." It sounded like a fistfight and made Jaycee pound my dash along with the beat. I lifted my phone to shoot her whipping her head back and forth in a blur of joy. Then the light changed, and I cut the music.

"You didn't *love* that?!" she asked out of breath.

"It's not that," I said. "I have to concentrate on driving you know?" But I was just jealous that music had never taken me over like that before.

\*\*\*

Jenna's party house was an old A-frame in this older rundown part of town. Almost all the other houses on its street were foreclosed or abandoned, but she swore that when she was a kid it was the nice part of town. The front of the party house was all glass, and it was pretty beat up inside. The first time she invited us over it was hard to believe how Brady Bunch it was. The walls were the color of traffic cones, the carpet was thick green shag, and the bathroom baby blue. The furniture sagged, and the book-shelves were empty. There was a dry swimming pool in the backyard behind the house, and past it was a fenced-in dirt lot. No one else seemed to live within blocks of it so we could do whatever we wanted and no one would ever know. A long time ago though, when our parents were still in diapers, it had probably been a nice place to live.

The party house belonged to Jenna's grandfather, but he moved to Florida after her baby cousin drowned in the pool back when it was full. I guess the house felt like a morgue to him after that, and maybe that's why her parents never sold it. Jenna was real young when he drowned so being around the house and that pool must not have weighed on her the way it did the rest of her family.

Hanna was going to teach tumbling at the Y so her Sweat Time was set. Paige had texted Jenna that she had a plan, but she had to learn French first. According to her, we would never see her again if everything worked out. Sweat Time had her pipe-dreaming like a fiend.

The front door was unlocked so Jaycee and I came in and crashed on this ratty couch that smelled like stale beer and body odor to wait for the others to show. She put her legs on my lap while I plugged in my earbuds to avoid talking in case she brought up the country club. Maybe it would've been better if I'd cut her out and let her be just another scholarship kid. Tyler was cold like that, but she was too sweet to drop like that. Honestly, she was the only one of my crew I trusted.

I heard Jenna complaining about her mom to herself upstairs, but since I was running on no sleep I didn't get up to join in. Instead, I thumbed my phone to drown her out. Discharge's "Sweet Suburban Dream" came on and made me imagine what the party house looked like when it had a lawn and none of the walls had holes punched through them.

Jaycee crawled over to pull out one of my earbuds and listen along. "Better than the music on the radio." She bobbed her head. Maybe her classes made it easier for her to hear the words true through the static and shots.

"I'm only listening to this for class."

"That's nothing." She took my phone from me and scrolled through the playlist. "I have to actually study for my electives."

"I am studying, right?"

"Whatever. Send me that playlist." She got up to raid the fridge. I was glad she hadn't made a move on me. There was this buried part of her that craved all this attention from me that we both played off. Sometimes I had the same issue for her too, like we both had half a heart inside us that fit together but wouldn't admit it.

***

Jenna came downstairs and flopped on the couch like Jaycee and I weren't there. I guessed that being interrogated about her mom's demons by the other kids had her beat up so I grabbed a Diet Coke from the fridge and brought it to her with a Klonopin to help her unwind. She took it and slumped with a sigh. Whatever she had going on at home had to be truly black if she had her mind set on moving into a dump like the party house.

"We should talk," Jaycee said, but I plugged my earbuds back in and got up to meet Tyler at the door. He had his gym bag loaded heavy with his latest loot. When Jaycee saw him she got up and went to the kitchen to read her forms alone while he cracked two bottles for us. Job hunting was too much to deal with sober.

Tyler started in about all his problems with Hanna before we got our scams together. No one had asked him why he broke up with her, but it was important to him that we had no doubts that he came out on top.

"It had to happen," he said. "I need space, and she's always blowing up my phone or begging to hang. It got pitiful, you know?"

Tyler told Jaycee to come over and toast to his freedom, but she only gave him the finger and kept reading.

"Why'd you come to the party house if you don't want to party?" Jenna yelled over her shoulder toward the kitchen as if Jaycee had broken a big rule. "Are we drinking or not?"

"Nah," Tyler said. "I don't screw around with drinking." Then he took a Swiss army knife out of his pocket and cut the foil off a wine bottle. "No wait a minute," he said after he popped the cork. "I said that wrong. What I meant to say was when I'm drinking I don't screw around." He sucked down half the bottle and held it up like a trophy. "Growing up with waiters has its advantages. They showed what was worth lifting and what was too cheap to bother with." He propped himself up on elbows and eyed Jaycee. "I've got taste."

"Yeah," Jenna said. "You'd never date a girl who couldn't drive."

"That would be *so* embarrassing wouldn't it?" Jaycee asked with a scowl. I don't know if she cried when she rushed off to the bathroom, but I should've followed her. If I'd been a better guy I would've forgotten about the forms and taken her home, but I was too busy forgetting about Paige then.

\*\*\*

Our Sweat Time forms had three sheets stapled together. We were supposed to bring them to work for our new bosses, but we'd all folded ours up so there was no way they'd give a good impression. Anyone who'd hire us probably didn't care about that kind of thing though.

The first sheet asked for the contact information for our job. It said that whoever hired us had to sign a form at the end of Sweat Time to prove we did our hours and that they also had to write a letter about what we did and rate us. I doubted the school bothered to check them, but I'd never heard of anyone who had completely faked theirs. Most kids slid into spots at their parents' law firms or ad agencies or whatever. They got by with doing real work half the time. The only thing you learn from real work is that you don't get to decide anything.

The second sheet was this personality test that was supposed to help us discover what job we were meant for. All the questions were like "Would you rather build a house or draw a house?" or "Is it better to pass a law, or protest one?" The back of the sheet had a website where we could plug in our answers to find our calling in life. We shredded it to give it purpose.

The last sheet listed businesses that wanted to hire us, along with their contact information. Some were decent, but most were dead-end jobs like pizza places or gas stations. No dream kid would ever work in a place like that since we'd never live it down.

Tyler's parents had him set up at the country club and Hanna was down with the Y. Paige had this great plan she wasn't sharing, but Jenna, Jaycee, and I were out of luck since we only had a week to find a job or else the school would assign us one. I was terrified to let them pick for me since they might've just thrown darts again.

"This is the last thing I need." Jenna drank and got hopeless. I read over the jobs I could score without a connection again, but they sounded like places where I could lose a finger if I didn't pay attention. Jaycee came back and sat in the corner away from us. I watched her read her forms as if they were one of those tests that told you to read all the instructions before you started, and the last line said to throw it away to get an A.

"I need some fresh air. Bryce?" Jenna took a J out of her bra. Jaycee glared at me, then went back to the bathroom when I followed Jenna outside. Tyler was already on his second bottle. There was no doubt his haul for the day was worth more money than we'd ever earn combined during Sweat Time. Jenna and I went through the kitchen, then out the back door. I'd hooked her up and it was her turn to do the same. Sharing was caring.

\*\*\*

Jenna sat on the edge of the pool and smoked. I pried one of the tiles loose and watched it skid down the slope of the pool. I'd never noticed how deep it was before.

"So this is where it happened, huh?" I asked.

She hit the spliff, then inhaled hard to force the smoke down. Her face puffed up as she held her breath then when she couldn't take it anymore, she leaned back and let it pour out of her mouth. "This is where it happened."

I drew a hit in and got that charcoal burn in my throat that always came when I didn't use a bowl, then hit it again. The weed started to creep on me kind, and I wondered if Paige was doing the same thing wherever she was. "Who found him?"

"I did," she said. It came out flat, the way doctors speak. "My mom told me to watch him, but I was only ten you know? It was her fault, not mine."

"He was a baby?" I wanted to stop talking, but couldn't.

"Mikey was two. Old enough to walk, but not old enough to swim." She ground the joint into the space where the tile had been and left it there. "I don't want to talk about it."

"Then forget it. We have to figure out Sweat Time." I rubbed her back, but she kept staring into the pool. I bet after her grandfather moved away he bought the only house in Florida that wasn't near a pool, and never swam again.

"Mikey was only two," she said. The winds picked up and lifted a cloud of dirt into the air past the empty pool. That turned me hopeless too. I felt like we were all on the verge of losing everything for no reason, and had to fix that.

"Hey Jenna," I said.

"What?"

I grabbed her bra straps and cheesed the way they make you do in school pictures. "I love your magic bra!"

"Hands off," she said and slapped at me. "Go check on your non-driving non-girlfriend. I'll be back in a second." I didn't argue since she needed the empty. All kids need space and nothing sometimes. That's why we came to the party house. When I opened the door I wondered if she was going to pray.

\*\*\*

Tyler had tipped over his second bottle by the time I came back, and the carpet had new stains to add to its collage of filth. He'd dosed until he washed out, and Jaycee stared at him lying there on the floor from where she sat on the stairs. If she'd wanted to get back at him she could have. He deserved it, but she was better than that.

My forms were gone, and I panicked at the thought of what he might've done with them while I was outside. There was no way I was going to ask for a new one since that'd only lead to a lecture about responsibility, the kind where a teacher acts like they're speaking to me like an adult but it's obvious they think I'm dumb. That was the problem with our school. No one in charge was ever honest with me. They acted like I was mature and special because I was this dream kid, but I knew they thought we were all brats. If a teacher was ever honest with me one time I would use their first name no problem, but fake got fake.

I was searching between the couch cushions when Jaycee came up with both our forms. She turned them over and slapped the backside of the last sheet all thrilled. "Read this," she said.

She put her arm around me as I tried to read this single paragraph on the back of the last page. It was the same as those trick tests after all, but I wasn't able to understand what the words meant since my buzz was too mixed to make them out. You can't always judge. You take what you take, and it works smooth until you get cocky. Then it turns on you. "What does it say?"

"Wait here," she said, then ran out back to get Jenna. Jenna's face was streaked when she came inside but we didn't press her about it.

On the back of the last page there was this paragraph titled, "Optional Entrepreneurial and Professional Development." Jaycee broke it down for Jenna and me. It basically said we could make our own business if we wanted to, and The Dream Academy would count it for our Sweat Time. They wanted us to have the chance to follow our passions. The last line said we should take risks, be bold, and chase our dreams.

If Jenna had prayed out by that empty pool alone it had paid off. We were free. All we had to do was come up with the right hustle. Night had fallen, and if the rest of us besides Jaycee hadn't been wasted or recovering we would've celebrated, but it's impossible to party when everyone's at a different stage. There's no rhythm to it. We kicked around ideas until Tyler snapped to, and left. Jenna curled up on the couch and tried to doze off. I wanted to leave, and I didn't.

"What are you going to do for your fake job?" I asked Jaycee. She twisted a straw between her teeth and didn't answer me. I let her find her own space to think, and zoned out beside her on the floor listening to the music beat against my brain. Maybe she was worried about making money or only stuck on the things Tyler and Jenna had said. When we had to go, she kissed me for real. I didn't fight her, but I didn't kiss her back either. I hoped Jenna didn't see. When Jaycee pulled away she acted like it never happened. It wasn't like I meant to be rude. I was just mixed up about which way to turn. While Jaycee got her coat on I wondered what Paige's great plan was, and hoped wherever she was that she was miserable too.

*** 

Jaycee had me drop her off at the diner where her mom worked, but she didn't leave when I parked. She was waiting for me to say the right thing, but my head was blank and pounding. Instead, I turned up the volume while Generation X sang "Kiss Me Deadly" so there was no room to talk. She didn't go, but she wouldn't look at me either.

"So what kind of business are you going to fake?" I asked again after the song ended.

"I'm not faking anything," she said. "I'm going to work with my mom at the diner for a while. It's less trouble to be honest."

"Yeah," I said. "I'm sorry about what went down at the country club you know? I should've stopped you."

"Swear to God! Don't apologize for not saving me from my stupid ideas. Thinking you have to *save* me is insulting you know? I'm not a kid."

"No, you're not," I said. I pulled her close and kissed her. "Is that better?"

"Only if you meant it." It was impossible to read what she felt as she stood, and watched me drive away.

The whole way home I listened to "Kiss Me Deadly" on repeat. Regardless of whether I kissed her to seal up those broken hearts inside us or to spite Paige, I meant it. It was the most genuine thing in the world.

"Maybe you need it. It'll be impossible to read what she felt as she read," and Vivid had to drive away.

The whole way home, I listened to 100 Mo Mouth, on repeat. By the time of whether I passed her to text up those texts instead of whe orth to miss Paige. I meant it. It was be more careful now in the world.

# Chapter 6
# Kids Who Fight

**PAIGE LET** us in on her plan the Friday we had to turn in our Sweat Time forms. She said she got the idea from this girl Riley who went to community college with her boyfriend. Although she never heard the words au pair before, Riley made the job out to be a non-stop party. She only knew Riley because she bought X from her, but she pretended they were best friends to make us jealous that she had all these college connections.

Paige was bound to go dubstep if she stayed on X, but there was no way to stop her. I wished my dad got samples of X so I'd win her attention, but he repped legal. She was nicer when she was on it though, all rainbows and hugs. The only meds I scored were like the buttons on a remote control. They made your brain fast forward, slow down, or pause. None of them made you want to romance the planet.

Riley said she'd spent her last two summers in Europe, and that had Paige dreaming of flying away. She swore she'd danced on a beach with foreign guys until the sun came up, and even after it did, the DJ kept spinning. She told Paige she'd slept in castles older than anything we'd ever seen, and that being an au pair was one long rowdy vacation.

Paige laid out her scheme over lunch. She was convinced the school would let put off her Sweat Time until summer once they heard her out, and if they did we would never see her again. Not even her college boyfriend could keep her from all that adventure.

"So you're just going to babysit?" Hanna asked, as she ate the crackers and Diet Coke she called lunch.

"I'm not going to be a babysitter," Paige said. "I'm going to be an au pair!"

"Isn't that just a fancy babysitter?" Hanna slid her sandwich bag of saltines back into her purse. If she'd smoked a cigarette afterward it would've counted as a big meal for her. She was on this "runway diet."

"No. I mean you watch their kids, but Riley said you mainly just lay out and shop. It's way different over there. You can do what you want."

"But you can't do your time in Europe unless the school approves it, right?" Jaycee asked in between bites of her fish taco. "Do you even speak another language?"

"I'm taking French so why wouldn't they let me go?" Paige pulled out this ad for this au pair agency from her purse to show she meant business. "Pretty soon I'll be working on my tan with a glass of Champagne, and you'll be a bunch of haters stuck here."

"Nobody gets rich babysitting," Jenna said. "What about your boyfriend?"

"I'm meant for Europeans, you guys. They're more sophisticated," Paige snorted. "Boyfriends can be replaced."

"Not all of them," Hanna said. "You never told us your boyfriend's name so he must be ugly."

"He's gorgeous, but it's not like he's going to hang out with a bunch of high school kids."

I had my plan for Sweat Time worked out too, but no one asked what I was going to do.

"Being an au pair isn't the point anyway. First I go to Europe, play nice with the kids, and hang out for a while. Then sooner or later some rich dad will hit on me since I'll be all young and foreign." She dropped her voice even though we were the only ones at the table. "Once we hook up he'll either have to leave his wife for me, or I'll blackmail him and bank."

"Is that what Riley did?" Hanna asked.

"It's a solid plan, right? I just have to babysit for experience, and get certified."

"To screwing rich husbands," I said, lifting my Coke for a toast.

"That's why I don't bring my boyfriend around you," Paige shoved the ad into her purse. "You're juvenile."

***

I drove to the country club after school to help out Tyler before my fake job started. I got the idea from Jenna when she was talking about her mom's volunteer work, and figured if the school believed she was a great teacher then they would believe anything.

I parked in the employee lot between cars littered with fast food bags and grimy car seats in the back. Tyler's Escalade was parked between them begging to get keyed. Those beaters made me feel sorry for the people who drove them. That was their life, driving junky cars to a dumb job to feed their kids. I bet the members at the club never learned their names or looked them in the eyes. Those beaters made me glad that I was still in high school, for once.

Tyler was by the entrance to the kitchen smoking a cigarette with a couple of the Mexicans. They were all dressed up in starched white shirts and bow ties like prom kids.

"Hola mi amigo!" Tyler shouted as the Mexicans tossed their smokes into a plastic barrel and went inside.

"Cut it out. They know you don't speak Spanish. It's embarrassing."

"Who cares what they think? They're the help." Tyler handed me his gym bag and told me to stash it in his car.

"This is why you texted me? Do it yourself."

"I've got to be careful around here during the day, but my side hustle is going strong." Tyler poked his head inside then put his arm around me. "It's for the Catholic girls. We're supposed to be earners right?"

"You work here."

"I'm only here for cover. It's not like I'm one of the hombres or anything. Plus the girls at Saint Mary's pay top dollar for the cheap shit. Paige turned me on to the idea."

"Dude, am I the only person she doesn't talk to anymore?"

Tyler stuck his hands in his pockets all nonchalant as I lifted the bag onto my shoulder. "I have no idea what your situation with her is if there is one, but if you're so thirsty for her you should stop trying, you know? Girls don't respect you if they can have you whenever."

"All I know is that you're going to get busted if you step up your game like this."

"Not with all the weddings and fundraisers they've got going on here. If anyone asks questions I'll just pin it on one of the dishwashers or waiters. Most of them work two jobs anyway. Besides, you never get caught and the government has to keep track of your dad's stock. That's federal-level heat."

"I stay low-key and don't lift much. I've got my prescriptions. Besides I'm not dealing or anything, just spreading the wealth."

"You should. Paper makes the world go round." He pointed toward his SUV like I had on a bowtie too. "And I'm a printing press."

"As long as you're in that shirt you're just another hombre."

"That's where you're wrong, man. I'm royalty here."

"Whatever. Go clean some ashtrays."

I carried the bag to his SUV to get it over with. He played lookout until I closed his car door, then gave me the finger and hit the button on his keychain to lock it.

I spun out while The Cockney Rejects sang "Join the Rejects," and figured he was bound to catch jail time sooner or later.

\*\*\*

At home, my mom's Zumba music blared from the basement as I waited outside Johnny's room listening to the crashing racket he was beating inside. His patch must've worn off, and I was glad he was wound up so he'd come off as a wild child in my "before" recording.

I'd turned in my Sweat Time form at school with this outline for my start-up charity that didn't exist. I explained how my art therapy non-profit was going to help kids with behavioral problems, but they acted way more stoked about the idea than I'd planned. The secretary hugged the breath out of me when she read my proposal, then took it straight to the principal. He shook my hand once he'd read it, and told me that he'd had me wrong. He asked me to talk to the other kids about my work when I finished, but I told him it was too personal to make a big deal about.

I took Jaycee's advice and drew a line through number 9 on my List of Fantastic Promises before stuffing it back into my pocket.

1. Find out what makes me happy.
2. Save the party virgins when I can.
3. Make Paige love me again.
4. Figure out things with Jaycee.

5. Listen to music that's not on the radio.
6. Lay low in school.
7. Don't get caught up in other kids' drama.
8. ~~Spend more time with my family~~.
9. ~~Learn to make movies~~.

I opened Johnny's door. If I wanted to learn to make movies I had to start somewhere, and the school always preached that we would learn more from doing than from sitting around in a classroom.

Johnny's face was covered with finger paint. By then he'd dropped his toy weapons and was busy painting a monster on this plastic table that sat low in the middle of his room. His creature was covered with claws and horns, and when he saw me standing with my flip cam out he raced to tackle me.

"Hold up," I said. "I've gotta shoot you."

"What you say?"

"I've got to shoot you for school."

"I shoot you first. Bam! Bam! I'm a tough guy."

"No, like for a movie. Go paint." I held up my flip cam for him to see.

"My monster will eat you up!" He plopped down at his table to show me the mutant he'd made. It was covered with teeth and its hair was on fire.

"Paint a new one that's even meaner!" The Latin music underneath us throbbed louder. I was relieved that my mom didn't do her hip bumping in the living room, and had the common sense to hide her gyrating from the public, unlike Jenna's mom.

I framed his paint-smeared body up for my "before" scenes and recorded him wobbling side to side as he splashed colors onto poster paper with two brushes at the same time. Specks of red and blue flecked onto his Roblox t-shirt and spotted his bare legs until he'd splashed out a devil with a mouth filled with fangs.

"What's his name?" I asked as I zoomed in on his baby face.

"Butt," he laughed. "His name is Butt!"

"Whatever works for you, man." I cut the camera off. "It's saved forever now."

"I want yogurt."

"Sure, but wash your hands and don't touch the walls." I never got why my mom and dad had another kid when I was in middle school. Maybe my mom thought it'd make my dad hang around more, or she wanted a fresh excuse to give her life purpose.

I heard the toilet flush and the faucet turn on as I waited outside the bathroom. The music cut out, and my mom made her way up the stairs. She'd sweated through her Lulu Lemon gear, and rested beside me to catch her breath. In the bathroom, Johnny sang "Happy Birthday" at the top of his lungs to measure the time he had to wash his hands like he'd been taught to do in pre-school.

"Did you take off his patch?" my mom asked me, and I shook my head. "He's not supposed to wear it after school. I'll never get him to sleep."

"I don't think it helps."

"His teacher says he's listening better," she said as Johnny walked out with his paint-spattered face. "It takes time though."

He put his hand in mine and walked me to the refrigerator. After I set him up he slurped his yogurt while my mom asked what the camera was for. I told her it was for school and left it at that.

"See," she said as she pulled down Johnny's pants and peeled a clear plastic triangle off his thigh. "You wouldn't be there if we hadn't taken care of your issues." She could've been glowing from all that dancing or just proud that I was doing school work, but either way it was nice to see her happy. She'd been so down lately that I was scared whatever she kept to herself was next-level trouble.

"Where's dad?"

"He's away at a conference, but he'll be home soon." She poured wine into her coffee mug. "I'm glad you're spending time with your brother. He needs that. I can't handle him all by myself." She tousled his head and left us alone.

I put my hands on Johnny's tiny bird shoulders and whispered "You are a tough guy. You don't need a patch. You can take it off at school and she'll never know. Remember that."

"I 'member," he said as he spooned yogurt into his mouth.

***

Tyler texted me after midnight, which meant at least a dozen other people must've blown him off. I couldn't blame them. No one wants to start their weekend with some other kid's drama.

NEED RIDE NOW! AT CC! ANSWER BCK!!!

It would've been easier to hit delete, but I figured helping him out would add to the good karma I'd been building. You have to balance out the bad with the good because the only way you get busted is if you spend all your time doing wrong, and never make up for it. I texted that I was on my way.

I found him standing by the gates of the country club with his pressed white shirts twisted between his fists. This is how Tyler told it, but he probably changed the details so he'd come off as the victim. He said his parents told him that he only had to show up, clock in, and hang out until his shift was over. It was supposed to be a breeze, but after a week the kitchen manager started making him run food and wash dishes which wasn't the deal. He'd went to his parents about it, but they'd changed their minds and wanted him to appreciate actual work for once. So he was stuck taking orders from this female manager he made out to be a total dictator.

"She's a bitch on a power trip who talks to me in Spanish half the time and acts like my parents don't run the place." He jerked at his starched shirt to try and rip it in half. "I had to let her know who she was dealing with." He rolled down the window and threw his shirt and bowtie out. Once they landed on the street he told me the worst part.

The worst part according to him was that all the members he'd known his whole life started treating him like a slave once they saw him in his uniform. They ordered him around and made a production out of forcing him to get them more ice or polish their golf clubs.

"They're just clothes, right?" He said, raw with rage. "What difference does that make? I'm one of them." He spat through his teeth like he couldn't unlock his jaw. "One of them called me Jose, and his friends fell out of their chairs like it was the funniest thing they ever heard."

"It's your first week, man. Forget it."

"I quit. My parents took my keys away, but I don't care. No one deserves to be treated that way."

"You've got to go back. There's no way you can make it two months without a ride."

"I can always find a ride if I have to. There are Ubers and buses."

"What about your Sweat Time report?" I asked, trying my best to sound sorry for him.

"My parents will sign that since it's for school. They'd be too embarrassed if their friends heard I failed."

He told me to drive him to Hanna's house. I didn't argue while he texted her, but I hated myself for not deleting his message. If I had I wouldn't have been dealing with his drama which was on My List of Fantastic Promises. He left his window down to let the air blow the edge off all that anger while I sped up. When I let him out he didn't say thanks, only, "I'll never call you Mouse again. Mouse is dead." That was enough.

Hanna waited on her front porch to tell him off as he stalked up to her. Maybe he had to fight with someone he could hurt to feel better. They were screaming at each other when I pulled out. I'd done my good deed for the day.

***

Jaycee text-bombed me the entire way home, but I didn't answer her back. Instead, I cranked up the heat, and listened to Gang Green's "Another Wasted Night." I liked the music more than before, even if I resented Mr. Klimax for trying to force his version of cool on me. Hitting his playlist had become part of my driving ritual. I get stuck in these patterns I can't break sometimes.

Johnny was asleep when I got home, and my mom was in the den drinking a glass of wine and watching this show where people tried to decide which house to buy. She didn't notice me. I wanted to talk to her, and I didn't.

Upstairs, my dad had made it back from the road but had already locked himself up in his office, so I crashed on my bed to read through Jaycee's texts. She must've been bored to blow up my cell that way. I deleted her first three messages but felt like a dick about it so I messaged her back to see how her Sweat Time was going.

"OK ☺," she messaged. "$ could be better. U?"

"At work. No $, but EZ."

"Send it?" she asked.

"Ltr. Miss hanging w U?"

"KK. Luv ur list. ☺"

I shut off my phone and laid it on my List of Fantastic Promises after I crossed off number 5. Then I popped two Klonopin to get eight hours straight.

1. Find out what makes me happy.
2. Save the party virgins when I can.
3. Make Paige love me again.
4. Figure out things with Jaycee.
5. ~~Listen to music that's not on the radio.~~
6. Lay low in school.
7. Don't get caught up in other kids' drama.
8. ~~Spend more time with my family~~.
9. ~~Learn to make movies~~.

\*\*\*

The problem with Paige's plan was obvious from the start. It's not like some people don't live amazing lives, it's that they're the exception. For most kids, everything is a pipedream, and if you believe in a dream where it's all you think about, you're going to crash hard. That's why I never told anyone the principal was so psyched about my project.

Paige quit her au pair training after three days. She heard from the other girls there that Europeans only hired Africans or Russians since they were cheaper and less trouble than Americans. They also told her that if she was lucky enough to get a job overseas she'd be treated like a maid. Life is like that. All these people make you believe you can be anything you want if you work hard. They promise if you apply yourself something wonderful will happen, but it never does.

When Paige dropped out of training she had to babysit McMansion kids for Sweat Time while their mothers went to hot yoga classes or dinner dates. She wanted to quit but had to keep the job for school. She also needed the cash for X since that way she didn't have to explain to her parents why she was using their ATM card so much. She was sick that Riley had lied to her, but she needed the connection. We all need at least one person we can't stand most of the time. My person was Paige.

It was Saturday night, and since Jaycee was at the diner and everyone else was off doing their own thing, I texted Paige to see how her job was going. I was surprised when she messaged me back and begged for company, but I guess she didn't want her college boyfriend to see her being all domestic. I drove over, hoping she loved me again so I could mark number three off my List of Fantastic Promises by the end of the night.

Marky Ramone sang "I Don't Wanna Grow Up," and I sang along. Paige was stuck at this McMansion in a fancy subdivision called Hickory Trace. All the McMansion farms had names that were *so* country although most were only big houses with tiny lawns. It wasn't like anyone there went outside anyway.

It took me forever to find the house she was at since they were all copies of the same dream home. If I'd had money like that I'd buy a place like the party house; one away from the rest of the world. I could find some peace in a place like that.

Paige was super pissed when she answered the door. "What's up, hippie?" I asked. "Where are the kids?"

"She did it again!" Paige shook a check in front of my face before stomping off to the living.

"Are you playing hide and seek with them?"

"The McMansion mom shorted me again! She owes me two hundred dollars, but only wrote a check out for seventy-five bucks. I was here until after midnight last night, and she didn't even say sorry!" She pointed at the amount line. There was a smiley face drawn on it.

"Do you even have a bank account?"

"You don't get it," she said. "She thinks she can rip me off because this is for school and she goes to spin class with my mom. She doesn't get a discount for that."

"Where are the kids anyway?" I asked, and she got this look like she hadn't thought about them for a long time.

"We should find them," she said.

We heard their little voices first, but since the mom was one of those security freaks there were baby monitors all over the house which turned it into a giant echo chamber. Squeals and shouts crackled behind every door as if the place was haunted by killer kindergarteners. When we finally found them they were squared off in a fourth-floor bedroom.

"Give it gurr!" a blonde in tights and Ugg boots shouted as she shook her finger at her sister who stood on the bed with a bouquet crushed against her chest. "They's mine!"

I held onto Paige to stand. "This is awesome! Is it always like this?"

"They're total brats," she said. "Last night they were biting each other in their sleep. You wouldn't think it's so hilarious if you had to deal with them."

"They my flowers!" the brown-haired munchkin on the bed shouted. "I won 'em." Both of the girls wore blue vests with patches. I told Paige they looked like evil Wal-Mart greeters, but she said they got them for being Daisies which were like baby Girl Scouts.

"Girls stop," Paige said with her hands out like a crossing guard. "If you're going to fight let's do this right. You know the drill. Come here."

The girl on the bed threw down the bouquet, then the two marched over to Paige and stuck out their palms. She told them to stay put, then went into the bathroom.

"I'm going to win this time," the blonde one said. Her sister mean-mugged her and shook her head. They didn't say another word until Paige came back with a stack of washcloths. She wrapped the girls' tiny doll hands with them until they were padded with pink cotton.

"You know the rules," she said. "Go to your corners." The girls walked to the opposite sides of the room while we sat on the bed. Once they found their spots they put their fists up. "Ready," Paige said. The girls snarled like Pit bull puppies. "Set." They paced to the middle of the room with small dead-set eyes. "Go!"

The two tiny fighters went crazy but didn't punch so much as hit each other with their whole arms while they let out this thin shriek that lifted higher and higher. It was so angry beautiful that I didn't want it to end, but in a second the flower girl was on the floor with her sister wailing on her like a boss.

I looked at Paige, and it seemed like the check didn't bother her so much anymore. "Okay! Go to time out now!" The girls pouted, then dragged their feet back to their corners. We left them there and went for a post-fight drink.

"She probably has nanny cams stashed all over the place," I said as I twisted the top off an Evian bottle.

"I doubt it. I smoke here. If she saw that on camera I'd get fired for sure."

"We're always being watched one way or another even if we're cheap help," I said to stab her for dreaming she could drop us all and run away. "Maybe the dad checks the cams, and likes what he sees?" I let that set in. "Maybe you could play blackmail with him?"

"Gross! He's like sixty, and not Euro suave you know?"

"I miss hanging with you."

"I miss you too," she said, "but I'm too busy for high school right now. I've got to concentrate on my future."

"Busy with what? All you do is get high and disappear. The school's going to catch on, you know? Why not stay with us and have fun? I miss our fun."

"I am having more fun than you'll ever know," she said, and patted the top of my head. "It's just not with you."

"But we've got history."

"That's true." She gave me this pity-face, "but history is in the past, right?"

"Look, don't text me anymore okay?" I said. "I can't take it."

"You texted me," she said, then rubbed my arms. "You're a good friend you know? You're always there for me. I won't forget that."

"I have to get out of here."

"Yeah, the mom will be home any minute, and she'll freak if she sees you here. I'm not supposed to have guys over."

"What are you going to tell her?"

"I'm going to tell her that I put the girls in time-out for fighting," she said as if I'd asked the most obvious question in the world. "I'm going to tell her the truth."

# Chapter 7
## Kids with History

**AFTER MY DAD** got back from Seattle with more pharmaceutical company love, I searched through his samples for a drug that would turn Paige on and add to my personal stockpile. Even though I had more prescriptions than a Walgreens thanks to my psychiatrist and my dad, I kept stocked in case things went truly dark. That had happened before. It wasn't that there weren't legit reasons for me to be on meds, but after Paige broke my heart my parents decided their mission in life was to make me the way I was before. That was on me though. I messed up and told them I wanted to die, and they didn't understand I only said that because I was grieving heavy and didn't have the right words to explain it.

By the start of my sophomore year, I had to go to see a therapist once a week because my parents didn't believe I was back to good, but the more I went the more he found wrong with me because that was his job.

I fought hard to stop going to therapy since talking about depressing shit led nowhere, so my dad got me on with his psychiatrist who only asked if I was eating okay, sleeping through the night, and had any thoughts of hurting myself or others. I gave the answers he wanted, and he wrote my scripts just like that. My dad saw him after me, and although we had different meds he passed his on to me. Maybe he figured they'd make me normal faster. Before long I had to dose on the daily. My mom begged him to take me off my meds, but he argued that they were completely safe. After a while, she gave up, and they stopped talking about anything for the most part.

I only shared a little at a time with my crew, to be safe. I had to have Xanax for when my anxiety hit, and Klonopin to sleep. Without my Adderall, there was no way I'd get any school work done. My Carbamazepine and Prozac kept me level. For a long time I kept my stockpile secret to myself to avoid being labeled a headcase, but once I started sharing, the story got around that I was this serious dealer. That was my fault for being nice.

I opened the boxes in his office, desperate to find some knock-off X or pharma-Molly buried in his samples, but it was hopeless. One box had upgrades for Vicodin and Norco that were cracked open, and the other had packs for migraine medicines. There was more money in pain than in joy. No drug company invested in making the world sing.

I closed the boxes and went to bed. My dad probably thought he'd checked them himself the night before when he found them opened in the morning. If he knew better he didn't have the guts to talk to me about it. That's what he paid my psychiatrist for, after all.

*** 

The last week of October, when our Sweat Time was almost finished, we were assigned our semester projects. We had to take the standardized tests for the state, but, other than our final exams, whether we passed or failed depended on these semester projects that were meant to show that we'd learned something. The Dream Academy said there was a difference between getting an answer right on a test and being able to use what you were taught. The semester projects weren't that bad unless you got stuck with a group project. If that happened you were doomed.

The worst teachers loved group projects. One minute they'd preach about how important it was to be an independent thinker, then the next they'd herd us together and lecture about the value of teamwork and cooperative learning. They couldn't keep their story straight.

All group projects turned out the same way. There'd be one kid who worked like mad but got weighed down by slackers. Half the group would swear to do their part but never come through, one kid would disappear, and by the end, there'd be just that one desperate kid stressed out and cheated for caring.

I tried to explain all this to Jenna's mom before she assigned our semester projects for English, but she argued that if our groups sucked then it at least showed us whether we were leaders or loners, and either way it had to get done. That wasn't fair though since leaders and loners got treated the same. Groups passed or failed as a team, even if that team was one kid who hadn't slept in a week because he was abandoned.

Jenna's mom let our English class choose our groups, and once we did she handed out a clipboard with a sheet we weren't allowed to turn over until she gave the word. My friends and I huddled up on the love seat and from the start, I was sure Tyler, Hanna, and Jenna would blow it off, and that Paige would disappear. That left either me or Jaycee to carry the load, but neither of us wanted to. By then I barely recognized Jaycee anyway. The playlist I'd sent her had totally transformed her.

"You're the boss this time," Tyler said. "I didn't fake my Sweat Time like you." His parents had forced him to go back to work and apologize to his manager the day after he quit. The members kept on treating him like a slave and calling him Jose, but no matter how terrible it was, it did him good. I hadn't heard him say one mean thing to Hanna after they got back together, and he'd stopped teasing Jaycee and Jenna too. It was as if he realized other people had feelings, for the first time in his life.

Jenna's mom told us to turn over our sheets and get started, but when I did there weren't any instructions for the project. A lot of the semester projects at The Dream Academy made us figure out what we had to do ourselves because the school believed instructions made us rule-followers instead of independent thinkers. The sheet only said to give our group a name, come up with a slogan, and draw a mascot.

"What is this? *Game of Thrones*?" Tyler asked.

"Just do it," Jaycee said. She'd cut holes in her jeans and stuck safety pins through her homemade concert shirt.

Tyler drew stick figures with Xed-out eyes. Our mascot belonged in a bathroom stall. Hanna asked him what it was supposed to be, and he said, dead kids.

"So what's the slogan for a bunch of dead kids?" I asked.

"I don't care," Paige said as she checked her phone. "None of this matters."

On the slogan line, I wrote, "None of this matters." That only left naming our group.

"How about The Break-ins," Tyler said. "Like not only because we rob the country club and all, but because we break kids in, you know?"

"Don't give yourself that much credit," Jaycee said all unimpressed.

I wrote "No Name Needed" on the sheet, and turned it back over.

"Time's up," Jenna's mom said. "Move. Don't think. Do." When she read our sheet she giggled, and Jenna told her to stop it.

"Let me make sure I understand," she said. "Your group is called No Name Needed, your slogan is 'None of this matters,' and your logo is a group of stickmen who are either dead or knocked out cold."

"Yeah. That's it." I waited for her to lay into us for not applying ourselves, but instead, she pressed our sheet against her heart like a love letter.

"I'm glad to see that your History of Punk Rock class is paying off. I told you that you never know what you'll love." Then she walked to the middle of the room and held our sheet up for the rest of the class. "This group isn't afraid to speak truth to power. They are free-thinkers. You should all do the same." The achiever kids looked confused and started to erase whatever they had written down.

"She loves to highlight me," Jenna said, although her mom had bragged on all of us. "She's dying to make me look as whack as she is."

"She just likes to be different," Tyler said. "At least she's wearing shoes to class now, right?"

"I *have* to get out of this place." Jenna winced.

"Are you sure you don't want to do this?" I asked Jaycee, but she only popped her bubble gum at me. Maybe she figured not doing anything was the most punk thing she could do, and it burned me that I'd given her that playlist in the first place. It was as if I'd handed her a Bible, and in no time she'd become a nun. I shot a picture of her rocked out on my phone when she wasn't looking so she'd never forget when the music swallowed her.

Jenna's mom went to her desk, pulled out a stack of index cards, and then handed one out to each group. She told us to keep them face down until we heard her out as if we'd burst into applause the second we caught on to her great plan. Jaycee took our card from me even though I was supposed to be the boss.

"Let me see it," I said, but she stuffed it down the front of her shirt and waited for Jenna's mom to give her speech as if it'd be so inspiring.

Jenna's mom rocked on the edge of her desk and held up a card like ours. "What do you think is on the other side?" she asked, but no one answered. "What do you want it to be? What will you do if it's not what you expect? How can you make it what you want?"

"Dude," Tyler said, "does she have to talk about every assignment like it's some kind of mystery?"

"Shut up," Jaycee said. "She's trying to make a point."

"Questions aren't points. Questions are what you say when you don't have a point," Jenna said, then left the room.

"Give me our card."

"Not until she says to," Jaycee said, and blew another bubble in my face.

"Fine. You can be the leader then. I don't need the hassle."

Jenna's mom got tired of watching us squirm over what she had in mind, and gave us the okay to flip over our cards. Jaycee winked at me, pulled our card out, and tossed it my way. "You're the leader. I'm too busy at work to deal with this. What does it say?"

All the other kids already had their hands in the air. "I don't know what this means," that achiever girl, Heather, said. "There aren't any instructions."

Jenna's mom had done it again. "If you have questions go find them, but don't think you'll find your answers online.

The solutions to your problems aren't on your phones. You have to go out and live to appreciate what you can create." Heather dropped her hand and studied her group's card as if it was a math problem that was way over her head.

"What does our card say?" Jaycee asked, and after I'd read it was clear why everyone else was twisted.

"Yeah. What did she stick us with?" Tyler asked.

I held up the card out for the others to read. It only said, "This is *Now*."

At the end of class, Jenna's mom said we had until the week before finals to turn in our semester projects, but she was going to check our progress after Fall Break which only gave us two weeks to pull together something that'd get her juiced. If we didn't pass our semester projects we were sure to catch summer school, at least for English. I was glad my stockpile was loaded. If I timed my doses right I could probably make it almost a week without sleeping if I had to, and if that wrecked me then at least I'd have an excuse for an extension. It was also a plus that I had Jaycee, punk or not, since there was no way she'd ever let me down or disappear.

***

After school, I got an email from Mr. Klimax about our History of Punk Rock semester project, but it only read, "Too wasted to think about school. Be sure to let the music leave scars. Details soon. —Kenny." I emailed back, "Rise above Kenny!" He had the balls to be straight with me, and that deserved a first name.

The leaves on the trees outside my house had turned shades of burnt orange and red as I sat in my car and thought about how awesome it was going to be to torture Johnny with my videos when he grew up. I rolled down my window and listened to the wind blow easy and cool,

silencing every songbird, as middle school kids stepped off
their bus without a word and hiked home. That great quiet
of autumn was full-on. The stillness of it hung on everything and made me feel peaceful for once. That's what I
liked best about the fall, the way the volume drops to the
point you don't want to think because even your thoughts
ruin that great quiet.

Joey Ramone sang "What a Wonderful World" as I drove
to see Jaycee at the diner, and his upbeat nasally voice
got me cheerful. She'd told me the diner was always dead
on Mondays, and I hoped that'd give us time to figure out
what to do about our semester project. More than anything
though, I wanted to see her again. Something about her
made me feel safe.

The diner where she worked was rundown and sat on the
corner of the turnoff to the housing projects. It was a small
concrete building with chipped white paint and pictures
of cheeseburgers dancing painted on the side of it. Inside
there were a dozen tables with cracked vinyl seats. I sat at
one by the entrance to watch leaves skitter across the street
and played with a plastic menu until she noticed me. She
tugged at her apron and glanced back toward the kitchen as
if I'd invaded a part of her life she kept out of sight.

"You shouldn't have come here," she said as the streetlights came to life outside to illuminate the bruise-colored
sky. "I'm supposed to be working."

It was after six, but there was no dinner rush to stress
about. The place only had one other table where two men
in coveralls sat eating bowls of chili while they watched a
baseball game on an old TV above the counter. "It looks like
you have the time."

She craned her head over to the counter where a woman
who could've been her mom read a magazine by the cash
register, then gave in and joined me.

"What do you want?" she asked.

"Nothing. Just came to waste time, and maybe figure some things out." Number four on my List of Fantastic Promises had been weighing on me ever since Paige made it clear that we didn't have a history so much as we *were* history.

"You have to order if you want to stay, or I'll get in trouble for slacking."

"So get me a milkshake."

"What kind?" She fished out a creased notepad from her apron, then slid a pen out from her ponytail. I told her it didn't matter, and she shrugged before walking back through the swinging doors to the kitchen. A bus hissed to a stop outside on the street as the rain began to drum against the pavement. The driver opened the door, then closed it and steered away into the purple dying day.

Jaycee sat a chocolate milkshake on the table in front of me, then picked the cherry off the top of it for herself. She licked the whipped cream off of it, then sucked it into her mouth in a flash. She said that was the best part.

"You want to talk about our semester project for English or something?"

"No. I mean I did, but school is the last thing I want to think about now. See, I just figured you were the only one I could talk to about this."

"About what?" She raked two fingers into the whipped cream head of my milkshake then pushed them into her mouth.

"You don't have a dad right?"

"I've got a table." She wiped her hand clean on a napkin and threw it to me. But she didn't leave.

"It's not like that. I'm being serious. You're the only one who can answer this for me."

"Answer what?"

I moved the milkshake to the side and leaned closer. "How do you stop loving someone?"

The television over the counter cut out, and the men rambled out, leaving dirty dishes and wadded dollar bills for Jaycee behind them. Her face was colorless as she left to clear their table, leaving me alone to listen to the raindrops beat gently against the window. She stuffed the wadded bills into her apron, carried the dishes into the back, and stayed out of sight for a long time. Maybe it hit her that I thought she was an orphan, or maybe she had to let a question that big hang on me so I'd appreciate how wrong it was to ask. I drank my milkshake, letting the rich syrup at the bottom settle me, and was about to leave, when she finally came back. The woman behind the cash register was gone, and the drumbeat of rain grew louder outside.

"First off, I have a dad." Her face had flushed red as the leaves hanging from the trees, but she said each word as if she'd practiced it a dozen times in her head. "I don't like to talk about him."

"Cool." I played like it didn't matter. If I apologized it would've only made her more pissed.

"Secondly, why would you think that if I'd lost him I'd stop loving him? I mean, I don't think anyone can *stop* loving anyone after they've started. It's like no matter how horrible they are there's probably always going to be part of you that is marked with them."

"My dad's gone most of the time too, but I wasn't talking about him."

"I'm not an idiot," Jaycee said, "but you are if you keep on dreaming that the love of your life is the girl you dated in middle school."

"Where is your dad?"

"That is none of your business." She looked past me toward the rain filling the potholes and gutters outside. "It's a secret."

"Don't you trust me?"

"It's not about that." The anger faded from her face in blots of pink and red. "He's in prison alright? He's in prison, and you probably think, 'Oh, that makes sense,' and are dying to say how sorry you are for that."

"No," I said. "I was just hoping you'd let me drive you home."

*** 

We sat in my car outside her apartment tower listening to 7 Seconds play "Young Until I Die," on repeat until the weather let up enough for her to make a run for her building.

"We're getting together this Friday at the party house to celebrate the end of Sweat Time. You're coming, right?"

"Do you want me to? You'd have to pick me up and I don't like being a charity case."

"You're one of us. I want you there." I snapped my seatbelt free.

"That's not true. You're the only reason the rest of those kids hang with me. They'd never say it, but they only see me as this kid with a free ticket. It's okay though. I don't need them. I've got my music and you to play hero, right?"

"You're giving me too much credit." I kissed her, not to make her feel better or forget, but because I wanted to. When I pulled away she froze and sucked her bottom lip like she had to make sure it happened.

"Why did you do that?" she asked, looking through me.

"Because I needed to."

"Does that mean you've decided to let go of your seventh-grade crush at last?" she asked, but something in her face changed when I didn't answer.

"You think too much," I turned away to watch the wiper blades slap clean trails on my windshield that were destined to get blurred, "and I never know what to say okay? Just say you'll come to the party with me. I'm no good alone."

Jaycee wiped her mouth on her sleeve and took a big breath. "I'll go," she said, "but don't tell the others about my dad, okay?"

"I don't know what you're talking about," I said. "We just talked about music."

"We did more than talk," she said, and kissed me before charging into the rain. It was easy to burn over her when she was around, but when she wasn't I couldn't help sliding back into wishing for that perfect middle school kind of love. Maybe the only perfect things are memories.

***

The storm made my drive from the river and through downtown the same as steering through a carwash at thirty-five miles an hour. The traffic lights swung back and forth on their wires overhead flashing three yellow globs on repeat. The people on the sidewalk were black and gray shadows, there and gone. Somehow I'd gotten turned around and the GPS on my phone wouldn't load. Its blue wheel kept spinning to show it was trying to connect but stuck. There was no way to go on without directions, so I parked in a vacant lot and listened to The Spits play "My Mess." My routines usually kept me steady, but the music didn't help my nerves. I unplugged my phone to restart my GPS and saw I'd missed five messages from Paige. I closed my eyes to forget about her as the rain battered my hood, but it's hard to get out of your head when you're stranded.

Paige's texts were desperate. "Need U" and "Plz!" The last one had this address for me, and I typed it into my GPS.

Part of me dreamed that she needed me again, and another hoped that the blue wheel would keep spinning. But it connected at last, and an arrow came on screen to lead me away. I promised it'd be the last time I'd come running. Chasing her made me feel like a freshman at forgetting.

Paige sat on the bottom of this staircase at an apartment complex a few blocks up from the community college. She was smoking a cigarette with a fist under her chin like she had something heavy on her mind but jumped up when she saw me running her way through the downpour.

"I was worried you'd blocked me," she said, "but you always come through don't you?" She hugged me tight like she hadn't seen me in years, then we sat and watched the rain make a waterfall between us and the parking lot.

"I made this promise to stop answering crazy texts," I said as she laced her fingers between mine. "This better be an emergency."

"Didn't you want some attention?" She curled against me to keep warm. "I didn't mean to bug you, but I had to tell someone. This is huge!"

"So tell your boyfriend," I said. I wanted her off me, and I didn't.

"That's what I'm talking about," she said. "He's taking me away, but you have to keep that a secret. You're the only one I trust."

"Away to where?" I asked, scooting away.

"Don't be like that," she said. "It's a good thing."

I imagined her mom crying on the news, her name flashing on those Amber Alert signs.

"You and Jenna forever talk about running away as if it's the solution to all your problems. Why now? You should at least wait until summer when it's nice, or next year when we're all shipped off to learn about the world or whatever."

"Frank doesn't want to wait," she said with these hopeful eyes, and I broke up.

"No wonder you never told me his name," I said after I got myself together. "You're dating a guy named Frank? That's a total dad name."

Paige's face knotted up, and she lit another cigarette. Maybe she figured I'd be stoked for her or that I'd at least beg her to stay, but her falling hard for a guy named Frank was more than I could handle. "He's got it all planned out," she said with hate shading on her.

"What's his wonderful plan?" I asked even though I didn't care. None of her plans ever worked out, we had that much in common. She only wanted me because a secret was worthless until you shared it with somebody.

"It's like this." Her voice went sunshine. "After he smoked me out last night we were lying in bed, and all he could talk about was Florida. He said he has friends there who live right on the beach. He promised we can crash with them for as long as we want. Pretty soon you'll be freezing to death in Ohio, and I'll be sunburned and free."

"No more European dreaming?"

"Forget Europe. I'm not going to bust my ass in French class to be a maid. Don't you get it? In Florida Spring Break goes on forever." She pushed her hair behind her ears and put her arms out for me to hug her congratulations. I did. It would've been so easy to rip her for buying into her pothead boyfriend's dreaming, but I played like she'd dropped the greatest news ever. That way when she got slammed with the facts she'd crash epic.

"Swear you won't let anyone know! I don't want anybody to stop me before I'm burying my toes in the sand."

"There's no way I'd ruin what you've got coming," I said. The storm clouds parted until only a drizzle fell. "Thanks for sharing."

"You're my friend, right?" She stuffed her lighter into her purse, and climbed up the stairs.

"Yeah," I said. "We've got history." I waited until she was out of sight, then went to my car. I was loose inside and cranked The Suicide Machines version of "I Never Promised You a Rose Garden" as the arrows on my phone directed me home. I shouted along, thrilled to dig on Kenny's cool, and eager for the disaster to come.

# Chapter 8
## Kids on Camera

I'D SCREWED around too much, wasted weeks, and despite My List of Fantastic Promises I'd gotten caught up in other kids' drama and my own until my Sweat Time project was almost up and I still didn't have my "after" footage. I felt sick when I pictured my teachers and the principal lecturing me for being a complete liar and slacker even if I was, and was sick over the prospect of getting held back or stuck in summer school if they decided to send a message. By the time the last Sunday before my project was due came, I had to turn Johnny into the poster child for finger painting rehab. If he was wired and determined to make monsters bleeding from their eyes I was dead. My laptop played The Dead Milkmen's "God's Kid Brother" until I closed it to take away my last reason to stall.

Johnny was in the backyard digging a grave for his Power Ranger when I found him. He jerked out clumps of grass, then clawed the dirt to make a trench deep enough to bury his favorite toy. It seemed like a lot of trouble.

"Where's mom and dad?" The sun had dropped low and streaked the sky with yellow and purple trails that matched the fallen maple leaves on our lawn.

"What'd you say?" he asked before stuffing his best friend into the ground and covering him with mud.

"You're going to miss him you know? I'm not going to dig him up for you."

"I'm big." He poked out his chin. "You can buy me Pokémon?"

"Do you know how to play?"

"Play what?"

I didn't know what had him stoked for Pokémon, all of a sudden, but the wanting was enough to turn him into a gravedigger. Maybe he figured burying his best friend would help him grow up.

I walked him to the kitchen sink and washed his hands before passing him a juice box. He sucked on it and swung his feet while I checked to see if he was patched up and chill. He hadn't listened to me about taking them off at school, and over time they'd started to work on him. I heard my parents talking upstairs, then a door slam. The scene was shifting. I had to move fast.

Johnny picked out his gear for the shoot while I played with my camera on his twin bed. He settled on a shirt that had baby chickens on it and read "Chick Magnet," a pair of camouflage shorts, and sunglasses that were too big for his face.

"You good with that?" I asked.

"Yep. I'm a cool guy. See?"

"No doubt. Now you've got to be my special helper, okay?"

"Do what now?"

"No monsters, okay? I want you to make a turkey for mom since it's almost Thanksgiving."

"Like school?" he spread his fingers out wide and tracing them with a finger.

"Exactly. But you have to paint real slow and smile the whole time."

"For Mommy?" he asked, and I nodded. "What about Daddy?"

"Sure, him too. Come on."

I laid out construction paper next to his kiddie paint set and framed him up. The camera zoomed in as he chewed his bottom lip before dropping his left hand, fingers fanned out, onto the paper. My parents got loud above us, not shouting but just below it, as he outlined his hand.

"Tom is my turkey's name," he said with satisfaction. "He beats the other turkeys up."

"No, Tom is a good turkey. Say that for mommy."

He huffed but delivered his line while my parents got more heated than before. His round face turned up at the ceiling as they laid into each other, but after I promised to score him Pokémon cards he got back on task and made a kindergarten masterpiece. Behind him, I zoomed in for a tight shot of his brush stroking Tom's feathers brown and gold until one last jab dotted a single black eye.

"He doesn't have a beak."

"What you say?"

"A beak. You know, a bird's mouth," I said.

"What does a turkey sound like?"

"Like this," I said, and clucked to cover the noise of my parents' fight. Johnny laughed and stomped a turkey dance around his art table, but my guts were acid. My dad could've noticed his samples were missing, or my mom might've heard a rumor that I was dealing at school from one of the mouthy moms in her spin class. There was no way to make out what they were at it about because every time they yelled loud enough to understand, they caught themselves and dropped the volume. I only got fragments like "You did," and "Help me then." It was about me or it wasn't, and either way, I had to run.

"You were a cool guy," I said. I stuffed my flip cam into my pocket. "I'm going to get your cards for sure."

"Not cards," Johnny said. "Pokémons."

"Right. Pokémon." It was sad to see him begging for a gift without any idea what it was.

"I'll get you a whole bunch. I swear." He grinned as he handed his painting to me. "What's this for?"

"For mommy and daddy," he said with this puzzled face. Upstairs another door slammed again and footsteps hammered against hardwood floors.

"Right," I said, "They'll be super impressed." I took the painting from him, then went to my car before my parents were finished with each other. The clock on my dash said it was eight o'clock. The sun was gone, but there was no way to find the peace I needed to edit my shots together and show what a giving heart I had until everyone was asleep and the house was silent. I drove for hours until I was alone again and safe.

***

It was after midnight when I came back. My dad was locked in his office. Once I asked him what he did in there all the time and he said "work," but it had to be a lie. I figured he was drunk or hiding from us. When he was home he never noticed me or my brother, and barely talked to my mom before he locked himself up. I bet he used the samples from work too when there wasn't anything to look forward to.

My mom was asleep in the living room with an episode of *The Bachelorette* playing on mute. She loved to watch those dull Hollister model-looking guys fight over some boring girl who forever talked about her heart. She'd watch them take helicopter rides or bike along the beach eager to find out who proposed to the dumb cooze like it was her Super Bowl. That show reminded me of Paige's plan because she believed those things happened in real life. I left the TV on in case she woke up. Turning it off would've ruined the only romance she had going for her.

Johnny was sprawled out in his bed with his sword across his belly. Pictures of monsters covered his floor. I dropped three packs of Pokémon cards on top of him, jealous at how simple it was for him to be happy, but was glad he had it that way. He had the longest eyelashes I'd ever seen on a kid and a mouth like one of those dolls that comes with a bottle. I hoped he'd be able to dodge the shit that comes when you grow up and start to think and feel too much, that'd he'd stay that innocent forever.

*****

That Sunday night Kenny finally emailed the instruction for our semester project for History of Punk Rock. It was three lines long. According to what he wrote all we had to do was relate the songs from his playlist to our lives somehow, and explain why they left marks on us. In the end, he said he had to go because he was bleeding. The holidays were coming up. Everyone was coming undone.

There was too much work to do for my Sweat Time project to sleep, so I popped an Adderall and uploaded the shots of Johnny to my laptop. The rush inside me lifted off slow at first while the "before" scenes of him wailing on stuffed animals and pouncing half-naked on pillows played. I stopped those after a minute and a half to insert a black screen so that those teachers had time to consider what a terror he was. Then I cut in this scrolling list of behavioral problems along with their definitions that I'd lifted from the web. I never said he had them since they'd assume the worst on their own. See, people take pictures and words magnify them on their own. Everyone wants a tragedy.

Next, I dropped in still shots of paintbrushes and coloring books and had the words "Art Therapy" scroll across the screen to signal the salvation to come. The idea that art could save a savage little brat was too simple to be real, but none of our eager-believing teachers wanted reality. They wanted confirmation that they were doing good work and that no kid was beyond help. I had cast myself in the role of redeemer sure they would eat it up since if I was a saint then they were too.

At the end of the movie, I inserted the shots of Johnny grinning like a dope while he painted his turkey. I'd missed it before, but he wasn't faking. Maybe his head was full of the Pokémons he'd score, or maybe it was because I was hanging with him, but his cheesy smile was true. For a second I thought about shaking him awake to see what a star he'd become, but by then day was breaking through the stripped branches outside. The rush in my brain had fallen to an aching hum. I was spent, so I emailed my video to Jenna's mom with the word that I'd be out sick. Jaycee would vouch for me. She always had my back.

I heard my family wake up and start their day as I laid motionless in bed until the house was silent again. It was nice to be myself surrounded by all that hush. I doubt my parents even noticed I'd missed school, or if they did they'd decided it didn't matter since there were only two days of school left before Thanksgiving break.

\*\*\*

I'd been out for most of the day before I texted Jaycee to see what I'd missed. In no time she messaged back that

Jenna's mom had my Sweat Time project, but said she'd probably dock points from kids who'd sent them via email since only the achiever kids showed up to discuss *Go Ask Alice* in person like we were all supposed to. I shot her a smiley devil emoji and wrote that's why I didn't bother to come, even though it wasn't the truth, and promised to pick her up for Jenna's Sweat Time party Tuesday night.

"U want 2?"

"Yeah. Why?"

"When? Where"

"10. Ur place. Look $"

"KK"

If my mom and dad hadn't given me grief for missing one day, two days wouldn't make a difference. I picked the card for our group project off my nightstand and read it over and over again. "This is Now." A vacation would do me good, but first I had to follow up with Paige to see how her escape plan was going. If she was going to bolt for real I'd have to stop her silly ass, but the only way to ask was not to ask.

"Whats up?"

"Dont start," she replied.

"U cool?"

"Dont H8 on me." She must've taken a hit I hadn't heard about, and that worried me.

"Goin 2 Jennas?"

"Maybe." Her replies came fast like she was in a hurry to lose me. "Dont tlk 2 me if I do."

"No luv?"

"Off!"

I didn't reply since she might've blocked me if I pressed her. I was sure whatever went down was out there, and the story would find me sooner or later. If she was broken up she'd come back to me even if she decided to blame me for it. I was thankful for that.

***

I slept the best I could manage, but by Tuesday I was edgy over the fact that no one had messaged me the details about Paige if they knew them, or texted to see if I was alive. When you're out of sight it's easy for kids to forget you exist. Most people only care about their issues anyway. Husker Du sang "Don't Want to Know if You Are Lonely," and it turned me gray. I wondered if my parents even wanted kids, or if Johnny and I were only the next step after marriage and buying a house.

After school, Jaycee texted to make sure I wasn't for real sick, and warn me that Jenna's mom sent my Sweat Time report to Principal Keys. I told her that was bound to happen and didn't want to think about school. Then she wrote that she missed me and I texted the same back, but mostly because it felt good to be missed.

"Cant W8!," she wrote with this string of smiley faces and hearts like some middle school kid. That ruined her good pity for me.

I sent "Going sleep L8r," and turned off my phone. I hoped she wasn't picturing Jenna's party like some romantic overnight. I didn't know what we were exactly, and with the mystery of Paige's latest crash hanging on me I had to stick to solid friends for a while. The party was meant to turn up and get lost, not to play dating show reveal.

As the day ended outside, the best or worst that could happen waited for me on the other side of my bedroom door. My eyes shut tight while the sound of my brother's feet slapped across the floor beneath me. I heard the rumble of my parents arguing again through my wall. There was no chance to rest before the night was full-on. My phone played Kenny's list on random as I pulled open my nightstand drawer. No time to play sick. No time to move; only time to burn through the hours left before the night got live.

Adolescents tore through "Self Destruct" as I double-dosed on Adderall to stay on point and let the music in. Later, alone and sweating in bed, I downed Nyquil to smooth the manic rush. There was no sound other than the screams and guitars pouring from my phone. Paige was bound to show up to hate on me. Jaycee was waiting with a heart like a drinking glass. The numbers on my phone changed until it was Wednesday night, and time to move. I got as straight as possible, grabbed my gear, and opened the door to make a story.

\*\*\*

I drove to Jaycee playing Kenny's playlist, despite myself. I breathed as slow as possible to level myself out since I'd left my meds at home to force myself to go slow. I should've been above the songs Kenny pushed, but they'd started to work on me, which was stupid. It was stupid to adopt someone else's image of cool, and punk belonged to burnouts and kids in Goodwill clothes. I was better than that but hadn't found a way to shut it out.

Jaycee was in the parking lot outside her building, but it wasn't her. Her hair was Smurf blue, and she had on a short black dress and fishnet knee-highs as if we were off to ball. I flashed my headlights and wished I'd dressed up more. I had my usual hoodie and jeans on while she'd gone all out. That had to be disappointing for her.

"How do I look?" She switched the overhead light on so I got the whole picture. I'd never seen her in her punk glam, but it was deadly. Her lips were cherry as Jolly Ranchers, and her eyelids were lined out like a Bratz doll.

"Expensive." I was joking, but she took it as a compliment.

"You said to look money right?"

"You're a whole bank Jayce." I drove to the party house with the brand-new Jaycee palming my knee with one hand and scrolling through Kenny's playlist with the other. I tried to keep my mind off both. Paige was waiting, and she owed me an answer about what I'd done that was so wrong.

"I'll keep it slow so we can talk," Jaycee said before putting on The Dead Boys' crawling "Ain't It Fun." "Is this okay?"

"It's fine," I said. "You didn't have to get Gucci for me you know? Tonight is no big deal."

"I'm with you," she said, then pulled her skirt over her pale legs. I turned the heat up and stayed quiet. "Do you like me, Bryce?"

"Jayce, come on. You're my best friend."

"And?" she asked, as if it was obvious there was something left unsaid. I mean, I stepped off from love for her sake. Inside I was sure that if I let myself love her back sooner or later I would fuck it up and lose a girlfriend and my best friend at the same time. There wasn't anyone I had to break down how to play it either. It's hard to know which way to turn when no one gives you any answers. Your parents say go to school, the school says figure it out for yourself, and in the end you are totally confused and want everything and nothing at the same time.

"And I'll always have your back." I sped up, and pointed toward the sky. "Look at the moon. It's like it's about to hit us."

"Pretty," she said, "but it's not full yet."

"It will be soon."

"I love our drives." She braced her cheek against the window and took her hand off me.

"I love them too. When we're alone, we're bulletproof."

She turned up the volume and stared at the moon so we didn't have to talk about the space between us anymore.

***

By the time we reached the party house cars I didn't recognize had packed the driveway and filled the yard. They weren't parked so much as left where they'd stopped. After I managed to wedge my car into an open spot, Jaycee draped her arm across my shoulders and told me to let the song finish before we went inside. I wanted to touch her, and I didn't, so I kept my hands on the wheel until I unplugged my phone.

"Do you like me like this or not?" she asked. Her fingers brushed my neck like she was checking for a pulse, but I pretended not to notice while I turned on the overhead light to shoot her.

"Did Jenna's mom say what we have to read next?" She frowned at me but posed anyway.

"Some Indian book called *Think on These Things*. She gushed about how it went over not conforming and how simple love was in her guru voice. You should read it this time. It sounds legit." Jaycee took my phone and modeled it so the title of the last song glowed between us in the dark. "So what do you think about the song?"

"Honestly, I've heard those songs so much I can't hear them at all. It's like no matter how loud they get I don't notice the words."

She passed my phone back, then studied herself in the mirror. "You should give them a chance. They matter."

"I've got time," I said. "They're not going to disappear or anything."

"They could," she said kind of low, then switched off the light.

***

The trouble started because the party was turned up from the start. See, a party should start mellow and build. It

142

should take hours for everyone to get hyped, and then the flow has to blow off in stages so that by the end of the night the floor is covered with shoeless kids passed out on their bellies. That way no one gets hurt. The right flow stops drama before it starts because everyone is in rhythm and no one thinks about crying or fighting. They're too busy living. When a party rages from the start, drama breaks faster than anyone can keep up with.

Maybe it was Jaycee's fault for dressing like some punk princess. She shouldn't have changed up her style for me or imagined I'd come at her like some TV hopeful begging for a rose. See, before that party, she was my best friend, the only person I trusted. I didn't mean to wreck that.

Maybe it was Paige's fault for coming in all angry tears. The only reason she'd texted me to stay away was so there would be no doubt I would be there. Shoving someone away makes them ache for you. Tyler had proven that at least a million times.

I wish I could blame Jenna for inviting her Cherokee Hill Bullies over like they were on our level since if they hadn't been there then Jaycee wouldn't have gotten it so bad, but it wasn't on Jenna. What went down was on me for being so desperate to start over with Paige. I was so thirsty for another chance that somebody was bound to get crushed.

\*\*\*

The party was way out of control when Jaycee and I walked in. Tyler was racing through a case of beers on the coffee table, and daring two CH Bullies to keep up with him. Hanna watched him go rowdy. I wondered if he lost his mind again would she still cared enough to rescue him.

"Oh my God!" Jenna yelled from where she was wedged between two of her CH friends on the ratty couch. "Look at Miss Teen Ohio!" Her friends broke down. The Bully on her right hooted and clapped his hand, while the other one yelled for her to turn around.

"Ignore them," I said, but Jaycee's eyes got wet and darted around the room as if she'd walked in naked and had to count how many kids saw her.

"Promise you will stay with me," she said as she squeezed her fingers against mine.

"I'm here," I said, but pulled my hand away and shirked behind her. It was a cowardly thing to do, but when the spotlight is on a kid it's hard to fight the urge to run.

The CH Bullies gave up on racing Tyler through the case of beer and circled Jaycee. Even though it was steaming inside the party house with the crowd and all, they kept their Cherokee Hill Bulldogs jackets on like they were a gang.

"Damn girl, give us a spin," one of the Bullies said.

"You're dressed to impress, right?" another asked. "Show us what you're working with." His teeth were as white as the fangs on Johnny's monsters, and I wanted to crack every one of them.

Jaycee didn't say a word as they moved on her, but she reached behind her back for me frantically.

"Leave her alone okay?" I grabbed her hand to pull her back. "She's with me." The CH Bullies stopped to size me up. They could've taken me easy, but I wasn't about to let them act up on Jaycee without checking that.

"You Bullies can't hang. Why do you have stripes on your sleeves?" Tyler shouted as he cracked two new beers and held them up high. "I guess Dream Kids are the real lettermen here yo!" He pounded three more beers in less than a minute, then crushed them to show what a beast he was. Hanna had this face on like she wanted to gag, but she played watchdog despite herself.

Tyler's challenging their rank was enough to bring the Bullies back to the table and lift the heat off Jaycee. Together, we wrestled our way through the crowd to the kitchen before they changed their minds.

"So this is what I get for looking money?" Jaycee asked as she covered herself up with her arms. "Take me home."

"Look, forget those pricks." I turned on the faucet and filled a Solo cup with water, then passed it to her.

"No thanks. I don't want Tyler to start in with one of his straight-edge rants. Can't we just leave?" She hugged her arms tighter to her chest and trembled. If I'd been a better person then I would have taken her away. We could've gotten milkshakes, parked under the moon, and talked about how small we were in space that goes on forever, but that's not what happened.

As soon as I saw Paige push her way through the crowd and jet out the back door with her face streaked black I forgot about Jaycee. I didn't mean to leave her, but when I saw Paige torn up and crying it was like the light went off Jaycee, like she disappeared.

*** 

Paige sat on the edge of the empty pool in this ridiculous granny dress and struggled to untangle the strands of beads from the hair that hung over her face so she could light a cigarette. Her hippie transformation was complete. The whole time I'd known she kept changing as if she had to try out lives to find the one that fit her, but after years she was still searching.

"I'm only going to talk to you because you told me not to," I said. She wiped her eyes and gave me this crooked expression, but didn't tell me to leave. "You only texted me that because you want me here, right?"

She blew smoke into the air, defeated. "You know Bryce, that's the best example of high school boy logic I have ever heard. I so told you to stay away from me because I am secretly dying for you. Classic." She sighed kind of sad, then took another drag.

"We're the same age, and I don't go around constantly bragging about my great plans in a costume. You're not so grown-up or special you know?" The moon was bright enough to make the trees glow. The night was cold and quiet except for the muffled bass and howls from inside the house. I stood to leave but stopped when she started to sob.

"You're right. That's the truth isn't it?" She sucked up the snot running out of her nose and tossed her cigarette into the dry swimming pool.

"Do you want me here or not?"

"Oh you've already told me what I want and who I am," she said. "I'm sure you're dying to hear what happened so you can tell everybody what an idiot I am."

"I've never told anyone anything about you."

"True." She wiped her eyes, and turned my way. "I'm not going to Florida. No sunny beaches are waiting for me now."

"Frank changed his mind or something?" I did my best to act shocked.

"He told me he only said that because he was high. Plus I'm sure he's hooking up with someone else."

"Who? Another girl from our school?"

"Riley. She's always at his apartment when I come over, and girls can tell you know? I swear to God I can smell her on him." She lit another cigarette and clawed at one of the cracked tiles beside her. I asked her what she was going to do, but she only shrugged.

"Love isn't like the movies where no matter what goes wrong you end up together because it was meant to be.

Most of the time it doesn't even end when it ends. Look at me. I still love you, and that doesn't mean a thing."

"I don't believe this!" Paige said. "You honestly want to make this about you? In case you are too childish to appreciate it, this is *my* bad time okay? Tonight is *not* about you. How selfish can you be?"

"It's not like that. Maybe it doesn't make you feel better, but I wanted you to hear that."

"Way to jump on the sad girl, Bryce," Paige tossed a piece of tile at me. "Here's a hint, if you don't know what to say just shut up."

"Whatever. Keep on being the victim. I'm done." I left her by that empty pool and hated myself for dropping Jaycee. I hated Paige more for coming over just to bleed her problems on me. The party house was where we came *not* to think. It was the best escape we had.

***

For a minute I was terrified that Jaycee had run off on her own to find a way home, or worse, gotten carried off by the CH Bullies. The madness in the living room had flooded into the kitchen until the entire first level of the party house was a riot of bodies moving fast without direction. I felt raked out and wished I hadn't left my meds behind. I was too clear to deal with a whirlpool of mindless kids.

Jaycee was at the top of the stairs when I found her. Her hands covered her ears as if she was sure the house was about to explode. That was on me. I eased her up gently and led her to one of the bedrooms to prove she wasn't forgotten. Once we were inside, when the dim night blanketed us and the party became a separate thunder, she curled into herself on the floor.

"You left me," she said. Chalk-colored shafts of moonlight sectioned her body. "I asked you to stay with me or take me home, but you left the second you saw her."

"Do you want some music?" I took out my phone. "There's probably no way to back my car out now."

"I only want to be away from you."

There was no right thing to say, so I took pictures of her on the floor. Her black dress in the dim light turned her into a ghost.

"Stop that! I can't stand the way you take pictures to ignore me. I'm not a joke."

"I never said you were." I put my phone into my pocket and lay next to her.

"I am though. You have no idea. I'm glad you don't know what it's like to want someone who can't see it or doesn't care if he does."

"You think you're the only one?" I asked. The air smelled like dust and smoke. "It feels like you've swallowed a cinder, one that got stuck in your chest and keeps burning. And there's nothing you can do but hide how bad it hurts. You think of them every day no matter how pathetic it is when you know for a fact that you don't matter to them. But you keep burning and believing there is this chance, tomorrow or next year or whenever, and you hold on to that hurting because it is the only part of their love you can touch."

"Yes that, exactly," she said as she took my hand, "but how do you make it stop if you want it to?"

"Once someone is in you that deep I don't know if you can. Maybe it takes time. Maybe you learn to carry it, or it gets too much to take. For me, I'm just going to stop reaching out. I only catch thin air, then feel dumb."

Jaycee kissed me as her fists curled into my shirt. I went into her, ran my hands up her money dress until I found her panties, and stripped them off. We weren't there, and we were. In the dark, I watched her lips part and her body tumble over mine in flashes until I closed my eyes not to be. Blind and smothered by love I inhaled the smell of her perfume and the sweat that hung over us. I heard every breath she took. When I opened my eyes I saw hers' staring up at me white and pure in the dim blue room as if we'd found the answer. We were opened up, and free. Our bodies moved together to fill up all that infinite empty space inside ourselves and erase our minds.

It didn't last long. The moments you steal when you're floating above everything that cuts you never do. Before long I felt myself getting tight and had to jerk away before it was too late. After it was over I cleaned up with my t-shirt and collapsed by her. When she put her palm on my stomach I felt like the worst person in the world.

"It's done now," she said, calm and distant. "That's it. No going back. I always hoped it would be with you."

"I'm happy it was me too," I said, glad she couldn't see the shame washing over me. "You're my best friend."

"We're more than that now. Friends don't do that."

"Sure they do. Friends save each other."

She leaned over me. In the moonlight, her eyes had shifted pale as concrete. "But we're more than *just* friends, right? I mean, that wasn't some random hook up."

I arched up, took her palms in mine, and focused on her. For a second we stayed that way, each of us hoping the other shared our version of the truth.

"Jaycee," I struggled out as kind as possible, "we saved each other from hurting for a while. You saved me, and I saved you. But I've got bad wiring. Most of the time I have no clue what I'm doing, much less why I feel the way I do, or how I'll feel five minutes later. I don't know how to be alone or with other people. You don't want to deal with that. You have to forget what we did so it doesn't wreck what we've got."

"It already has." She dressed in a hurry to leave before she screamed or started to cry. Seeing her that way stabbed me, left me pinned to the floor.

"Don't let it. I've been twisted lately and need to get better. You understand, right? I love you. You're my best friend."

She jerked the door open and light poured in on me. "Don't ever say that you love me or that you're my friend! You're right. I'm going to forget everything about you. You don't have to worry about me. I'm not going to be your tag-along or charity case anymore. I was right too you know? It's done now." She disappeared, and I was more stranded than ever.

Paige crushed me, and I crushed Jaycee. Abandoned with nothing to do or say, no one to do or say it to if I had, out of place and time, I wished I'd had enough meds with me to go numb as all that nothing filling the galaxies above. The riot downstairs beat on. I wondered how she'd get home, or if she would. I should've chased her, driven slow until I figured out the right words, but I only closed the door to hide.

Outside the window, kids danced by the pool as if it was the best night of their lives. It amazed me, the idea of all that joy. I made myself small by the window and waited for the party to end. I wanted to text Jaycee and make sure she was safe, that she'd found a way home. I wanted to tell her how sorry I was, but sorry wasn't the right thing to say. The worst thing you can do is let someone love you just because it feels good to be loved.

# Chapter 9
# Kids Who Change

**THE FIRST** time I saw Paige I thought she was a boy. I was in line behind her on our first day of seventh grade. Her hair was shorter than mine, and she had on khaki shorts that went past her knees and a guy's t-shirt. While I tried to hide in the crowd she was determined to show the other kids what she was all about. It wasn't until she took her class list from the lady at the end of the line and turned around that I saw she wasn't a boy. She was a skater girl.

Her skater girl phase lasted most of the seventh grade. She came to school in Airwalk shoes that she had scuffed up with a nail file to give off the impression that she could grind, and wore a chain wallet instead of a purse. The other girls tried to dress like pop stars or their older sisters, but Paige was determined to be the opposite of pop star hot. She never learned to skateboard, but that didn't matter.

We had most of our classes together, and by the end of our first semester we were going out as much as you can go out in seventh grade. She told me she liked the way I made the teachers mad by always asking them to explain what the point of everything was, but I wasn't trying to be a rebel or anything. I only wanted to understand why we had to do what they told us to. Still, she was sure I was a bad boy and loved me for it.

Even though she dressed all skate park, she was a total kitten inside. After school, we'd hold hands on the curb while we waited for our parents to pick us up. On the days when they were late and the buses were gone, I'd eat the rings off her candy necklace. She smelled like Aloe Vera and sweat, but she tasted like sugar.

One day near the end of the school year, her mom caught us making out, and went off on her because I had my hand up her shirt and all. Paige didn't come back the last few weeks of school, and nobody heard anything. It wasn't until I saw her over the summer that she told me her mom sent her to a church camp with promise rings. That was the first time she told me she didn't want to see me anymore.

She was the first girl I did pretty much everything with, so it was hard to ignore her. When a girl's your first they're always in your head no matter how old you get or how much they change.

We both got selected for The Dream Academy halfway through eighth grade. My parents were super proud of me, but Paige's mom only kept her out of Saint Mary's Girls' School under the condition she started to act like a lady. She was a stranger from our first day of high school. She'd grown her blonde hair out and wore the same jean skirts and Hollister tops that the other girls did. One time I sat with her at lunch to catch up, but she pretended that I didn't exist while she went on to her girlfriends about how she wanted a little dog she could carry around in a purse. I called her a fake princess in front of her new friends, and she didn't talk to me for the rest of the year until we ended up in the drama club dressing room together during the Spring Formal.

Her date for the dance was this senior kid from another school who'd bailed on her to hook up with a girl from his school. She was drunk on wine coolers and crying when she came to me. I only pulled her into the dressing room so the other kids wouldn't see her that way, but as soon as the door closed she pulled off her dress. I listened to the music or voices outside while we had sex for the first time surrounded by these costumes from *Romeo and Juliet*. Afterward, we came back in time to catch the last slow dance, and I was sure she loved me. I didn't know better back then. Maybe I still don't. The next day she got back with her senior boyfriend like nothing ever happened.

Whatever happened to Paige the summer before we were sophomores, broke her up. She came back to school a total goth: black hair, black eyeliner, and black dresses. I asked why she turned goth, and she punched me real hard. She told me I'd never get her. I stayed away from her for months and waited for her to change again, but she stayed Hot Topic and started to smoke cigarettes between the buses when she could sneak out. It wasn't until I heard that she was cutting herself up that I'd had enough, and got the courage to call her out.

I found her between two buses smoking a cigarette and asked if she was turning into a razor kid. She told me to fuck off and said I was too young to understand her life, that I'd always be too young for her. After that, I wrote her off and figured she'd be dead or different if her mom even let her come back.

Last summer she started hanging around Jenna and the rest of us, and we kind of made up. She said she was sorry for treating me bad, and I apologized for calling her out even though I wasn't. When the days were hot she'd come over to the party house to lay out with the girls and smoke. Tyler and I drank while we watched the girls all oiled up and blazed, and the world seemed kind. Her hippie shift started when she met her college boyfriend at the end of summer. Maybe the bud she got from him caused it, or maybe she was still trying out lives, but either way she was a burnout by the time Thanksgiving break finally came.

But the fact that she was a stoner wasn't the reason she got pulled from The Dream Academy. It wasn't because of her community college boyfriend either. She got pulled because of what she did to escape the tutoring center her mom stuck her in.

Thanksgiving Break was almost over before I got the story. There were questions I'd never get the answer to, but I had to let them go.

*** 

The Wednesday after the party, after I crushed Jaycee true, I was so wracked with regret that every sound in the house felt like a shove. I dosed more than I should've and buried myself under my covers. I had to hide out and get my mind back together. A million thoughts ran through my head. I worried that Jaycee never made it home. I pictured Paige back with her boyfriend to stay above us in her mind. I wondered if Hanna had mothered Tyler home, or left him to party himself into a coma to teach him a lesson. When I'd left, the party house was trashed. That felt right.

On Thanksgiving Day my mother ordered a huge spread for us and kept up this happy hostess routine the whole dinner. Johnny went on about what he wanted from Santa and how he saw a horse with horns while my dad and I sat quietly waiting for dinner to be over. Mom said it was nice to have her family together again as if she didn't get that my dad and I weren't really there. I mean, she should've put our pictures on the table and saved herself the trouble of pretending.

After dinner, my dad went to his office and locked the door while Johnny shadowed my mom and asked if turkeys were real. She told him they were, then shooed him off to watch cartoons before grabbing her coffee mug and a bottle of wine. Every hope she'd had for a sentimental holiday was lost. If I'd been a better person I would've told her that I loved her, but the sight of dirty dishes reminded me of the diner and Jaycee and made it impossible for me to love anyone, especially myself. I went upstairs and waited for Thanksgiving to end so there'd be no reason to feel like a dick for not appreciating the things I hadn't lost.

\*\*\*

The Friday after Thanksgiving, I woke upbeat. Two days of fighting not to think had left me scraped thin, but I had to move. They have hospitals for kids who can't get out of bed when the dark times hit. Our semester project was coming due, and for the first time in my life, I was glad to have homework. It's easy to want to die when you don't have any reason to be.

I grabbed my camera and texted everyone except Jaycee to meet me at the party house late at night to put in work. If Jenna's mom wanted to see what it meant to be a kid at *Now* I was down to give her more than she could take. First, though, I had to check on Jaycee. She could hate me or love me. I'd deal with either as long as she was safe.

On my drive over to the diner Generation X's "Kiss Me Deadly" played, and for the first time, I heard it clear. It was like Jaycee was riding right next to me. The sky was gray and cold as I remembered the ghost of her, all sugar and trusting, in the moonlight of that bare room. I was determined to make sure nobody ever heard the story about that night since nothing said meant nothing happened. Kenny was waiting to see the bite marks his songs had left on me, and every scar had Jaycee's name on it. I swore to make her an icon for broken hearts when it came time to turn in my semester project for History of Punk Rock. Those are the only real heroes anyway. The ones who bleed out and keep living.

***

I guessed Jaycee would be at the diner since she had no other place to be with school out. Maybe that was a jerk thing to believe, that her life was only school and work, but I hoped that even if she did have something fabulous going on that she'd gone to work to avoid remembering that night. She could rip me up, I deserved that, but she had to be there. If she wasn't I'd be too sick with stress about what might've happened to leave my bed.

Jaycee came out of the kitchen when she heard the bell above the door ring, but stormed off once she saw me. I settled into one of the cracked vinyl seats and waited for another customer to show so she'd have to come out whether she wanted to or not. I put my earbuds in and closed my eyes to game plan. I'd let her talk first to get it out. Saying sorry from the start was the same as saying it was no big deal. I was tranced out good when she yanked my earbuds out to ask what I wanted.

"I had to see if you made it home," I said. "I was scared."

"No you weren't. If you were so terrified about me you would've tried to find me. You were my ride. Do you even know how far I had to walk that night? Who does that?"

"I was trying to give you space," I said. "I thought you wanted to kill me."

"I did, but I still had to get home. Didn't you think about what could've happened?"

"All night, and every day since. Sit down okay? We should talk."

"I'm working," she said, "and you already said what you had to."

"But I have to get you for our group project. I figured maybe you could talk about what it's like to not have your dad around." I showed her my flip cam, and her face flashed hot.

"That was a secret! Do you think I want anyone to see me up on screen talking about that? How stupid are you? Don't you know how to keep a secret?"

"Yeah," I said, and put my camera away. "I didn't tell anyone about us."

"Why not? You could use that for our project. Want to shoot me talking about how I lost my virginity to a prick who said I should forget it, and that we're awesome friends?"

I pulled a chair out for her and kept quiet until she gave in. "I'm not good at explaining how I am, and I didn't mean to hurt you. I was twisted over Paige still, then we clicked so quick that there wasn't any time for me to think about what to say or how I felt, you know?"

Outside a crosswalk beeped like a timer running through the second left for me to line out a solid case, but honestly, I was still lost. All I knew was that I needed her and she needed me, but there was too much static between us to figure out who we were. "Let's talk about anything else, and get normal again," I said. "Did you make any money today?"

"Money is a normal talk for you huh? And no. After Thanksgiving, everyone is either off work or stuffed. I should've stayed home."

"I'm glad you didn't. I don't get how this place stays in business." I scanned the cracked floor and chipped tables, the bent plastic menus, and the security camera above the cash register.

"People come in all the time. This place has been around forever. It's a legacy. That means a lot. This was the first diner on the block." She took my phone off the table, pushed the earbuds in, and hit play. "'Damaged Goods'?" she asked.

"Yeah, Gang of Four. I know what I'm going to do my project for Kenny about."

"I've been listening to that track a lot lately," she said.

"Does that security camera even work?"

"No," she said as she handed my phone back. "The weird thing though, is that I feel like I'm forever being watched and judged anyway. Like there are cameras everywhere."

"There are, but no one pays attention to anyone except themselves." I tried to hold her hand, but she slid it off the table.

"At least now you're making sense. What do you want, Bryce? I mean, for real?"

Her eyes were still searching me for a reason to believe, and I wanted to be the kind of kid she could believe in. I wanted her to love me again and deserve it, but there was some defect in my brain holding out for Paige from seventh grade even if she was buried and gone. Jaycee opened her hand on the tabletop and I took it.

"I want to be who you think I am," I said. "I want to be good." She stayed still as she sorted out what that meant.

"You will or you won't," she said. "But I want you to swear to me that you'll always tell me the truth. Don't say you love me if you don't. Be my friend, love me or drop me, but promise you'll be honest about whatever we are."

"I promise. And I'll never leave you alone again either."

"So we're friends?"

"No," I said. "More than that."

***

I didn't go home after getting things straight with Jaycee, or as straight as they could be. Instead, I drove around until it was time to meet up at the party house. I figured the others would show if only because there is nothing more that kids want to do after a holiday than get away from their families. Driving kept me from stressing about what I'd said, and how Jaycee heard it. I turned up the volume and wished love stayed as simple as stealing kisses in middle school.

Tyler and Hanna were busy helping Jenna clean up when I joined them to wipe away the reminders of the night I'd failed so hard. After we finished I showed them my camera, then gave them the rundown of what I had in mind.

"This has to be like straight confessions so don't hold back." I sat a chair against the wall to frame them up for the interrogations. "Jenna's mom needs to hear what it's like to deal with the shit we have to, right? Let's drop the real on her about the *Now* so she will never dare to push kids to get real again."

"Ugh, why do we have to do this? She doesn't know anything about anything, and nothing's going to change that." Jenna flopped onto the couch and covered her face.

"That's what I'm saying. This is our chance to teach her. Don't sweat. I'll blur our faces and scramble everyone's voices so it plays witness protection."

"Whatever," Tyler said. "Can't we just write an essay or something?"

"Do you want to write an essay?" I asked, and he shook his head. "Me either. So who's going to get real first?"

"I will," Hanna said, and took the hot seat. "You said you're going to hide us, right?"

"This is about the truth, but I got you covered. No one wants to deal with their story getting out so trust me, nobody will be able to tell who you are." I got on one knee and held my camera steady. "Quiet on the set. Rolling."

"This is me *Now*. You can't see me or anything, but here it goes. Okay. My whole life everyone always told me how pretty I was. I did these baby beauty pageants when I was little and everything because my mom made me, or I wanted to. I don't remember. I just remember that I was sure that I was this princess until two years ago when I posted this 'throwback Thursday' pic of myself at the beach. I thought everyone would die over how cute I looked, but this girl, Alyssa, commented that I must have always had a belly roll."

Tyler shouted "Boring!" behind me, and Hanna's face knotted up like shoelaces.

"So that was two years ago," I said. "What's that got to do with now?"

"This." She opened her mouth wide for me to zoom in. When the camera focused on the roof of her mouth it looked like she'd tried to swallow a stray cat alive. "This is me now," she said. "Those scratches are from my fingers, from making myself barf. I can't eat without throwing up or else I feel like a balloon. It's like every time I eat, my body swells up, and I get terrified that if I don't run to the bathroom I'll stay that way forever. My mom made me go to her doctor last week."

"What did he say?"

"She. I tried to lie and say I was just stressed out, but she didn't believe me. She told me about this girl who had to have her gall bladder removed because she did what I do. She gave my mom the number for the therapist too, but I'm not going to do this forever. I just want to take a selfie without seeing my belly roll you know? I want to be pretty again. That's worth staying sick for, right?"

She walked out of frame, and I paused my camera.

"That's sick," Tyler said. "Why didn't you tell me?"

"Don't even start," she said. "You had to know."

"Your turn Tyler."

Tyler sat with his elbows on his knees so that only the top of his head showed. "What do you want me to say?"

I didn't answer. When you stay quiet people always share too much.

"Now I'm lying low I guess," he said. "I used to be straight business though."

"Tell me how you operated?"

"I had more games than Playstation, man. I used to lift free golf vouchers from the country club then sell them for twenty bucks apiece since it's all profit." He laughed to himself but didn't look up.

"Boring. No one feels sorry for rich golfers. Get real. What's on you now?"

"I messed up," he said. "I used to steal liquor, and sell it to these girls at a Catholic school." He raised up and cocked his head to the side for the camera. "I banked like Bill Gates until I tried to cut them off."

I paused my camera and asked him what he meant, but before he could answer Hanna shouted that she'd made him stop drinking and dealing before she took him back. Tyler shook his head and said, "What can I say, man? The things we do for love."

"So now you're out of business?"

"Yeah, no, I don't know. The girls I used to hook up keep hassling me, threatening to turn me into the cops if I don't come through since they saved my texts and all."

"Do you think they're telling the truth?"

"Of course they are," Tyler said with this face like he wanted to puke too, "Wouldn't you? There's nothing I can do, man. I'm trying to wait it out since you can't erase your past, right? It was my fault for acting so boss. They'll either wreck me, or they won't."

"So now you're what?"

"Screwed or saved. No way to tell which yet. I just have to play it off, and hope they find a new connection."

"Maybe they'll just get tired of hassling you," I said.

"I doubt it. I got like two more crazy texts today. They won't leave me alone until they get what they want, even if that's just to make me feel awful for fun."

I stopped filming as he slumped off to crash next to Hanna, then waved Jenna over. "You're up," I said as she sat down in a huff.

"I don't want you to blur me out, okay?" she said. "I want my mom to see my face when she hears this. Promise?"

"You're the one who has to deal with the video," I said. "Go."

"This is me now mom. I had a great Thanksgiving. It was *just* the best. I came home, and there was no dinner, no parade on TV or anything, only this moving truck parked in our driveway with two guys loading up my dad's stuff. He had finally had enough of my mom, and was out. Do you hear me? You blew it. I'm moving in with Dad, and you can keep your weird school, your ugly paintings, and your bad poems. I'm going to Cherokee Hills where things make sense, and you can keep teaching nothing. That's what you taught me. I'm over this!" Jenna stormed off, but we didn't follow her. The shoot was supposed to be one big finger in the air for her mom's class, but she'd gone nuclear.

"What do you think will happen?" Hanna asked. "I mean, you can't turn that in."

"I have to. She set herself up when she handed us 'This is *Now*.' I'm done being fake. You think we can still come here after Jenna's gone?"

"No way," Tyler said, but Hanna argued there was a shot since the party house had been like our second home for so long. It would be cold to leave us without a place to belong.

"We should go," Tyler said. "Jenna needs time to cool off."

"You two go. I'll wait here so she's not alone."

"Sure you're not expecting anyone else?" Tyler smirked.

"No," I said. "No one else cared enough to show." I moved the chair back as they walked out with their arms around one another. I doubted Tyler would stay sober and quit scheming, but love made people do stuff they wouldn't if they had their own way. So did fear.

***

I went slack on the couch, plugged in my earbuds, and played Dwarves' *Everybody's Girl* while I waited for Jenna to come back. Paige showed up instead. That killed the music.

"You missed the excitement," I said as I held up my camera.

"That's why I'm always late. It lets me skip high school drama. What happened?" She put her feet in my lap, then took my camera away.

"Like I texted you. We worked on our semester project tonight. It got real confessional."

"What'd you learn?" She pointed the camera at me, but the red light wasn't on. I was safe. "Hanna is a skeleton kid, Tyler's going clean and might be screwed for it, and Jenna's going to Cherokee Hills since her parents are splitting up."

"What about you?" The red light turned on. "Tell me about being a drug dealer."

"Put that away. I'm not a drug dealer. I just share you know? I help friends in need."

"Isn't giving away drugs the same as dealing?"

"I don't know. Ask my dad. Ask my psychiatrist."

"You're funny," She shut my camera off and passed it back. "Want to hear my confession?"

"Sure," I said, definite that she was going to cut me up with some lame story about how great her boyfriend was, but that's not what happened. It would've saved so much heartache if it was only that.

"Okay," Paige tucked a leg underneath herself as she closed her eyes to decide how best to let it out.

"By this time next week I'll be at Saint Mary's if my mom can transfer me this late," she said with a laugh that wasn't. "You think Tyler will hook me up if I get sent there?"

"Don't joke if you're telling the truth. What happened? What's the story?"

This is how Paige told it. The Dream Academy had sent a letter to her mom the week before Thanksgiving Break that said she was in danger of failing. That seemed impossible since most of our classes didn't have grades, only closing letters from our teachers that went over how we did and whether we passed or not, but Paige said she was over high school and had checked out a long time ago. She didn't think her teachers noticed, but they did.

Her mom went ballistic and stuck her in this tutoring center filled with these super-motivated Asian kids who wanted to call a lawyer whenever they got a 98 on a test instead of 100. What could she do? She hated it, but her mom had taken away her keys when she found out she was dating a community college guy. Paige's mom drove her, and she went. Simple as that. But Paige knew how her mom talked about the other kids at the tutoring center, and came up with a plan.

She went to the tutoring center every day, and every night when she came home she changed a little. She didn't make one big shift because that would've been too obvious. She did it a little at a time. On Monday she started wearing her hair up in a bun with pencils stuck through it. By Wednesday she'd drawn these lines out from the corners of her eyes. Not big ones. You'd have to stare to notice them. When Thursday came she covered her mouth and bowed her head all shy every time she laughed. It wasn't until Friday when she came downstairs during one of her mom's parties dressed in a bathrobe with a paper fan that her mom realized what she was doing. Paige had painted her face like a Geisha and spoke with this bad Japanese accent to underline what her mom had turned her into. She told me her mom sent her to her room and wouldn't speak to her until her friends left. Then, when they were gone, she screamed at her for being a total racist. Paige was sure she'd get sent off, but she was also positive that she'd never have to go to the tutoring center again.

"Why didn't you tell me at the Sweat Time party?" I asked.

"I told you that night wasn't about you," she said. "That's why I came here tonight."

"You don't have to do the project if you're getting transferred you know?"

"I didn't come here for the project," she said. "I came here because tonight *is* about you. Let's go upstairs. I have *got* to tell you something."

I followed her because the defective part of me wanted to, even though the good part didn't.

***

We sat on the carpet in the same bedroom where Jaycee and I had hidden when we were falling apart. Somehow every celebration that week had turned into a funeral. The moon had gone away, and inside there were only shadows and the sound of Paige rummaging through her oversized purse. I pulled at the shag carpet and waited for what came next.

Paige sparked her lighter and lit a candle that sat inside a tin. I asked if she wanted to tell me a ghost story, and she said those were the only kind she had. Light danced in yellow waves across her body.

"You ever wake up and realize you were wrong about everything? Like the person you are isn't you, but only this part of you trying to be important." She let her fingers inch over the flame until she had to pull them away.

"I guess. I mean, I wish I had this instruction manual for life instead of being left to find my way." She let the flame touch her fingertips.

"Stop that! You're scaring me."

"I'm scared too." She blew on her fingers and tried to smile. "Come over here."

I crawled across the floor until we were pressed together by the candle. "You've never been afraid of anything."

"That's because you don't know me. No one does. I'm totally afraid of starting over with a bunch of Catholic girls. I won't fit in there. I'm not all 'Hail Mary' like they are. Plus, my sister thinks I'm the devil so she's probably already told everyone there how awful I am."

"You'll be a rock star." I nudged her as the candle wax melted and made the room smell like strawberries. "Tyler told me Saint Mary's is a school with two hundred girls and one virgin."

"Who's that?"

"The statue of Mary on the lawn that prays for the ones who aren't."

She snorted, then wrapped her arms around me. "You're the only one who's always there for me, you know?"

"You don't care about friends. This entire year you've either been planning to take off or treated me like I'm beneath you."

"I can't do that anymore. Besides, Jaycee has you now. Everyone saw her doing the walk of shame the last time we came here."

"Is that the story?" No one had told me, probably because I was the hero for scoring on her. Kids can't keep a secret, especially if it was juicy with sex. Jaycee was set to get crushed again once she heard the rumor, and I'd be a liar regardless. No matter how hard I tried to tie things together, they always came undone.

"The gist of it. The official version has way more details," she said. "I was jealous."

"Nobody has any idea what we did or didn't do, and why would you care anyway?"

"I came here for you." She leaned forward until her lips were inches from mine. The heat from the candle passed through the space between us. "You're always there in the end."

She came closer than before, daring me to move. I wanted to, and I didn't. Our lips met before I had the chance to decide who to be, and in no time I was back in that drama club dressing room with her in the dark. For a second it felt good to go back in time.

The room flashed white as Jenna yelled "Smile!" I had covered my eyes in the glare and saw the outline of her holding her phone. "You two are hot!"

"What is wrong with you?" I tried to find my feet, but knocked over the candle and caught a spray of hot wax that torched my arm.

"Don't be so dramatic, Bryce. I'm just playing. Finish what you started, but leave the lights on!" She coughed like she couldn't take it, and shut the door.

Paige swatted her hand in front of her face and laughed so hard I was sure she'd set me up.

"Funny huh? One big prank." I blew on my arm and hand while she shook her head and pointed at me. "What?"

"Bryce, you totally got caught red-handed." She choked for air and held up my arm to show me the splatter of strawberry red wax that plastered me from my elbow to my wrist.

"Forget it. Jenna's going away, and so are you. She's right though, let's finish what we started."

Paige wiped her cheeks on her sleeve and packed the candle back into her purse.

"No matter where you go I'll be with you," I said. "You don't have to be scared or wonder who you are with me."

"Bryce, that means a lot, it does, but you know I have a boyfriend. I'm not going to let my mom ruin that too." She was still there, but she wasn't the same girl who kissed me less than a minute before.

"You said tonight was my night." I picked the wax off my arm. "I thought we were starting over."

"Don't think like a high school boy." She stroked my hair. "This was your night. I wanted to kiss you goodbye."

"But we're friends."

"We are friends," she said as she opened the door, "and more than that, but it's not the same. You get that, right?" She gave me this pitiful look as if I was a dog about to get put down.

"I only get that I don't *get* anything."

"That's because you never change. Grow up, Bryce. You're too old to live in a dream world."

***

Once Paige left I focused my camera on the window, that black square of night hollowing out the white walls around it, and waited for it to swallow me. I heard my phone buzz and wished the other side of the door led out into that endless black nothing forever and ever. But buzzing and lights brought me back into the present where I was dumb and beat with no way to make things right.

My phone had thirteen messages from Jaycee. I touched her name on the screen, sick that our story was out. I didn't tell anyone about us, but it was on me for using her to disappear. I tapped her name to explain what I'd heard, but her messages weren't about our story if she even knew. You can take a story, but you can't take pictures.

"U R SOOO TRU!!!" Jaycee texted underneath a pic of Paige kissing me. The messages were at most ten seconds apart: "WHAT A FRIEND!" "LIAR!!" "WHY?" and on like that. I read them and trashed them, but she sent them faster than I could thumb delete so there was no doubt how low I was. I shut my phone off and fought to breathe. My chest felt like it was cracking open. Jenna had to pay.

I searched the party house for her, but she had bounced. I cussed her name at the top of my lungs out back where the stars had left. All that rage set off a panic attack and left me shaking on the dirt until the night chilled me still.

***

How I got home is one of those things I can't remember. When my nerves hit I lose myself. I lose time. I came to in my room with my phone on my chest. My earbuds were gone, and The Germs sang "What We Do is Secret" directly into my heart.

Jenna came first.

"U up? Why send that to JC?" I hit send and prayed she'd reply.

"4 fun Shes rachet FAKE She never belong."

"That's crazy bitch shit and you got her and me wrong I was wrong but you know the rules don't talk/didn't happen glad you're gone," I responded, then went to Jaycee's messages. They'd stopped after midnight, so there was no use in trying to hit her back. Falling asleep was hopeless. I was so wired that it was either move or end up in a hospital.

There'd been so many nights when I'd begged God for sleep, or did more than I should to go out. I didn't want to die. I just didn't care if I did when the heavy times hit me. Most kids aren't afraid of dying, since they can't imagine forever, and death is one of those things that happens to other kids. I opened the picture that Jenna sent Jaycee again. It was a real nightmare. See, most kids aren't afraid of dying. They're afraid of being found out, or staying who they are.

# Chapter 10
## Kids in Stories

HERE'S THE thing about stories. The main reason kids can't keep them to themselves is because the first person who tells a story becomes *the* authority on it since they were the source. See, if any kids hear a different version of the story that sounds too out there to be true, sooner or later they're bound to backtrack the telephone game to the first person who put the news on blast. That makes the first person super important, and if you know something is about to get out, if you're smart, you'll have one of your friends put the story out first. That way you can control which way it spins before it gets demented. The downside is that if the wrong person spreads the story first, and this happens most of the time, you've got no shot at convincing anyone that what actually went down is different than what they heard from that first gossip queen. No matter what you say it only comes off like you're trying to cover your tracks, take the heat off a kid you like, or make the whole deal seem like a huge misunderstanding. The more you explain the worse you look, and the more convinced everyone is that you're lying. The first person has the official version. Nothing can change that. Unfortunately for Jaycee, the first person to spread the story about us going upstairs together at the party was Jenna. Maybe she figured pissing me off by making Jaycee out to be a skank would keep her from daring to keep trying to fit in, or maybe she hoped it'd get her mom in trouble since she owned the party house. Either way the Monday we came back from Thanksgiving break she'd totally poisoned Jaycee's rep and had me ready to get major payback.

I didn't hear the story until after homeroom because Jenna's mom walked in like a zombie, and dropped her head onto her desk which made a big scene. Jenna was out and so was Paige. I prayed I'd never have to see either of them again.

"Carol do you want our updates on our semester projects now?" that achiever kid Heather asked. She had this thick binder in her lap with different colored tabs sticking out from it which made it obvious that she'd worked way too hard over break. She was juiced to show off and quaked in her seat like she'd downed a dozen Red Bulls.

"Not today," Jenna's mom said. "We'll revisit your semester project later on. I'm not feeling well today." That was a relief since I still had to get Jaycee on video if I could make her stop wishing me dead.

"But I *really* think you're going to want to see this," Heather pleaded, but Jenna's mom told her to be patient, then burrowed her head into her folded arms like some kid in detention.

"What's up with her?" Tyler asked.

"I guess the whole divorce thing," I said. "Let's bounce."

"Library?" Hanna asked, and with no better option we followed her out. Jaycee trailed behind us and ignored me whenever I tried to make eye contact. It made no sense that she tagged along if she couldn't stand the sight of me.

Maybe she only came to remind me what a dick I was in case I had forgotten.

\*\*\*

The Dream Academy's library wasn't like other schools. It wasn't stacked with books and outdated magazines. Instead, it was one giant computer lab with rows of desktops, tablet computers in racks, and things that had no business being there like a popcorn machine and old video games like Double Dragon and Galaga that we could play for free. It didn't even have a librarian, only these help screens that would transfer whatever book we needed to our phones or computers. The second level had a walkway that overlooked the tech-loaded first floor with these sound-proof study rooms that looked like miniature racketball courts furnished with yoga cushions.

We found four seats together, but the second we started to play online something was off. The other kids weren't scrolling the net all slumped and dead-eyed. Instead, they kept glancing over at us and whispering. I told Jaycee that I thought we should bounce, but she said she was totally over whatever I thought.

"Let's go upstairs to the study rooms," I said, but Tyler blew me off since there weren't computers there and he was updating his fantasy football team. "I can't stand everyone watching me."

"No one is watching you," Hanna snickered. "They're scoping Jaycee out."

"What do you mean?" she asked with this honest surprise that gored me. I was sure she'd heard by then, but when you're the story you're always the last one to know.

"Oh my God," Hanna said. "You *have* to know. I mean, it's been a week."

"Know what?" She shrank into her seat.

"Are you going to tell her?" Hanna asked.

"Can we please go to a study room already?" I stood and begged Jaycee to follow me. Hanna came along too if only to make sure I gave her the complete version.

As we made our way up the stairs some kid shouted "Light her up pimp!" I didn't look back to keep from coming off proud.

Once we found an empty study room, I waited for Jaycee to settle in. Hanna joined her to play moral support, but I was sure she only wanted to jump in on the story. The next best thing you can be besides the first kid to tell the story is to be the person who leaks what's going around to the star of it. That way you get to watch the news hit them, and pretend you care no matter how many people you've already told.

"Do you want to give her a clue, or should I?" Hanna asked. It was Jenna's fault, it had to be, but since Paige hadn't given me the details I had to let Hanna drop the story on Jaycee. No matter how bad I wanted to be the one to break the story going around, Hanna had the official version. Girls always hear more than guys do anyway. We never care enough to learn more than who scored.

"Tell me," Jaycee said. "It can't be any worse than what Jenna sent me anyway." The idea of tearing me apart was painted across her face. I turned and scanned the kids below us typing, texting, and talking, and pictured each one spinning the story they heard or half-heard into the sluttiest version possible. None of them cared that they were destroying the best girl I had ever met just to have something to say.

Behind me, I heard Hanna take a deep breath and say "Okay," before she gave Jaycee the entire evil rundown.

This is how Hanna told the story, and she swore it was official. Last Tuesday when we all went to the party house to celebrate the end of Sweat Time Jenna said Jaycee walked in dressed like a stripper and tried to hook up with three of her friends from Cherokee Hills who blew her off since she was such a skank. Then she tried to hook up with me, but I wasn't having it until I went outside and got way stoned with Paige. When I came back she was still desperate to get used and begged me to bang her out. Jenna said that Jaycee didn't even bother to close the door, and like half the kids there were in the hall watching us get it on and cheering. When it was over Jenna said I told Jaycee to get to stepping because I was through with her trashy ass, but instead of leaving she went downstairs and started pawing on some CH Bully until he gave her a ride home for a blowjob. Hanna said that was the story. That was the truth.

Jaycee sat iced in her seat. "So that's who I am now?"

"No. Don't be like that," I said. "That's all Jenna. You're not like that."

"I'm not?" Jaycee asked, as her body tensed up.

"No. You're sweet. It's on me. It's on Jenna for making everything up."

"She didn't make everything up though," Jaycee said. "Some of it's true, right?"

"What are you talking about?" I asked as she went for the door. "How did you get home anyway?"

"Does it matter?" She shoved me out of her way. "You don't care about the truth. You have no idea what that means!" Then she ran past me and rushed down the stairs.

Hanna put her hand on my back and we walked down to the library together. "You don't think she did that, right?" I asked, but she only shrugged and said that's the story.

Downstairs, Tyler asked if I'd lost my party favor without taking his eyes off the screen.

"Don't start," I said. Jenna's story was barely true, but it shredded my guts wondering what was real. I imagined Jaycee trading herself for a ride to spite me, and got acid. It was impossible to believe, but she didn't set me straight. Maybe that's the way it went down, or maybe she only wanted me to hurt long and deep the way she had.

The bell rang as a kid I didn't recognize shouted "Playaaa!" my way and cheesed. While the rest wandered to class, and I skipped out and drove home. I was bursting to lock myself away. No one could touch me in my room. The bad times only came when I opened my door.

\*\*\*

One day is a long time for a story to go around, and the word on Jaycee had been out for at least a weekend since Paige heard it last Friday. By the time I came back to school on Tuesday, still full of what-ifs and grieving, the pressure had gotten to Jaycee. She didn't have to say anything, and wouldn't have to me anyway, but it was obvious the story had taken her. The second I saw her in our English class it was clear what she planned to be.

See, when you're on the wrong end of a story you only have three options. The first, and best one, is to wait it out. No matter how awful a story is it gets old sooner or later, especially if something even more heinous goes down like a kid gets pregnant or ends up in a wheelchair. The second option is to try and explain what actually went down and turn on the mouthy kid who started it. The only chance you have to flip the script is to turn whoever spread the rumor into a bitch with an agenda. I prayed Jaycee would deal with it that way, but she wasn't built to play offense. No, she decided to take the only option left which was the worst one. She decided to be what everyone said she was so they'd have nothing to talk about. You can't hate on someone for being who you said they were.

Jaycee came in dressed like she was going to a club or something. It was the first time I'd ever seen her wear makeup to school and she had it on thick. She'd cut a slit halfway down her shirt and wore a skirt too high to ignore. Snow covered the ground outside, but she wore high heels that she could barely walk in. While Jenna's mom handed out packets Jaycee bit her thumb and twirled her hair like a nympho. It made me heartsick the way she broadcasted her damage and waited for more to follow. That's the thing about hurting. If you get hit hard enough you start to like it, belong to it, want to stay down because you know how it feels and in a messed up way that makes you feel safe, like you belong.

"You can open them now," Jenna's mom said once she'd finished handing out the packets. "Take the rest of the period to consider where you'd be happiest, where you can set your feet firm, reach your arms toward the sun, and grow taller than you ever imagined." The words were from her usual 'follow your bliss' script, but she said them as if she was reading an obituary.

"What the hell is she talking about now?" Tyler asked.

"College." Hanna opened her packet and dumped out at least fifty more college brochures. "I guess she wants us to think about where we want to go."

The achiever kids sat at their desks and poured over the latest brochures as if they were planning a dream vacation. I heard them talk about pre-tests and grants and all those nails inside me went pointy side up. I hadn't thought about college since my crew took shotguns to our boxes. The achiever kids went on about application deadlines and letters of recommendation. It's easy to forget the future exists when you aren't sure you can live one more day.

Planning for college was stress I didn't need, but if I didn't get busy I'd get left behind while the achiever kids went to Big Name Old Buildings Happy Multi-Racial Students University. I had no idea where to start, and doubted I'd make it to Christmas.

Paige came in late and sat by herself on the other side of the room. When she got her packet she pretended to read through the brochures as if no one else was there. Maybe it was too late in the semester for her to transfer, but I hoped that wasn't the case.

Tyler shuffled his brochures but kept glancing over at Jaycee as though I didn't notice.

"Whatever you have in your head forget it," I whispered. "She's mixed up right now. She's got issues."

"Hey man, the ones with issues are the most fun, right?" He jabbed me with his elbow, but I held off on hitting him back.

"Seriously, man. She's just putting up a front." The pictures of rolling lawns where happy students beamed as they walked beneath magnolia trees sent jolts of electricity through me and made the glossy print run together.

"Her front is banging though," Tyler said under his breath so Hanna couldn't hear. "How was she? You've *got* to tell me what it was like when that good girl went bad."

The current inside me spit lighting through my brain until I couldn't take it. I twisted away from Tyler's bro hug, grabbed my bag, and told Jaycee we had to talk. She gave in and followed me out the second Jenna's mom turned to write a list of famous college dropouts on the board. I doubt she even noticed we'd left, but the sight of me taking her away definitely made the story juicier.

Out back, snow drifted on the breeze. I took off my coat to cover a bench so that Jaycee had a place to sit that she wouldn't freeze to in that skirt. She didn't have to stay, but the whole time we walked out she never asked me to let go. Maybe she wanted to see if I cared enough to stop her.

"It's freezing out here," she said. "Don't you *ever* boss me that way again!"

"I'm watching out for you. What's your plan? You want the entire school to think you're an easy score?"

"They already do, thanks to you," she said. "Want to see what they've been snapping me?" She stuck her phone in my face so I could read all the DMs from dudes hitting her up, and the others that said she was a whore who should get a disease and die. "This was saving each other right?"

"That was Jenna, not me! I've always stood up for you."

"Like at the country club?"

"I didn't want you there. I even went to make sure you were cool."

"Yeah, I came home wasted and drenched in a tennis outfit that my mom won't stop asking about. I was so cool. Thank you!"

Goosebumps covered her blue skin, and for the first time, I loved her completely without worrying about Paige. We had the same kind of lost. Neither of us had any idea who to be anymore.

"Look, it is my fault for not being straight with you, but I am now, okay? I want you to be with me. Forget everything that's gone down. I don't care what anyone says. I need you. You're the only one who sees me, who *really* cares."

Jaycee stood and pulled my coat around her as class let out inside. "You remember when I asked you what would make you happy?" she asked, and I said yes. "I used to think it was me, but I was wrong. I'm not even the same person. You saw what those kids wrote right? We're who kids say we are."

"No, we're not. I'm not a drug dealer and you're not a slut. We're just messed up. I want you to be with me. It'll kill the story."

"Kill the story?" Her cheeks flushed hot. "Do you think I care about what anyone says?"

"Yeah, that's why you got wasted at the country club, right?"

"No! I went there to be with you, okay? I figured if I partied with you you'd see me as more than this good girl who had to beg rides to hang. God, you're *so* dumb sometimes."

"Don't say that. Paige always says that. How did you get home from that party anyway?"

The heat drained away from her face as her lipstick smudged mouth fell open. "Jesus," she said, "you believe that? After all this time you believe that I'd do something like that?" Before I could say another word she rushed inside with her head down.

I chased after her, but one of the secretaries snagged me before I had the chance to say the right thing for once.

\*\*\*

The secretary asked me to call her Grace, then planted me in Principal Key's office to wait. Inside. I tried to forget about Jaycee and focus on every reason that I could get kicked out. When I was sure I was alone I popped a Xanax, and after it smothered the jerking inside me I scanned his office to get a read on him.

There were pictures of Einstein, Steve Jobs, and Shakespeare in frames. His bookshelf had a dozen copies of *Keys to Success*, along with books on child psychology, Buddhism, and poetry. I could tell a lot about a person from their office. When I went to a new therapist I knew right away whether they were going to ask me about my dreams or my parents, but his office was this mess of influences that didn't fit together. That made trying to read him the same as working a jigsaw puzzle made up of pieces from different sets so I gave up and zoned out on the logo for The Dream Academy engraved in the dark wood above his desk. The more I stared at it the more I wished I had spray paint.

Principal Keys came in with his phone against his head and acted as if I wasn't there. I'd already missed the first half of my Abstract Art class, and if he held me any longer I'd have to go see Jenna's mom during study hall instead of strategizing how to get Jaycee to want me again. I never understood how I was supposed to learn anything when there was never any answer and my mind was upside down most of the time.

"I agree. It is exceptional," Principal Keys said as he paced around in circles. Whatever a principal does must screw with their body the same way being President does. He was younger than my dad, but his hair had gone completely gray. I'd given up on making it to class when he said, "Yes. I'll make sure he's on board. No, I think this will be our best campaign yet."

"Am I in trouble?" I asked, but he only pushed his phone back into his pocket before studying me the same way I'd scoped his walls. "I'm going to be late for class."

"You are Bryce Hughes?" he asked although he had to already know.

"Yeah," I said. "Did I do something wrong?" The lighting storm of nerves in my head shot flashes of a hundred things I'd done big and small which would've qualified me to get expelled if not arrested.

Principal Keys put his hand on my arm before taking a seat behind his desk with this poker face. "I'd like to talk about your Evolution through Labor project. I hear it was inspiring. Where are you on that?" He folded his hands together as my mind went blank. "How is your art therapy work going now?"

"Things are good," I half-stuttered, sure that I'd start mumbling my words too if he kept staring through me. "A kid painted a turkey and it kind of changed his life."

"That is impressive," he said. "That is what this entire experiment in education is meant to foster. I would like another update by next week. Can you do that for me?"

"What for?" I asked. "Wasn't it good enough?"

"That is why you're here," he said. "It is exactly the kind of work I'd like to showcase on our new social media campaign. I've got serious corporate donors on the line, and want you to be the faces of our school, Bryce."

"How long does it have to be?"

"Don't be narrow. Ideas are better than limits. Be honest and show me what you have accomplished. I am counting on you."

"Whatever you want, Principal Keys," I said all dry-mouthed, even though my brain was flashing No! Trying to turn Jaycee back to good was heavy enough. The whole point of faking my Sweat Time was to play charity and lay low until I could mark off number six on my List of Fantastic Promises. Now he was pressing on my fake to a level that would blow his mind.

*** 

Principal Keys didn't let me bounce right away, but instead got up and locked the door. "Call me Rich. You know we use first names here?"

"Why?"

"Because that is one of the things that sets us apart. It is integral to our brand." He started to walk circles around me, then stopped and put his hands on his hips like my mom when she got real. "This school is the dream of some very important people. That's why it's called The Dream Academy. We are all working together to prove that high school can be reinvented through technology, innovative approaches, and corporate partnerships. Didn't you read my book?"

"Sure," I said even though I hadn't, "but most of the time I don't know what anyone wants here."

"Our school wants every student to become their best self, but to do that we have to raise funds. It is a sorry fact, but it is the truth. This is a gamble, and people only put their money down when they are betting on a story that can change the future. The story is more important than the odds. Everyone who buys a lottery ticket believes in the story that one day they will win no matter what the statistics say. I want your work to drive our new story, Bryce."

"I'll do my best to help you score. There's no way I'm transferring now."

"I am sure you will, Bryce."

"Can I go now?"

"Yes, but I want to meet with you on Friday to see your progress. I hope you are excited to work with us on this. It is a rare honor." Principal Keys opened the door. Abstract Art was over and my Computer Science III class had already started.

"I'll be here."

"And Bryce," he said as I brushed by him, "whatever else you have going on that I don't know about, keep it that way." I gave him a hang loose sign and he closed the door.

I was glad that anything he heard about me or my friends was covered while he needed me, but pissed to be caught in another story beyond my control.

I skipped my next class after meeting with the principal to meditate on how to make Jaycee believe that I wanted her to be with me, and to figure out a way to play like a genius changing lives with crayons and watercolors. The problem was I didn't have the words for either. Words change, lie, fall short, get misunderstood, or ignored. That's why I loved pictures. They were open windows. Watch the worst movie in the world with the sound off, and it's a hundred times better. All the chatter and sound effects vanish, and if you pay attention in that quiet you can see right into the characters' souls. It sounds lame, but it's true. The biggest problem in the world is that people spend so much time talking and texting that they go blind. They can't see anyone honestly after a while, not even themselves.

I hit the gallery icon on my phone and brought up the picture I took of Jaycee before I crushed her at the party house. When I looked close all I saw was faith gushing out of her.

*\*\**

There was no point in going back inside until study hall when I could ask Jenna's mom how to play the whole art therapy thing up, so I hid out in my car. I opened Jaycee's Twitter feed on my phone to take in all the hateful swipes and lame come-ons she had to carry. Cock Sparrer played "Suicide Girls" while I scrolled through the poison she was catching until it was too much to bear. The song beat on, and for the first time I worried that she might try to end herself to escape all that shit.

I scrolled to Richard Hell's "Blank Generation," and let it ease into me while I checked my email. There was another message from Kenny reminding us to get to the bones and show him how the music marked us up. I forwarded it to Jaycee so that if she ever spoke to me again we'd have something to talk about besides how fucked up our lives had become. Once I hit send I texted Paige and told her to never speak to me again, praying that she'd text back quick so that I could tell her what she'd done to me. Then I popped two Klonopins to get slacked, but the best I managed was that half-sleep that dipped me out for twenty minutes or so, then brought me back just as worn as before. When I came to I wished that I'd told Jaycee that I wanted to kill myself over what I did to her so she could see how sorry and throbbing I was for her. Maybe that would mean something, let her appreciate how defective I was for real. I slid out of my car into the drifting snow and wondered if Kenny understood what he was doing to me, and if that was the point.

*** 

Jenna's mom was alone in the art studio room during study hall, and she didn't turn around when I came in. Paintings that were only blocks of red and yellow still hung on the walls and the smell of oil paint filled the air like always, but the room felt off. I picked up the instruction sheet for our Abstract Art final project off a table by the door but didn't leave. She was tranced out, and that made me stay.

"Mrs. Lovins," I said. "What do you want for our final art project? I got held up."

She looked at me as if she wasn't sure who I was even though she'd known me for years. "Carol. Call me Carol. Why is that so difficult? And you have the instructions in your hand."

"Right." She turned back to the frosted window while I read the sheet. It was a list of these abstract artists who'd either died homeless or made it. Nothing else. The school must've banned instructions, but that's all any of us wanted; a clear idea of what we should be doing with our lives. I wadded the sheet up and tossed it on the table. "I don't get it."

"What don't you get?"

"I don't know what I'm supposed to do."

"None of us do," she said. "We're left to go on and discover that out for ourselves. Would you like something to drink?" She went to her office to get coffee. Maybe she hated being by herself or was hoping for advice I didn't have.

She drank her coffee as the snow picked up, and zoned out. I held mine until she found her way back. "Winter is early this year," she said, but mostly to herself. "You are friends with my daughter right?"

"You know that," I said. At our school, there was no way to hide drama, especially if even the freshman knew. The teachers heard all the stories but didn't let on most of the time.

"Have you seen her lately?"

"No. I should head out." I tried to go, but she asked when I saw her last. "I don't remember. At the party, I mean, at your other house I guess." That scared her, and I hoped Jenna hadn't gone completely off and reported all the underage madness that went down there.

"I already checked the party house," she said, "I stayed there the last two nights, but she never came. You don't have to pretend that I don't know it's your party house. Just because I'm older doesn't mean I'm ignorant. People don't change that much anyway. Do you want to know something? The person you are now is pretty much who you'll be the rest of your life."

"I hope you're wrong about that," I said. "That's what therapy is for, isn't it? Anyway, I need you to lay out how that art therapy thing you do goes."

"You're Jenna's dealer though right?" It wasn't a charge. She said "dealer" as naturally as "friend." I was sure she'd lost her mind.

"You've got bad information. I've never sold drugs in my life. Honest."

"Don't be like that. I'm not judging you, or her, or anyone else. I only want to know if you gave her anything dangerous." For the first time, I felt like she was a real person instead of a pixie.

"I share okay, but it's cool. Besides I haven't given her anything in forever since she's not into what I've got."

"What *is* she into?" She propped her head on her hands and waited for me to get real. Most of our parents were terrified of the newest drug destined to melt our brains. They got that from the news, but then they'd load us up with tons of prescriptions and never think about what hypocrites they were.

"Nothing dark. Just warm fuzzy junk like Molly, you know?"

"That's good." She sighed as if I'd lifted a car off her chest. "At least she doesn't take after her mother."

"She's been off the whole semester. She's super tight with these kids from Cherokee Hills. It's all she ever talks about. She's a Bully groupie or something."

"That's her father talking. He is still a booster for Cherokee Hills. Can you imagine wanting to stay in high school at his age? I begged him to wait until after the holidays to mention the divorce, but he said she was old enough to see it was for the best. Girls are delicate." She smoothed out the assignment sheet with her hands. Touching things must've helped her think the way walking circles did for Principal Keys. They should've learned that not thinking was the only way to feel better when days get dark. "I'm sure she's told you all by now."

"Yeah," I said, "but it doesn't matter. I don't think she cares about us anymore."

"I'm sure that's not true," she said, and for the first, she came off angry. "What are her friends from Cherokee Hills like? Why did you call them Bullies?"

I thought about what Jenna did to Jaycee and me, how she said it was a joke, but I couldn't rat her out without mentioning names so I only said, "They call themselves that. Like instead of Bulldogs I guess. I don't trust them."

"It probably fits," she said. "That school manufactures assholes." I put my coffee down as she pressed the wrinkles out of the assignment sheet. "Why did you ask about my volunteer work?"

"For this deal I've got with Principal Keys."

"What does Rich want with you?" She stopped like I'd hit an invisible pause button.

"It's dumb, but he wants to use this art therapy thing I did for Evolution through Labor for some ad campaign. I guess it's supposed to be flashy and inspiring to score money."

Carol crossed her legs under her tie-dyed skirt and faked a laugh. "You've come to the wrong place for flashy and inspiring, Bryce, but you have to impress him. He might not be good with kids, but he's amazing when it comes to fundraising. He's the reason this school is still here, you know. Without him, we'd all get kicked back into the real world."

"You have to help me though. I've got work for school, and all these crazy rumors to put down. I swear I'm going to end up in a hospital."

"Do we ever get too old for high school rumors?" she asked, but mostly to herself.

"Principal Keys wants me to deliver for this social media campaign he is stoked over, but I've never seen actual art therapy. Give me a visual to work with."

"It looks like making art," she said. "Why would it be any different?"

"I can do that."

"Whatever you do has to be amazing. If he's focused on you, then you have to be a star. I'll give you a book for inspiration, but forget everything else until you deliver." She paused like she was trying to swallow words she couldn't hold down. "Everything else except for one thing. Bryce, can you help me out?"

"Sure. What do you need?"

"Can you get me Xanax or something? I'm a nervous wreck. I can't sleep." It must've been rough for her to be all those people at once: a pixie poet/painter, a dancer, a mother, a teacher. I couldn't be one decent kid no matter how much I dosed. "Anything you can drop off would help, but promise to keep in secret."

"Don't worry. I'm tired of stories. Your place or the party house?"

"My house is the wrong place to be alone now. I grew up in the party house before it was the party house. It feels like home."

I told her to give me some time and made her swear not to tell Jenna. She gave me that same sorry fake laugh again and said she couldn't rat on me to Jenna if she tried. She'd even given up on texting her.

"I know how that hurts," I said. "I've got your back."

"Thank you. Go make something that will thrill Rich, and I'll find my way," she said. "You might not understand this, but even though girls are delicate that doesn't mean we're not unstoppable."

\*\*\*

No texts from Jaycee by midnight. No holler back from Paige. The true dark times always started the same way. One terrible thing happened that set off a chain reaction. I tried to ride it out, but that was useless. I told myself to focus on one thing until it's done to stop the thinking, but it didn't work because when I tried to start editing the shots for the semester project in English or figure out what to with Jaycee a hundred other things raced through my head. Every minute I spent stressing about school or worrying about my future I had this thundercloud of anxiety blistering me up with pictures of my mom drinking herself to sleep in front of the TV or Principal Keys waiting by his computer for me to be a genius. I was positive there was something out of sight and terrible coming for me.

I locked my door, turned off the lights, and sweated through my sheets in waves of shame and stress. No hope for sleep. No way to love. Sleep made me hate myself for everything left undone. Love made me burn for never having the right things to say.

# Chapter 11
## Kids in Heat

**JENNA STROLLED** into our first-period English class on Friday like nothing had happened. She squeezed in between Tyler and me on the loveseat, and, before I had the chance to ask what she thought she was doing playing innocent after what she did to Jaycee, she handed us cards like we were at a Christmas party. I stuffed mine inside my coat and didn't open it. I didn't look at her, and she didn't look at her mom who glowed at the sight of her in class again.

It took a minute for Jenna's mom to take her eyes off her, but before long she realized that she still had a class waiting for her to stop mooning and get on with whatever it was she had to lay on us. "I hope you've all made progress on your semester projects by now," she said. "I want you to use this class to discuss your successes and challenges with them, and I will tour around to check on you." I doubted she'd planned to turn the class over, but when teachers get rattled they always switch to class discussion so they don't have to talk.

Jenna's mom sat on the arm of the loveseat by Jenna, not going so far as to touch her, but close enough to put on display how badly she wanted to be by her side. I did my best to watch Jaycee without coming off stalker. I was glad she'd worn a sweater but sick over the way she left it half unbuttoned to show off what she was rocking. I swore to set things right between us before she got caught in real trouble.

"Please keep in mind even though this is a group project. I want to see evidence that you've truly considered your prompts and taken them in an exciting direction. Don't tell me what you plan to do. Show me what you have done so far. That is the great divide in life, the things you dream about and the things you do." Her arm rested behind Jenna, but she was smart enough not to touch her. Otherwise, there was no doubt Jenna would bolt again. I was ready for that, but she went to the other groups first to give Jenna her space.

"What are the cards for?" Hanna asked.

"Screw that." I pointed to where Jaycee sat alone singing to herself to have something to do. "You've got a lot of shit to answer for you know? She's totally twisted now."

Jenna gave me the most bored face in the world. "Whatever. I didn't slut her up. She did that herself. I'm not her stylist, Bryce."

"I mean what you said about her and your Bully friends. About sending her that pic of Paige and me. That's way over the line you know?"

"You can be salty with me if you want, but that's what they told me. And it's not like I Photoshopped you kissing Paige. You always made a big deal about how you weren't together so why do you care?" Jenna rolled her eyes, then took another card out of her backpack. "Give her this to make up." I took it from her, but just so Jaycee would know that she was still one of us.

"I thought you were transferring?" Tyler asked.

"Too late to do it now, but next semester. Are you going to open your cards or what?" We did, and inside were invitations. It was weird for her to go formal about throwing down, but I guess she wanted to make it an event. "It's my going away party," she said. "You all *have* to come. It's going to be epic."

Jenna's mom came back over to ask how we were faring with our semester project. When the others kept quiet I promised we were making progress. That usually wouldn't have satisfied her, but with Jenna back she wasn't about to press on us.

When the bell rang, I went to Jaycee. There was no use in trying to talk to her since she wasn't herself, so I passed her the card. Whether she came or not was her decision, but I prayed she would choose to be with me one more time.

***

Grace tracked me down at lunch to talk with Principal Keys. Hanna and Tyler leered at me as I followed her since talking with the principal alone was snitch-level suspicious, but I let them think whatever they wanted.

When I got to his office his desk was covered with file folders, magazines, and DVDs as if he'd built an office supply fort. When I sat he pushed the stacks to the side to eyeball me.

"What's up?" I put my feet on his desk to see how bad he needed me. He glared my way until he finished his coffee. By the empty cups I counted on his desk, it was number nine.

"Are you serious?" He swatted my feet off his desk. "You only have the weekend left to give me something special. I want you to appreciate what a rare opportunity this is. I have a team of designers and influencers waiting for you to deliver. Bryce, this matters."

"I've started, okay? But I've got semester projects to worry about, and all this college stuff going on that I forgot about, plus there's a lot of other drama weighing on me right now."

"Forget your projects and your classes too for now. I'll write your damn review letters myself if I have to," he said. "I have to meet with two of our largest corporate partners in a few weeks, and can't do my job until you do yours. This is the real world, Bryce."

"Can you write my letters for Abstract Art and History of Punk Rock though? I mean, they're not like normal classes."

"Do you really think those classes matter? Do you think that is what the real world cares about?"

I told him I didn't know, but the truth was our group project motto wasn't a joke. None of my friends figured anything we did made a difference. No one ever told us why it did, at least.

"Well, they don't," Principal Keys said. "Sure they are fun and they help our school make the news, but they are nothing like what is waiting for you in the real world." He pointed at the stacks of paperwork on his desk. "That is the real world."

"What's the point then?"

"The point is they make a better story and grab attention. They let me tell the public that our students have access to a wealth of experiences that will allow them to shape the future with fresh ideas. It's a good story Bryce, and you didn't hear this from me, but no one wants to hire a kid with a head full of their own ideas."

"So this is just another big program to score checks?" Maybe he was being honest because it felt good, or because he felt like we were in it together. Whatever the reason, I was glad he was straight with me.

"Not entirely. It's an investment in your future too. Colleges like to see that our students have lived a life, and staying on the cutting edge makes it much easier to recruit donors. The press loves anything they can tag 'new' and 'surprising.' Here, see for yourself." Rich handed me a magazine that had his picture on the cover underneath the words MR. OUTSIDE THE BOX. "That was last year. We need new blood. I want the press to see you, to believe in your work."

I looked at the magazine and admired Principal Keys for the first time. On the cover, he looked like a total badass, money like Jesus.

"These are for you." He dragged a storage tub out from behind his desk, then packed it to the top with the folders on his desk. Then he piled DVDs on top of it. "They'll give you an idea of what's trending right now."

"I'm not reading all that."

"Get through what you can." He frowned. "Your last film was too artsy. You have to find a balance. What do you have so far?"

"I shot some footage," I said. "I need a cart for this though."

"Good to hear. Video is the way to go. Streaming content owns text. Have you considered memes? Regardless, make whatever you come up with succinct and compelling."

"Or if one of the janitors can follow me out and drop it in my trunk."

"For Christ's sake pay attention!" He put the tub back onto the floor. "What did you shoot?"

"I shot a kid painting a picture. Stuff like that."

"A different kid than before I hope." He started to pace again. "Do you work with any females? Little girls evoke more sympathy in general. Especially if they are orphaned or handicapped."

"I don't know any girls like that," I said, which seemed to disappoint him. "Is that true?"

"Yes. Do any of your friends have a sister you could work with?" For the first time I got that fake didn't matter, that fake was the point. A kid was who you said they were, even if they didn't exist.

"I'll figure this out," I said. "Can I go?"

"One minute." He knelt next to me. "Bryce, whatever you turn in has to break the hearts of whoever sees it. It has to make them positive that if they give enough they can make the world a brighter place."

"Got it."

"I am trusting you," Principal Keys motioned for me to stand. "I'll have one of the staff take the boxes to your car, but first, there's nothing in your vehicle that shouldn't be is there?"

"My car is clean," I said, "and even if it's not, it is."

"Now you're beginning to understand the real world," he said.

\*\*\*

The snows had passed, and the sun broke through the clouds for the first time in days to light up all the trees and houses where a few of my neighbors were already busy hanging Christmas lights and sticking plastic candy canes in their yards even though it was only the start of December. The Queers' "Punk Rock Girls" played sweet as I pulled into my driveway and saw two missed texts from Jaycee. She was going, ready for me, and for a minute the world was a joyful place to be.

196

The storage bin full of DVDs and research was too heavy to lug out of my backseat, so I left it there. For a while I idled behind the wheel, ready to forget everything I'd been told to show and tell. I shot Jaycee a text to say I'd pick her up at ten, then went inside to turn Johnny into a wonder kid.

My mom was wrapped in a blanket on the couch with a bottle of Chardonnay wedged underneath her arm. This show where brides argued with their moms over wedding dresses was on the TV. "How was school?" she asked because that's what moms say when they don't have anything to say.

"Good."

"Good," she said. "Do you have a minute?" Normally I would've made up some reason to leave again or go upstairs, but she had that same cloud on her that Jenna's mom had in the art room, the kind that made leaving her feel like a crime.

"No Pilates today?" I asked. "Where's Johnny?"

"I took him to the sitter. Your father and I have an appointment tonight." She glanced down at the wine bottle but didn't have it in her to drink in front of me. "There are some issues we are working through, ones that have been going on too long."

"What kind of issues?"

"It's not for you to worry about now. I'm not sure what will come from all of this, but I want you to understand that no matter what happens we both love you very much."

"If you can't tell me then why stop me to say nothing?"

"I said I love you," she said with a sniffle. "Love's not nothing."

"Are you getting divorced or something?"

"Don't say that," my mom said. "That's terrible. And no one knows what will happen to anyone. I only wanted to say I love you."

"I love you too."

\*\*\*

Iggy and the Stooges played "Search and Destroy" while I waited outside Jaycee's apartment tower. I wondered if Kenny was ready for me to unload how his songs had scarred me up. Maybe he thought music was this great tool, or like a weapon to cut into kids like me. I worried about how Jaycee would take being the star of my semester project for his class. I wouldn't use her name, but there was no way to put into words what had happened to her in the last three months. Pictures were heavier than words. I switched on my light to make sure I had meds in case the scene went wrong and the lightning inside me sparked electric arcs again.

Jaycee was dressed more Gucci than ever when she got in. Her skirt disappeared under her in the seat as her shirt fell open to put her bra out there. I didn't know if she was trying to bait me into ordering her to change, or if she was set to bring on more pain. It gets like that sometimes. You feel like you're drowning, but instead of trying to reach fresh air, you end up pushing yourself down deeper until there is nothing left. It's like you're convinced you deserve it, but it never gets bad enough to fill you up.

"I didn't think you'd come," I said.

"You gave me the invitation. If this is what everyone wants then that's fine with me. It doesn't make a difference anymore anyway."

At the first stoplight, I unplugged my phone and took a picture of her. She caught me, but instead of hiding she leaned forward so her shirt parted wide, then she pushed her lips into a duck face. I shot her because it wasn't her.

"I'm going to delete that," I said. "You're playing with me."

"No. I want you to save it. That's what you wanted right?"

"Don't say that. I told you what I want. Look, I'm sorry about everything that happened. I get that saying sorry isn't enough, but I mean it."

Jaycee plugged my phone back into the jack and scrolled through the playlist. "I don't feel like talking," she said. "I want to sing." Out of the corner of my eye I saw her turn the volume dial all the way up, and thumb my phone. In a flash, I was bombed deaf by the wailing vocals and power chords from The Misfits' "Children in Heat," in the shouts of Jaycee screaming along and slamming her palms against my dashboard while she pumped her legs mad. Two minutes later the song cut out and sent her scrambling to keep the music alive. Her hair stuck to her face as she tore through Kenny's playlist and danced for herself. The longer I drove the more I disappeared.

***

Once we got to the party house there was no space left to park, not even in the yard. Jenna was serious when she said she was going to make it this party of the century, and by the swarm of cars that surrounded the place, there was no doubt she'd not only invited us, but also every CH kid she knew. Any chance of the night going off casual and kind was lost. I got out, then ran around to open Jaycee's door.

"You going to tell me you love me now?" she asked. "Do it. Say you love me."

"I love you," I said.

"It's that easy. It's so natural for you to say things like that."

"I wish you'd tell me what to say to make things right again."

"Forget it. The more you forget the better you are, right?" She stomped ahead of me so that I couldn't try again.

Out front, a dozen guys I didn't know in CH gear drank and barked over each other. For a minute we stood at the end of the yard and watched them. Neither of us was eager to take another step, but we couldn't admit it.

"What are you holding?" Jaycee asked.

"My anxiety meds in case it kicks. Nothing you'd want."

"Give me some." She cocked her hip to the side and stuck out her hand. "Sharing is caring."

I passed her the two Klonopin I'd brought, like sharing to care was hardwired, then tried to snatch them back in a flash. "I shouldn't have done that. You don't want those. They're too much, plus you can't drink with them either. Seriously, give them back and stop acting crazy."

"Mine now," Jaycee pushed the pills into her bra. "I'm going in. Don't try to play like my bodyguard either. You suck at it." She turned and took off across the yard while I chased after her, feeling as if I'd lit a fire there was no way to smother dead until it burned us both alive.

***

When a party is raging out of control it's impossible to walk like a normal person. There are no straight lines that go from where you are to where you want to be. The best you can do is wedge yourself between kids and try to avoid knocking someone over while you worm your way through. You have to find a friendly face fast if you don't want to get stuck in a maze of body odor and bad breath. If that happens, before long you'll have to force your way back outside just to breathe again. Luckily for me, Tyler was posted on a barstool in the kitchen, so I had a spot to land once I rubbed my way past the backs and butts of at least a hundred drunk kids.

"One for the records," Tyler said, as he took a slug from his Solo cup. "No way there'll be a window left in this place when this is over."

"Crowds make me edgy," I said. "And I thought you were going sober."

"Special occasion. Besides, Hanna's out back blazing. If she pops up I'm blaming you."

"Go ahead." I hopped up on the counter to look for Jaycee. "Everyone else is."

"Sorry man. Maybe you should throw a party? No one's salty at Jenna anymore, right?"

"I guess not." I took Tyler's cup from him and downed it. "Staying twisted over girls is too much effort." He agreed, then took a liquor bottle he'd stashed behind him to fill us back up.

"Where'd that come from?"

"Come on, man. I am blessed with the chance to boost the best."

We toasted, and I wondered if what Jenna's mom said about people never changing, about me staying this confused kid my entire life, was true. Maybe the person you are in high school is the person you're doomed to be for your entire life; like you don't grow up, you just get older.

I kept scanning for Jaycee while Tyler killed the bottle by himself. Before long Hanna came back, and jerked him away to fight over promises broken and all. I'd lost track of time, and Jaycee. The sparks were starting to kick inside me. Too many people. Too much noise and motion. I dove into the mob determined to locate Jaycee before another lightning storm of anxiety hit harder than the first and left me twitching on the floor.

Once you're in the middle of a crowd the first thing you do is go blind. There are only flashes, and you're too busy concentrating on staying upright to see anything. You have to depend on your ears and listen for war cries when you're buried in people. They're easy to pick out because they're not like talking so much as chanting. That's how I found Jaycee.

Five CH Bullies had formed a line around her by a bookshelf they'd flipped over to make into a bar. They chanted "Shots! Shots! Shots!" as they set her up. Jaycee couldn't stand on her own so one of the Bullies held her upright and helped her shoot from the Dixie cups they'd poured. After she was done, the Bully holding her steady lifted her arm into the air, and it fell limp the second he let go. She was drowning in love, too deep to see how close she was to the bottom. I did what I had to.

"Chill alright? I've got to take her home." I played it cool since if I tried to steal her away like a hero there'd be no hope of springing her without a fight.

The Bullies pushed me back and told me to chill, that she was with friends. Then they asked her if she wanted to go, and she slurred "Nahhh."

"See man," one of the Bullies said. "She wants to hang," I remembered the pills I'd given her, that kid on the floor last summer, and all the stories about girls who got carried off. My only hope was to find Jenna. No matter what she had against Jaycee I was sure she wouldn't let her get used that way.

"Jenna wants to talk to her. That's her cousin," I said while two of the Bullies ground up against Jaycee. "Watch her okay? She's only thirteen." They stepped back while I rammed my way through the crowd to track down Jenna before Jaycee went victim.

\*\*\*

I searched the first floor then wrestled my way out back where kids blazed, but didn't see her anywhere. The bolting inside my head hung halos around every face I saw by the time I was back in the kitchen. I was crazy with fear, but I talked myself through it. I concentrated on each move until I was on the counter again scoping Jaycee slumped on the floor. The Bullies were ignoring her, but that wouldn't last. I had to get upstairs.

The hallway upstairs was jammed with kids desperate to pee who stared me down as I pushed open the door to the first bedroom. In it, the floor was covered with kids on their backs making out. My anxiety arched live wires across my brain as I stumbled into the second bedroom. A girl was balled up in the corner. I slid to the floor for a second to wait out the storm. In the dark, the jerking inside my body eased a little until I heard my name.

"Bryce," Paige said across all that black. "Take me home with you."

I told my legs to stand, but they weren't listening. Sometimes when the panic hits true it leaves me paralyzed like that. I heard myself ask what happened, but wasn't sure the words got out until Paige crashed beside me, and laid her head on my chest. I was panting, but fought to take back my lungs. She still smelled like Aloe Vera and sweat.

"Frank left. He's with Riley. It's so unreal, like one night he was completely in love with me and the next he said he felt trapped and wanted to be free. It has to be Riley. You've got to get me out of here. Take me home with you, okay?"

She burrowed her face into my shirt. The volume dropped inside my skull as I held on to her to keep us both together.

"Take me home with you, and we can get back together forever," she said. "You've got to get me out of here and never let me leave. If we weren't supposed to end up together you would've forgotten about me a long time ago, but you never did, right?"

"No." She kissed me, and no matter how badly I wanted that young stabbing love to go through me deep, it was gone. I moved her away, tied up with all those things she said that weren't true. She'd always leave because she was the girl who disappeared. "I can't take you home with me," I said. "I've got to find Jenna."

"Don't bother. She left like an hour ago."

"Where'd she go?" This is her party."

"It's her going away party. She went away," Paige said, then tugged at my jeans. "Stay with me."

Jenna was gone. Tyler and Hanna had probably ditched by then, too. There was only me and Paige inside that dusty room outside the talk and music, and Jaycee stranded on the floor. "I can't now," I said. "I guess I grew up."

*\*\**

At first, I figured the hall had cleared out because it'd gotten late enough for everyone to weave home, but downstairs a swarm of kids pointed their phones where the Bullies were posted up as if they were at a concert. I shouldered my way through the crowd to see what everyone was snapping on.

See, it'd never happened to someone I cared about before. It'd always been some no-name kid, a party virgin trying to hang. Jenna wasn't gone. She was directing the scene and laughing with her Bullies friends. They all had their phones out. They were eating her alive. They shot her as fast as they could.

The Bullies had gotten Jaycee hardcore. Her legs and arms bowed like wires. Her clothes were missing except for her panties, and kids had written every slutty name possible on her naked skin. I threw my jacket over her before the crowd could steal any more of her away.

"What's your problem?" Jenna asked. "You know the game."

"You're sick. She's one of us."

"No, she's not." Jenna crossed her arms. "She's just a scholarship kid who can't hang. Oh, and thanks for lying about her being my cousin. I *really* appreciate your claiming that we're related."

"Let me get her out of here. This is way too heavy."

"Why bother?" Jenna asked. "She got what she deserved for trying to act like she's money instead of trash."

"This is on me." I tried to pry her off the floor. "And if you want to save yourself and your friends' asses she's got to get home. Her mom's dating a cop."

"You're lying," Jenna said, but I'd said the right thing to make her friends get paranoid.

"You want to find out? I mean, since you know her *so* well."

Maybe she bought my story or maybe she only wanted to get rid of us both, but she didn't fight when two guys came over and helped me carry Jaycee to my car. None of us said anything. She swayed limp between us. She fell into my passenger seat, covered with her wadded-up clothes, and I spun out for anywhere away.

The streetlights highlighted the words marked on her skin in red and black until there was no way to look her way. Paige text bombed my phone with messages that said I'd lost out and should've stayed, but I deleted them at the first stoplight. She was right. I should've stayed, just not with her.

\*\*\*

205

I stopped at a gas station to dress Jaycee and try to clean her up. Even though I was terrified to leave her alone that way there was no way to get the words off her without help. I bought baby wipes and hand sanitizer, did my best to wipe her clean, but the red stains of "SKANK" and "WHORE" wouldn't bleed away. Instead, they only stretched across her belly and thighs until they were bigger than before. That ink wasn't going to fade for days, I knew that from experience, and those shots would outlive every kid who took them. Girls who get exposed go eternal. See, nobody cares about dick pics since they're dumb, and guys are disposable. But girls get saved and shared. I got sick over the idea that her nudes were flying through the air to get off assholes she'd never know and let girls hate on her one night dreaming she was special.

The stink of alcohol mixed with the guilt of my leaving her for the whole drive back to her place until I had to fight back gags. I should've stopped her. I should've warned her that if you try to get everything you want you always get too much.

By the time I made it to her place she was able to stagger beside me. I pulled her key out of her purse to find her apartment number. She was knocked out and mumbling, but zombie-walked as best she could, mindless, until I got her to her door. I turned the key and slid her inside. Then I ran.

She was home, but she wasn't safe. There was no doubt those pictures of her were already going viral, and by the next day every kid at Cherokee Hills would have a piece of her to gawk at and jerk over. You can forget words, but pictures last forever. I drove home and wondered if I'd been able to see Paige in that dark room, had truly seen her for real lit up and thirsty for me if I would've stayed. I didn't want to believe I was the kind of kid who would have, but I wasn't sure.

# Chapter 12
## Kids in Pictures

**NO KIDS WHO** grew up like me and my crew had ever actually been alone in their entire lives. When we were little our parents made sure of that. They came to every one of our junior league soccer games, met with our teachers, and took us to therapists when we had questions they didn't feel like answering. They put parental locks on the television and had the passwords to our computers so they could make sure we weren't watching porn or about to run off with some online pervert. Up until high school our parents were constantly hovering over us, but it must've gotten boring after a while or maybe they just decided it took too much effort. But our constant surveillance didn't end after they lost interest. After a lifetime of being watched, we must've missed feeling special so we started posting every detail of our lives minute by minute. I woke up in the morning and checked my Snapchat, Instagram, Telegram, texts, and more before I got out of bed. It was standard. Every kid did it. Companies banked on that.

Sunlight streamed into my room like a searchlight when I woke up the Saturday after Jaycee got shot. I'd slept in my clothes, greasy and worn, but sprang awake to see how virus she'd gone in less than a night. Every kids' feed had those virus pics of her stripped and tagged. The CH Bullies had shared their work with the kids from our school, and in no time the whole planet was passing her around and commenting on what a stupid slut she was. Kids had even started tagging their comments and pics with #DEDTHOT as if that was hilarious. Kids love to rip the girls who get caught apart so they can feel above them.

I should've hated those kids, but it wasn't their fault. It's what you do. Sometimes it's the only way to be proud of yourself and forget how screwed up you are. I checked my texts to see if she'd been tipped off, but there weren't any. I prayed she'd hit me up soon so I'd know she hadn't drunk a gallon of bleach to end it all forever.

***

There were two days left before I had to turn in my footage for Principal Keys' social media blitz. My group project for Jenna's mom was still not finished, and my work for Kenny was looming too. It's easy to get buried when you have to say yes or don't say anything at all. I took My List of Fantastic Promises out of my nightstand and counted out five Adderall. Then I popped one and pocketed the rest before adding a number 10 to it.

1. Find out what makes me happy.
2. Save the party virgins when I can.
3. Make Paige love me again.
4. Figure out things with Jaycee.
5. Listen to music that's not on the radio.
6. Lay low in school.
7. Don't get caught up in other kids' drama.
8. Spend more time with my family.
9. Learn to make movies.
10. No more dosing.

I read the words over and over to hypnotize myself into believing they were true.

I pulled a notebook and pen, flipped to a clean blue-lined paged, and wrote out everything I had to get done: make Johnny a prodigy, show Jenna's mom what it's really like to be a kid now and hook her up, prove to Kenny that his songs left scars, and get with Jaycee to make sure she hadn't gone total dark. It was way too much, but I had enough meds to stay in motion until everything was finished or I washed out. If I couldn't hold it together there was no chance I'd survive.

The rest of the notebooks spilled out onto my bed as I opened the drawer to my nightstand to trash my stockpile. I had to get sober no matter what. If I kept on there'd be no telling how loaded I'd have to be just to function when I grew up. More than anything though, I wanted to prove to Jenna's mom that I wasn't doomed to be who I was in high school. I stashed a bottle of chill pills for her, left a few for myself, and then flushed the rest of my stockpile. When it was gone I felt more naked than I did when I was dumped face-down in my mom's flowerbed, like Jaycee must have.

***

Johnny was on his bed making bomb noises that sent sprays of spit into the air as he launched his Pokémon cards at the ceiling. He threw his cards like ninja stars at me as I dropped the art book Jenna's mom had loaned me onto his table and left.

In the medicine cabinet over the toilet I found the box with his patches in it, took out a couple, then went back to tranquilize him. He tried to show me his cards while I stuck the patches to his skinny butt and waited for them to dial him down. After they hit him I opened the art book for him to see, and did my best to hide how bad my hands were shaking when he tromped over.

"You got stories?" he asked.

"No," I said. "Stories are trouble. These are pictures for you. This one looks like a big mess right?" I traced the splatters of a Jackson Pollock painting on the glossy page. He followed the spills with his tiny finger to be like me before turning the page. "And this one looks like a bum who got beat up right? But then God made him an angel for it." He circled the halo on the Basquiat painting and smacked the white and yellow wings on it as if that'd make the man in the picture fly away. We went through the book together like that before I got out his paint set.

I shot him painting over the mistakes he saw on each page. When he came to a Julian Schnabel painting with a pretty girl who had a black bar over her eyes he painted two giant white eyeballs onto it and moved on. Stars and moons covered pictures of broken men and political graffiti. He fixed each masterpiece without waiting for the paint to dry before he moved on to the next. There were too many problems to worry about time. I left him there to set right the messes he discovered and went upstairs to edit my video of a child prodigy at work.

There was no need for stacks of research to make the hook Principal Keys' social media campaign. I was set on doing it my way. I uploaded the video, played drag and drop, and started with a scene of Johnny throwing cards at the camera. I filtered the scene Hawaiian Punch red when the music started, and put Zero Boys "Amphetamine Addiction" in the background, then cut to a shot of him smashing his paintbrush's bristles flat against the page.

Next I made the screen go black, and had the words "Art" and "Therapy" take up the frame the way they did in our programs, but made them pulse electric before they shorted out with the music.

I followed with a shot of Johnny painting a moon that covered a whole page while G.G. Allin sang "Pick Me Up on Your Way Down." I filtered the scene blue so it looked like he was trapped on the bottom of a swimming pool.

After that I had all these abstract paintings flash across the screen faster and faster until they blurred into outlines and colors. Bad Religion's "21st Century Digital Boy" came on, but I sped the track up to where even Kenny wouldn't recognize it. I kept it up for twenty seconds before I slowed everything down. The paintings inched across the screen, and lyrics to melted syllables.

The last scene stayed the way it was shot. A little kid painting over the pictures in an art book said it all. Maybe it was too arty, but it was true and if it didn't hit then at least I could say I did what made me happy. I wasn't going to explain it. My brother destroyed de Kooning and Kandinsky while Circle Jerks played "Leave Me Alone." One minute and twenty one seconds later the song and film ended. Black screen, and done.

I sent the file to Principal Keys, and left him to turn it into money. It wasn't fair that he'd made me prove the school was making us into geniuses and saints, but it was hard to hold it against him since, if he really knew who I was, he'd have chosen someone else. Maybe the older you get the less know.

When I was done with my work for Principal Keys I uploaded all the shots I'd recorded of my group getting real onto my MacBook, then got busy laying out what trying to survive now actually meant. See, Jenna's mom probably thought kids like us got lost, but found our way back to romance. She must've had this picture of us doing our best and turning wise regardless, but that's not real life. That's not now. *Now* was Paige almost killing herself trying to share a pic on her phone. *Now* was Hanna's mouth bleeding from shoving her fingers down her throat too many times after one wicked comment a kid made two years ago. *Now* Jaycee was exposed more than anybody ever with no way to erase that night. I uploaded the pic of Jaycee that everyone was tagging #DEDTHOT, cut off the letters and her head, and then blurred her naked boobs so that she was a billboard for what it was like to try to make it through, and failing epic. After I finished I burned the video onto a DVD, and put it in my bookbag.

Two thick black lines cut across my to-do list and left me ready to get on with Kenny's project, but after seeing Jaycee like that again my stomach was filled with batteries that had been sawed in half. She hadn't texted me yet which caused my nerves to kick like Bruce Lee, so I texted "HIT ME UP ASAP." There was no way she'd ignore me if I went all-caps, but if she did I'd have to track her down. I dosed again to get lifted as the sun faded into crushed orange clouds, and I hoped that the three pills I had left would carry me to Monday.

I put on Stiff Little Fingers "Bad Time" as I swiped through the pics I'd taken of Jaycee. It would've been easy to give Kenny the standard achiever kid essay about how his playlist had widened my appreciation of music and let me understand his generation, then drop in a few important-sounding quotes I found in like two minutes on Google, but I was too sped up and spiked to play model student. If Kenny wanted to see teeth marks on my brain Jaycee was the best evidence I had to offer.

My laptop pulled the pictures of Jaycee off my phone, and I arranged them into a slideshow video like the ones for the commercial kids.

Underneath the picture of Jaycee in my car from the night we saved the kid on the floor I wrote, "There is this girl who told me to listen to songs that weren't on the radio."

I moved on to the picture of her from the country club when we'd all opened our presents, all sweaty from cleaning up to protect us all, and typed, "She let me torch her presents, but her metal was white-hot."

The picture of Jaycee slumped on the couch with a wire running from my phone to her head came next, her eyes were closed like she was praying. "She wanted to hear the music you sent, and when I gave it to her she heard more than I could."

Jaycee in her ripped jeans, blue hair, and safety-pinned shirt followed. I filtered it in black and white like a cheap concert flier. "It took her away. She wanted me to feel like that, but I only heard what wasn't there."

I pasted in Jaycee holding a bottle to her lips, turning it up to be with me and belong. "She kept listening until she gave up."

The last picture I put on screen was of Jaycee in her trashy dress from our English class. Her eyes were off to the side, not daring to see who was taking her in. "I crushed her, and she's in trouble. But she will rise above. She's unstoppable. Together we're bulletproof." I promised myself that was true.

Once I emailed the video to Kenny, I grabbed my backpack and closed my laptop. The night was full, and I was ready to burn out to bring back who Jaycee used to be when she was all hearts and pop songs. She deserved to be happy more than anyone I'd ever met.

Downstairs Johnny was asleep. Paint covered his hands and his cards fell off his sheets and onto the floor. My mom must've been too tired from her own problems to clean him up, or maybe he looked so happy with his mess that she didn't bother to wake him. I kissed his forehead, then went to the living room.

My mom was on the couch under a blanket that covered everything except the top of her head. The TV played this show where famous wives who were friends who hated each other got into fights at fancy dinners, and that made me sad for her. If I had been a better kid I would've asked her about Dad, about how she was feeling and all, but Jaycee still hadn't answered my texts. I had to make a stop, then see how she was coping. While some woman who'd had a ton of plastic surgery yelled at her ex-husband for giving their kids his new girlfriend's number, I snuck out the front door and eased it shut behind me. Maybe leaving her alone and dreaming was the kindest thing I could've done.

\*\*\*

Jenna's mom sat on the couch picking at a box of Chinese takeout with a plastic fork. The empties and trash from the insane party the night before covered the floor. I knocked on the sliding glass door so I didn't come off as expected in case she had someone else over. The party house had never felt more like a funeral home.

"You came!" She sat her carton of take-out on the floor and greeted me like a long-lost son. "God I was afraid you wouldn't come, that I had scared you to death or asked too much. I spent the whole day wondering if I should text Jenna for your number to call it off."

"But you didn't, right?"

"No. She wouldn't have answered anyway." She went to the kitchen while I pulled the DVD and bottle of Xanax out of my backpack, and wondered how long it would be before she started pressing me for details about what had happened to the party house. Jenna could've ratted her mom out to the police. Jaycee could've found out about the pics and shit going around, and thrown herself out a window. I put three of the chill pills in my backpack in case things went totally dark. Life's like driving at night most of the time. You can only see so far in front of you, and sometimes you wonder if the dark is all there is ahead.

"Would you like a drink?" Jenna's mom asked. "A real one?" I said yes since there was no reason to play innocent. She filled two glasses with Coke and bourbon. "Not too stiff for you?"

I sat the bottle on the kitchen counter in front of her. "I can hang."

"How much?" She asked with this whiskey face showed that she was out of practice.

"Free. Like I said, I only share." She took another drink and tried to decide if I was serious. The second one hit her better.

"You should charge, Bryce," she said as she counted out twenties and tens. "No one appreciates anything they can have for free. Not art. Not poetry. Not love."

"Jaycee's an artist," I said because it felt rude to stand there without making an effort to talk. "She can sing, you know?"

"Then make sure you tell her what I said about giving herself away." Maybe she knew what happened or was only trying to help her out, but either way, it made me want to run. "You're an artist too, you know? We all are until the world convinces us that we are wasting our time."

"I don't know. I mostly stay in my room anymore." I slid the DVD across the counter. "For my group's semester project."

"I can't pass your group on your semester project just because you helped me out," she said as if we were in class. "That has to be clear."

"Pass us or fail us, but this is what we did. It's not an essay or anything."

"Who said it had to be? I am not supposed to be watching over students' shoulders and ordering which path they take. That only trains them to be soldiers in someone else's army."

"You get that from Principal Keys?"

"Yes. You know he actually signs his emails 'Risks over rules.'"

"No," I said, "but that's probably one of those things that sounds better than it is in real life. It's just advertising."

"Then we are lucky we're still in high school," she said. "At least that way we get to lose ourselves once in a while."

"I've got bigger problems than playing poster boy for the school, right or whatever, and seriously sometimes I envy those CH kids Jenna loves so much. At least at their school they're told who they should be."

"Do you like who they are? Look, what Rich says may sound like it belongs on a bumper sticker, but it is true. There is no secret survival guide to life. There are only a lot of lonely people trying to get by." She finished her drink, then shook her head. "Jesus, what happened here anyway?"

"I don't want to get into it," I said, "and you honestly don't want to hear it first-person anyway."

"Don't tell me." She left to collapse on the couch. "I have more to figure out now than I can take." I was almost out the door before she asked if I'd seen Jenna.

"No."

"If you do, tell her I love her. It won't matter to her since she blames me for the divorce, but let her know anyway, okay?"

"I'm sure she knows," I said. "She just can't take it right now."

*** 

The map on my phone traced a red line as its arrow directed me towards Jaycee's apartment and its electronic voice announced each upcoming turn. I was lucky my phone stored the directions I'd typed in before or else I would've been lost in the ghetto since I never watched for signs myself. While an electronic woman called out the turns I wondered if anyone kept track of where I went, like if I was even alone when I was driving by myself. Every pic, text, tweet, snap and post I made went out into the sky and got filed away in a computer for eternity. What chance does anyone have when their biggest fuck-up is saved forever?

It was past midnight by the time I made it to Jaycee's building. There was a group of men standing outside in bubble coats who smoked cigars and eyed me as I parked. I thought about turning around and going home, but I had to find out if she was solid or at least coping. I sucked in a breath, pulled my hood up, and hustled inside before anyone called me out.

No one answered her door when I knocked so I hit it harder, hot with fear over what she might've done to herself with nobody around to talk her down. Time loses all meaning when you're scared and speeding. I could've banged on her door for five seconds or five minutes before she opened it and squinted at me like she wasn't positive that she wasn't dreaming.

"What are you doing here?" she asked.

"I came to make sure you didn't go suicide kid. What do you think?"

"I have no idea what you're talking about. You have to go."

"I told you to hit me up, right? But you never texted back so I had no choice."

"My phone's gone. Some kid must've thought it was hilarious to rip me off last night on top of everything else. Usually my mom would've gone ape shit over that, but I guess she got distracted by how wasted and marked up I was." Jaycee tugged up the sleeve of her sweatshirt to show me how raw her arm was where she'd tried and failed to scrub the word "BITCH" off. It was like it was printed under her skin, a permanent stain. "Why would they do this to me?"

"It's worse than that." Maybe it was the way I said it, or the fact that I'd showed up in the middle of the night, that made her realize something heavy was going on.

"Bryce," she stuttered as she yanked her sleeve down, "What do you mean? What happened?"

"Look, we have to talk, okay? It's on me so you should hear it from me. Can I come in?"

"No. My mom's working late at her other job, and if she comes home and finds a boy here she'll go throw me out for real. She already threatened to. What did you do?"

"Get dressed. I'll wait. Swear I won't leave." She closed the door, and I tried my best to figure out how to fill her in on the fact that she was virus, tag bait, and worse than dead. You can live with grief, the commercial moms taught me that, but you can't take shame. It rots you from the inside out. It'd been three years since I got caught, but whenever I heard the word "mouse" part of me still winced and turned to see who said it. Three years later, and that one word made me want to die.

***

Jaycee and I stomped our way to this playground behind her apartment tower. The moon was bigger than I'd ever seen, and made the frost on the ground sparkle like diamonds while we cut long shadows underneath it. She took the only swing on the swing set, and scrunched her pink bunny nose as the wind picked up. "It's all blank after I left you," she said. "You have to tell me the real story. Be honest. I want to hear it all."

"I'll try, but what matters now is what you do. Swear that no matter what you won't run off or go suicide kid."

The chains above her creaked as she swayed back and forth, dragging the toes of her sneakers against the dirt. "Everything," she said. I shoved my hands into my pockets, and told her the entire story. The more I talked the less it sounded like me, like her, and the more it came off like this awful news report about how evil kids can treat each other. When I was finished she kicked her legs up and drew them back to swing, but her head hung low as if it was too much struggle to face me.

"See, I did my best. If I hadn't said your mom was dating a cop it could've been a lot worse." I stepped closer, but she wouldn't look at me or stop swinging.

"Do you *really* think it makes any difference what you did after they had their fun? They got proof that I'm who they said I was. I'm done. Even if the school doesn't take away my scholarship there's no way I'm going back."

"Don't be like that. I got it too, and I'm still here."

"You were a dumb freshman when you got caught. I'm a junior. There's a huge difference between the two. I can't believe you said I was thirteen!" She stopped swinging long enough to dry her nose on her fleece jacket. "I wish I was thirteen. Seventeen is old enough to know better."

"Listen, my life was hell for an entire year when I got shared, but I survived," I said to keep talking without any encouraging words to offer. "Every story gets dull once you've heard it enough, and pretty soon we'll be out of school. It'll be Christmas. Everyone will be way more focused on what they can score than on you."

"You were a boy. People expect that from boys. You're all *so* predictable." She twisted her body in the swing around to turn her back on me. "Girls who get it are total whores. That's what everyone says. I'm not even worried about the boys at school you know? Girls are way more vicious. They're going to torture me."

"Stop it! No matter what happens tomorrow or the next day or the week after that I'll be with you." I spun her slowly back my way. "We can outlive this together. I'm not going to let you swallow alone. It's too much."

"Why would I believe you?" she said. "You always leave me."

"Not anymore. I'm done being the boy who leaves." I lifted her and held her tight against me. Her jacket felt soft and warm against my cheek. "I love you."

"Don't," she said. "I can't take that."

I covered her icy hands with mine, then squeezed them tight to remind her that I was there, that there was an actual person with her outside all the darkness surrounding us. "Listen." I brushed the wet off her face. "Sometimes in life you don't get to choose what makes you happy."

# Chapter 13
## Kids with Purpose

**JAYCEE WAS** up on the story going around, but had no clue how the other kids would move on her when she came back to school. Not knowing what's coming for you is the worst feeling in the world. See, if you have an idea what's coming down then you can get ready to act hard, ignore it, or figure out what you'll say. It would've been better if she had to answer to the principal since she could just sit in his office and cry all victim. It would've been easier if she only had her mother to deal with since moms have to love their kids to avoid living with the guilt of writing them off. Adults have rules, but you can't escape kids who've got juice on your story. They're not like adults. They don't have limits on how far they can go.

I stood outside of The Dream Academy the Monday morning after Jaycee went virus with my hands in my pockets so no one could see how bad they were shaking. My feet wouldn't stand still while I waited for her to step off the bus that drove the scholarship kids in. My guts felt like I'd swallowed lighter fluid and chased it with a match, but if she had the balls to show up I didn't want her searching for me, or stressing that I'd backed out. It would've been safer for me to let her take the hits alone, but I was sure if I dropped her she'd never make it through. The only way to help her survive was to grow up and do what was right for once. Maybe you can only save yourself if you save somebody else.

A bus pulled up and emptied out, but there was no sign of Jaycee. Parents drove up, then away. Kids ran inside. I squeezed my fists inside my pockets to bring the blood back and prayed she was ready to take the beatings waiting for her. Another bus rolled up and I sized up every kid who stepped off until I saw her.

"Come on." I hooked an arm into hers and turned toward the parking lot.

"What now?" she asked. Her skin was the color of sticky rice except for these purple blotches under her eyes that showed she hadn't slept. "You were the one who was against hiding."

"We're not going to hide," I said. We walked to my car half-blind from the wind freeze-drying our faces, "but we've got to get ready for war."

***

Jaycee tied her blueberry hair back into a Samurai bun, then patted her cheeks until they looked human again while I cranked up the heat and plugged my phone into my stereo. When I went to hold her hand she brushed me away and practiced making this bad bitch face in the rearview mirror.

"Do you think I should dye my hair?" she asked.

"No way. It fits you." I scrolled to find a song that would psyche her up for whatever was coming for her.

"I don't even know who I am anymore. This entire year it's like I've been trying to be someone different, someone the other kids want to be around." She reclined her seat back but kept her eyes trained on the school.

"Maybe nobody knows who they are. I mean we have these ideas, right, but they get twisted by what everyone else says we are. Maybe you have to forget yourself to figure out who you are."

"I don't know why you picked now to play philosopher." Jaycee she slid lower, "But it's not helping."

"You're right. You're better off pissed off anyway." I turned up the volume on The Pillowfights' "Talk Shit, Get Hit," but she wasn't listening. Her head was already inside the school.

"What do you think they'll do first?"

"Only one way to find out." I nudged her fingers apart until I could hold her hand. It was slimy with sweat. "Let's get this over with."

\*\*\*

That scene you see in movies where some high school kid walks down the hall while everyone else talks under their breath and shoots them dirty looks plays like some stupid cliché, but it's not. That's real life. If I hadn't marched beside Jaycee with the same say-something face she fronted I never would've believed kids were so predictable, that we operate under this worn-out script when the drama is hot. The entire walk to her locker I wanted to lay into every kid who stared us down, let them hear what robots they were, but they wouldn't have heard me if I had. They were way too busy showing off how disgusted they were at the sight of Jaycee, asking each other "Why is that slut here?!" and stuff loud enough for us to hear. It was like they had to be shitty to fit in.

"You only have to make it two more weeks," I said as she sped up. "One of them will fuck up over Christmas break,

and then you can get rip them up. Nobody makes it through
high school without scars, right?"

"I don't *want* to be mean like that," she said through her
teeth without slowing down. "I want to get back to boring,
too good."

"You will," I said, "and I'll be boring by your side."

Jaycee opened her locker while I played lookout and felt
bad about convincing her to come back right after being
put on blast as a total whore. If any other girl had gotten
broadcast that way I would've let them drop out, but school
meant something to Jaycee. It was her ticket to being more.

"Did you stuff a card in my locker?"

"What? No. Hurry up. We're going to be late for English."

"I guess Christmas is early this year," Jaycee said with a
sniff.

"What are you talking about?"

"See for yourself." She passed me an envelope covered
with Santa Claus stickers. Inside it, there was this card that
had this picture of little kids singing around a Christmas
tree. I didn't understand what got her so acid until I folded
it open, and saw someone had posted those pics of Jaycee
on the inside with the words HO! HO! HO! printed in nail
polish.

"Jayce," I started to pass the card back to her but didn't
want her to have a souvenir to get sick over.

"I guess I'm everyone's Christmas present," she said.
"Everyone gets a thrill."

"This isn't you. It's only paper."

She slammed her locker shut and jerked the card from my
hand. Then she ran to class, ripping it apart until a trail of
shreds followed her. I stayed for a second in case someone
stepped up to take credit, but no one did.

Jaycee was balled up on the love seat as English class started although there was plenty of room since Jenna was out again. Tyler and Hanna shared a beanbag on the floor as if Jaycee was coughing up Ebola. I motioned for them to sit next to me, but Tyler blew me off and Hanna kept her eyes on her phone. Lines had been drawn.

Jenna's mom hopped onto her desk all cool-teacher and crossed her legs. She was more relaxed than I'd seen her since Jenna took off, but there was no hope of her good times lasting once she found out what Jenna and her Bully friends did to Jaycee.

"First," Jenna's mom said, "I want each of you to understand what an honor it has been for me to guide you for these past few months. While it doesn't matter in the end whether you remember my name a year from now or not, I hope that in some small way I have helped you find your place in the world. So let's get started. Would anyone like to present their semester project for the class?"

"You turned in our project in right?" Tyler asked under his breath while we waited for one of the achiever kids to jump up. From across the room Paige smiled at me and Jaycee. She had gone back to dressing like a prep and didn't have the class to turn her head when I caught her doing it.

"I can't hear you down there," I said, so Tyler slid up despite the risk of being seen sitting with Jaycee. He sat on the edge on the opposite end from her to avoid getting his picture taken by some kid eager to Snapchat proof that he was tight with the new virus.

"I said did you turn in our project, or did you trick us into confessing for something else?" He grabbed my arm when he spoke as if I had some payback in mind for what he'd said about Jaycee or how he clowned her that night at the country club. When pics go virus every kid can't help but shake over what else might be out there.

"You're psycho. I turned it in over the weekend," I said, as Jenna's mom put a hand up.

"How?" he asked as he let go of my sleeve.

"I dropped it on Jenna's mom at the party house."

"What?" Tyler leaned forward to scope out Jaycee. "Why were you with Jenna's mom?"

"For this thing, I've got going on with the principal, alright? There's a lot going on you're not in on."

"Dude, I don't even know you anymore." Tyler dropped back down to sit with Hanna.

Heather and her group of achiever kids strutted to the front of the room with these binders and poster boards, right off. She cleared her throat as her friends held up the posters they'd made. On each they'd had charts and graphs for their "This is Purpose" project. Even though it was clear my friends and I weren't listening, she opened her binder and went on about how her group had already chosen the colleges they would attend, the majors they would enroll in before grad school, had decided where they would live after graduating from med school, and whether or not they'd have children. While she droned on about their collective lifetimes of bliss, her friends held up graphs that broke down their projected yearly incomes ten years in the future.

"As you can tell from our careful research," Heather said, closing her master plan, all bloated with satisfaction, "we have each defined our purpose in life, and one day we will prove that, if you have a plan, dreams can come true." I swear she bowed like she expected applause, but Jenna's mom only thanked her before asking her group to take their seats.

"I appreciate your efforts, really I do, but please under-stand that a purpose is not a plan." It was nice to see that at least she'd gotten her guru vibe back. "A purpose is a reason, a calling. A purpose is why you exist, not a minutely detailed agenda for what you intend to do. It doesn't matter where life takes you if you stay true to the spirit that guides you."

Heather scowled and asked how a purpose was different from a plan with this poison voice. It was like she'd expected to be crowned queen of the class for scrounging all that data but instead failed because she answered the wrong ques-tion. It was nice to watch her get crushed like that. I hoped that she'd lost a little faith in the system. It would've done her good.

Jenna's mom strolled over to Heather's desk and put her hand on her binder full of statistics and facts. "A plan is only a set of steps and intentions. Plans fail. Plans change. Plans come undone," she said. "Life is not made for plans. It is made for living."

"What about their group," Heather snarled. as she pointed to where my crew was sacked out unimpressed. "Did they fail too?"

"You don't fail for trying. If you do what you can, if you earnestly try to create something that never existed before, no one can say that you failed. And more importantly, failure often teaches you more than success."

With that said Jenna's mom lifted this stack of books off her desk, and passed one to each of us. Every book was wrapped in black velvet and tied up with a ribbon so there was no way to tell what we got.

"Don't open them yet. You will ruin the surprise." She positioned herself on her desk and gave us the lowdown on what we had to do for our final essay.

"Close your eyes and touch them," she said. "Hold them up and feel their weight. Appreciate that they are real objects and not just lights on a screen. They hold worlds inside them."

My palm slid over the velvet jacket of my book. It felt like a kitten's belly and reminded me of Jaycee's fleece, of my purpose.

"Now open your eyes and untie your ribbons. It's time to see what fate has given you." I untied the ribbon and stripped the black fabric off my book. Its cover had a picture of this blurred-out man running away. It was called *Brave New World*.

I held mine up for Tyler to see, and he showed me his with this look like he wanted to vomit. It had a waitress on its cover and the words *Nickled and Dimed* printed in white.

"What am I supposed to do with this?" he asked like he'd been handed a welfare check.

"Maybe you'll learn something," Hanna teased, then modeled her book for us. It had a toy woman on the front of it holding a mirror and was called *The Beauty Myth*. Tyler rolled his eyes and told her being hot was not a myth.

Jenna's mom made her way around the room to write who got what before explaining that she expected us all to turn in a ten-page essay about what our books meant to us for our final assignment.

I asked Jaycee what she got, but she only tossed her book onto my lap and told me to find out for myself since she'd had enough surprises.

The bell rang and we got up to leave. I went to set Tyler and Hanna straight, but before I could that achiever kid, Heather, and her friends pushed past me and surrounded Jaycee with their gorgeous futures pressed against their chests.

"Women like you are the reason it's so hard for women like us to succeed," Heather said with her head held high. "You're the reason we have to fight to be taken seriously!"

"What does that mean?" Jaycee asked as the achiever kids filed out behind Heather like baby ducks. "What did you say?!"

"Trash," Heather said as she took out her phone, then she left without glancing back.

"Don't let her get to you." I put my arms out to catch Jaycee, but Tyler bumped me sideways to be a dick. By the time I was able to get my gear together she was already in the hall.

*** 

Fights don't happen the way you see them go down in movies. Real fights jump off before anyone gets what's going on, and turn into this madness where kids swing their arms furious until they're all doubled-over and frantic. They're never these fair one-on-one deals where everyone else backs off and lets the kids beefing settle whatever got them heated. They end like a horror film, and the hits that do the least actual damage, in the long run, are the ones that leave the most blood on your face.

Jaycee's fingers spread out like claws and had almost reached Heather's perfect blonde hair before I wrapped my arm around her waist and lifted her off her feet. She let out this wild hurt scream while I struggled to hold her back, the whole time kicking at Heather and digging her nails into my hands to break free.

"Say what you said again!" Jaycee squealed as kids rushed to the scene thirsty to get front row for a serious girl fight. "Say it!"

Heather smirked to show how beneath her Jaycee was, like it was this great chore to consider her. She looked so pleased with herself, so safe, that I debated letting Jaycee go for a second, but I'd seen what happens when girls fight. See, when guys fight they only want to land a few good shots so somebody says they won. When girls fight they go wild, and do their best to mutilate each other.

"What did I say?" Heather asked as her friends giggled behind her. Jaycee heaved for breath and wrestled like an animal to get free. "I said you're a little white trash slut."

Once Heather spoke that last syllable I felt something break inside Jaycee right between my arms. When it did she went limp, and let out these bubbling cries that sounded like choking. Then she lost her balance to where I had to hold her up. Kids pushed against each other and cheered. Some shouted, but I only saw their mouths opening and closing like wind-up toys. Heather's face went sour over the sight of Jaycee blubbering before she walked away so she didn't have to watch what she'd done.

\*\*\*

Jaycee sat on the tile floor with her face between her knees. For a minute I stood over her without saying a word. I just listened to her sob and cough until she calmed down enough for me to rub her shoulders without risking getting hit. She looked up at me as I stroked her blue bangs back from where they stuck to face, and it was obvious that she wanted me to say something to make her feel better about what went down. If I'd been a better kid I would've, but I was too pissed at her to play all roses and there-there.

"You're going to get kicked out of school if you jump like that," I said with my back against the door. "You want that?"

"Where are we?" she asked.

"The teacher's bathroom. Wash your face off and chill, okay?"

"We can't be in here." She sniffled as she stood to turn the faucet on. "We'll get in trouble."

"Teachers never leave class to go to the bathroom, and we're only going to get in trouble if you go berserk whenever a kid tests you. You want to lose your scholarship?"

Jaycee filled her cupped hands with cold water, then splashed her face. "Who cares? I've got nothing to sing about anyway."

"Why'd you come back then?"

"Because of you." She wiped her hands dry on her sweatshirt, then touched her chest like she was trying to locate whatever had snapped inside her. "I promised my mom that I would never scare her that way again, too."

I pressed my forehead against hers. "Only two weeks. You can do this."

"If I can't deal with this," she whispered as she braced herself against the sink, "if I go back to public school or take off, will you come with me?"

"Where you go, I go. You're with me from now on, like scar tissue."

"Thanks, I guess." Jaycee picked up her books off the floor before opening the door. "You're the weirdest guy I've met in my life."

"Yeah," I said, "that's why you love me."

"No way. I'm just using you for rides." We laughed, and for a second life felt kind again.

***

By the time lunchtime came, my nerves sparked like cut power lines. I sweated over the fact that Jaycee hadn't shown up at our table. While Tyler and Hanna bitched about having to read an entire book in a week I scanned the lunchroom hoping that maybe she'd decided to eat by herself to avoid the drama, but all I saw were kids on their phones or laughing. There was no point in asking what they were dying over since the story was so fresh. I tried to let the scene go, but the static between me and my crew was too much to bear.

"You're so pathetic you know?" I said. "Jaycee gets caught hardcore and it's like suddenly none of you want to be seen with her."

"I've got my own problems," Tyler said as he held up the book Jenna's mom gifted him. "I just want this year to be over."

"Yeah," Hanna said, "and I didn't say a word to her."

"Exactly," I said. "But I'm sure you shared whatever you heard a hundred times by now. What's the latest anyway?"

"You didn't *hear*?" She glowed like it was the last day of school.

"No. Go ahead and tell me before you pee yourself."

The problem with a story that's steamy and new is that whatever actually happened is never awful enough to satisfy the gossip addicts. See, kids change the details until the story is all raunchy gore. Maybe they do that so they're part of the story, or because the worse a story gets the better they come off by comparison. Either way, the official version is never the truth, but like this monster made up of what went down and everyone else's nightmares. Hanna always had the official version since sharing the latest drama was her favorite thing in the world.

This is how Hanna told it. She said that the CH Bullies got Jaycee wasted and were about to bang her out when Jenna showed up, frowning. She said Jenna told them they were too good to waste their time with a skank like Jaycee, and that it was time for her to learn what happens to party virgins who can't hang. So while her Bully friends stripped Jaycee down Jenna went scavenger and came back with this box of her mom's art junk so they could paint her up and show her where she belonged. But Jaycee woke up in the middle of their art project, like out of her mind and thirsty, and started begging them to do her like some sex zombie. They turned her down at first, but eventually they were like why not? Guys are guys. It turned into this orgy like in front of everyone. Kids swear she was crying for more the whole time you were carrying her away.

"That's total bullshit. I was there remember? I saved her, and she was out cold. Why can't you all just leave her alone?"

"That's the latest." Hanna leaned across the table so that the other kids couldn't hear what she said, not because it was a secret so much as because you have to pretend that a story is secret so it seems way important. "Isn't that what you wanted to hear?"

"But that's a total lie! We've got to set this straight," I shouted, and some kids across from me broke down over their lunch trays.

"Relax," Tyler said. "You probably missed it."

"It doesn't matter if she doesn't remember it, right?" Hanna asked.

"Yes, it matters! Look, when I found her she had her underwear on. Kids were taking pics even though she looked dead. You've got to set whoever is saying that correct."

"No one will believe me," Hanna said, annoyed that I didn't appreciate how cherry the latest version was. "Besides, don't you think the fact that she's jerk-off material for every guy here is way worse?"

Tyler grinned. I wanted to kill him.

"Swear you'll delete whatever you've got. It's not right. She's our friend."

"Already gone," Tyler said, then lifted up his book to fake reading. "It's not like I was impressed."

"Sometimes I think you only let her hang with us so you can screw with her."

Tyler sat his book down and sized me up all phony gangster. "Whatever you've got going on with her, Jenna's mom or whoever else that you're hiding from us has warped your brain, man! She's a nice girl, but she's got issues and I don't want a subscription, alright?"

"You should try pretending that Jaycee is more than a scholarship kid for once. It might do you good to care about someone besides yourself."

"You'd know," Tyler got up and signaled for Hanna to walk, "You're the expert on fake charity."

\*\*\*

I didn't see Jaycee for the rest of the day. Maybe she spent it hiding out in the bathroom the way I did sometimes when my nerves made the voices around me feel like needles, or maybe she heard the latest and hated me for not telling her about it. Either way I couldn't wait to find her or to lock myself away in my room.

On my way to my car, I saw Paige waiting on the sidewalk. Her arms were bundled underneath her coat, and she danced a little to keep warm while she waited for her mom in the cold. She didn't notice me, but the sight of her stranded on the cement with snow dusting her hair made me go to her.

"What happened to your Earth Mother get-up?"

"It got old," she said. "When I got dressed this morning it felt like I was wearing someone else's clothes."

The buses and cars were almost gone. The parking lot was spotted with dry circles in the snow that showed what had been there and disappeared. "So who's the next Paige going to be?"

"Hopefully a girl with a car for starters," she said. "Any ideas? You're the one who claims to understand me so well."

"That's not true. I only know who you're not when you're fronting."

"Maybe I always am," she said. Her hands had gone white, but I was afraid to hold them. "This is kind of like old times huh?"

"A little, but we're older now. It's not the same."

"Before long it's going to be Christmas. After that, I'm off to the land of Our Fathers and plaid skirts. Not a lot like Europe, right?"

"No," I said, "but that was a fun dream. You keep imagining those castles and clubs waiting for you."

"Nothing stays fun forever." She sniffled. "Especially dreams. You'll all definitely forget about me next year, but I'm going to miss you."

"Don't be that way," I said. "Maybe this is your chance to find the Paige you've always wanted to be. Endings don't exist. We're all saved forever in some computer."

"I miss being wanted," Paige said, as her mom's Mercedes crested the hill.

"You will be," I said. "There's no doubt you'll break a dozen hearts next year. I just can't be one anymore. I'm with Jaycee now, but she's in deep."

"Yes, she is. She doesn't deserve you."

"I don't deserve her, and you're the one who kept teasing me, keeping me thirsty over you like it was a game. I'll remember that when you're gone."

"Just make sure she's worth all the trouble."

"She is," I said, as Paige jogged to her mom's car. I watched it move up the hill, get small, and vanish. It was like reading the last line of a book and feeling it close.

\*\*\*

I spent most of that night in my room with the lights off wondering what I could've done differently to save Jaycee from the flood of dirty looks and gross come-ons that were fading her since she got stripped, tagged, and posted. I prayed she didn't hear about the latest version of what went down, and that she'd somehow find a phone to text me. Being locked up in my room had always been my escape from whatever was weighing on me outside my door, but that night I only imagined the beating Jaycee was taking alone. I should've stayed with her. I should've found a way.

It was late at night by the time all those imaginary disasters made it impossible to stay alone in my head, and with no friends I felt like dealing with I snuck downstairs hoping that my mom was awake. I figured if anyone understood what it was like to be on your own and terrified about the future it was her.

My mom was on the couch watching the news with these dead eyes that showed she'd been thinking too much too. For a second I stood at the bottom of the stairs and tried to think of the best way to start. What I wanted to say I couldn't. What she wanted to hear was a lie. The news was on when I went to her, sure that she'd say something if I didn't.

"You never sleep do you?" she asked.

"I wish I could, but my mind won't shut up when everything goes black and quiet," I said. "How's Johnny?"

"Better, but he's lost two pounds. I don't like those patches your father has him on. What is the good in helping him pay attention if he never wants to eat?"

"He's too little to care about his grades you know? And I like him better when he's clean."

"Everyone is better when they are sober," my mom said. "What is on your mind tonight?"

"Nothing. School's rough, but I can transfer or drop out if that doesn't change."

"No you can't." She sat up straight. "Wipe that thought out of your head. My situation with your dad is bad enough. I don't need to lose sleep over you too."

"What *is* your situation exactly?"

"What's yours?" my mom asked, then stood up and made for the kitchen. The news was doing another feature on The Dream Academy, but the sound was off. There was just the clink of glasses behind me, and the pop of a cork. I didn't want to stay, and I didn't want to move.

When my mom came back, she tousled my hair like I was still Johnny's age, and asked if I'd gotten into a fight.

"You watch too much TV," I said, as my phone vibrated over and over again in my pocket.

"Maybe I do," she said, trying her best to keep her wine glass out of sight, "or maybe I've just been fighting too much myself."

"So give up."

"I hope those aren't my only choices. If they are, maybe I should have done more."

"More what?"

"Maybe I should have made one big move instead of waiting for things to work out."

"Get some rest," I said, as I left to see who was text-bombing me. "One of us should."

From the stairs I watched her settle into the couch. Her wine glass caught the light from the screen as she put on this show where all these storybook characters live together in a small town and are never happy.

*\*\*\**

I sat on the end of my bed and went through the dozens of texts I'd gotten while I was busy being a good son. They read like a total scam. The messages came from a number I didn't recognize but were written like Jaycee had sent them. That's the danger of standing up for a kid who's gone virus. You're fair game. That's what Tyler and Hanna were trying to dodge.

For a while, I scrolled through the texts from the first to the last, and imagined kids huddled up at some party, drooling for me to answer back. I was sure if I did they'd play Jaycee, and message that she was about to jump out a window or beg me to marry her. Every message was more desperate than the last. One said she was homeless. Another said she was outside my house. If I'd slept more I would've hit delete, but I was too worn through to go out and ready to believe in a fairytale.

I laid back on my bed and answered the last one in spite of myself. I wrote that if it was her then she had to prove it. In no time my phone lit up "KK," and I shot to my window. Jaycee was in my front yard waving like a castaway.

In the living room, my mom's nightly ritual had turned her into Sleeping Beauty. In a minute Jaycee was up the stairs and safe from whatever sent her running. For the first time in weeks, my room felt peaceful again.

"I'm sorry," Jaycee said. "I didn't know where else to go except maybe a Waffle House. The bus stations get sketchy when it's this late." The white lines from tears ran down her red cheeks.

"How'd you even get here? Whose phone is that?" I asked as I swept tiny ice crystals from her hair.

"Relax. I lifted my mom's cell and used my tip money for a cab after I got your parents' address off the school's website. We're all online right?" She fidgeted on the bed like there was something swelling inside her she had to let out.

"Why?"

"There wasn't anyone else around to talk to. My mom told me that she wasn't going to have another criminal in her house. She must've got a text from one of the moms." She paused, then toed off her shoes. "It's okay though. I stole her phone so she has to make up eventually. I just need a place to crash tonight."

"But you were the victim?" I helped her fish her arms out of her coat. "You didn't commit any crime."

"Underage drinking. She didn't want to listen to anything I said after she saw how gone I was." Jaycee scooted under the covers, and I joined her without offering any advice. It was enough that we were safe together. "Just hold me," she said. "Hold me and everything will be okay."

We pressed together, still dressed and exhausted. I felt her body get soft again as she went out. I stared at the ceiling with this sense that I had to make the big move my mom never did. I didn't want to give up. I searched for the local news' anonymous tip-line's number on my phone, then forwarded those shitty pics of Jaycee going around with the word that she was getting it hardcore from the other kids at The Dream Academy for being a victim. I didn't think about tomorrow. I only hoped that if the news found out then the story would change for good.

After I made my move I turned off my phone and cuddled Jaycee. "Two more weeks," I said softly. "I promise we can survive that long."

# Chapter 14
## Kids on Blast

**THE MORNING** after Jaycee caught more hate than any kid I'd ever known, after she got kicked out of her house for being a criminal, I woke up from a sleep so thick I wasn't sure if I had the strength to push down the blankets. I listened for the everyday noises of my mother hurrying my brother to get ready for school, for the sound of Jaycee creeping around my room to find her shoes, but only heard my own breathing. I pushed the blankets onto the floor with my feet and concentrated until my eyes opened slow as garage doors. My room came into focus. My door was closed, my phone was face-down on my nightstand, and for a second it was like everything that had happened before had vanished. When I tried to remember what went down the day before, what I dreamed, my mind stayed blank. It's hard to tell the difference between a dream and a memory. Sometimes they're the same thing, this collection of pictures you barely remember, lines you heard or said that don't fit together. For a while I lay still and wondered if I was an alien sent to Earth who didn't have to learn or do anything. It felt amazing.

Once I stretched and focused on bringing back everything that had gone sideways the day before, all that might still fall apart, the present flooded into my brain. I rolled over to where Jaycee had slept, and put my hand against the sheet to make sure she'd really come to me. It was still warm, but she was gone. I wondered where she went, and got scared.

At first I guessed that maybe she was playing a game hide-and-go-seek style, but I checked under my bed and searched my closet without finding any trace of her. The bathroom was empty too. I went back to my room to see if she'd left a note, but the only paper lying around was My List of Fantastic Promises. I prayed she hadn't read it. I checked my phone to see if she'd at least sent a text and found the message I'd sent to the Channel 9 news. That's when I remembered my big move. I panicked and was dying to stay home but there was no way it was going to be safe at school now. I stand by her. I made a promise. It was time to be the kind of kid who kept his word.

\*\*\*

Downstairs my mom had cooked breakfast for Johnny and me. It wasn't like her to bother with that on a school day, but she'd sat the table with glasses of orange juice and plates stacked with bacon and toaster waffles as if it she was eager to be this all-American mom. Johnny ate with his hands while I watched her drink her coffee. Maybe it felt good for her to be the kind of mother she saw in sitcoms for once, or maybe she blamed the distance between us on her not doing the usual mom things like forcing us to eat healthy. I hoped she hadn't seen Jaycee sneak out.

"So you still planning on dropping out?" She laughed as if joking about what I'd said made it go away. "I'm sorry I didn't listen better last night. I've been losing a lot of nights lately. It's not fair to you."

"Why would I ever want to drop out of a school like mine?"

"You are fortunate. We all are to have each other. Nothing is more important than family."

"You're right." I watched Johnny swing his feet without a care in the world, and envied that the world hadn't left a mark on him yet. "You ever think about taking in another kid, wonder what that'd be like?"

"There's no way we could now," she said. "Besides, you are almost grown."

"We can do anything we want if we don't care about failing. That's what my English teacher says. Last night you told me a person has to make one big move or give up, right?"

"That is terrible advice. That's my fault. I'm sorry."

"Stop apologizing all the time."

"I'm..." she started, then switched on the TV so she had an excuse to stop talking. There was this shot of The Dream Academy on the screen, but it was only a graphic with the words "Cyberbullies" and "Live at Five" printed over it. My mom's eyes got wide, and I shoveled food in my mouth like I hadn't noticed.

"Bryce," she said as she pumped the remote with her thumb to catch what the anchor said before the station cut to commercial. "Does your school have cyberbullies?"

"I don't know. I mean, we have the internet, so probably."

"What did they do? I missed what the man said."

"No idea, but don't sweat it. We're not public school kids. We're Dream Kids remember?"

"You're right." She switched it off, "but isn't it a shame that a handful of bad kids can cause problems for students like you."

"There's always going to be someone who makes your life harsh for everyone else, you know? I'm sure they'll get checked." She smiled over her coffee because she wasn't listening to *me* at all.

***

Before I backed out of my driveway to search for Jaycee I read the message I'd sent again. Looking at her pics was gross enough, but snitching to the news about what went down made me feel like a traitor. My friends and I had always handled our own business no matter what. If I'd been thinking straight I would've figured out a way to get revenge undercover. That drop to the news made me lower than a pervert. It made me a rat.

NOFX sang "My Stepdad's a Cop," as I geared into reverse. Jaycee sprung up out of nowhere, and shouted "Whoa! Whoa! Whoa!" I hit the brakes, and she jumped in.

"You're crazy! I could've killed you."

"What was I supposed to do? Stroll to the breakfast nook and kiss your mom good morning? I had to hide."

"Right." I turned off the music and cranked the heat so she'd stop shaking, then headed off to school.

"When the kids see me wearing the clothes I had on yesterday they're going to die. Let's go back to your house so I can change. You're probably close to my size or I could lift something from your mom if she's gone."

"No one is going to hate on you for your clothes. There's something giant on its way. It's on me, but if it goes right it might bury this shit for good."

"What did you do, Bryce?" Jaycee asked like she'd walked in on me mopping up blood.

"I'm sorry. It was late and the only thing I could think of. See when a story won't die the only way to ruin it is to make any kid who shares it an asshole for digging it up again."

Jaycee cut the heat, and grabbed the wheel. "Tell me what you did or I'll crash this car and murder us both. I swear to God!"

I eased off the gas and steered onto the breakdown lane to confess. It was her story. Since I put in on blast I at least owed her an explanation why.

This is how I told it. Her mom was right. Not about partying being this serious crime, but about the underage part. I told her that since she was underage every kid who shared her pics was basically trading kiddie porn, and that was a *real* crime. Once that set in on them they'd shit themselves, and delete everything. I told her I dropped word with the news so they'd have proof that The Dream Academy wasn't filled with these perfect leaders of tomorrow, just regular kids who'd destroy a helpless kid for the fun of it. Once the news hit no kid would dare text her name or slide a nasty card in her locker. It'd be too risky to try. I told her the whole school was probably trashing her pics and their posts right that minute since nobody holds onto evidence that they're a piece of shit.

Jaycee froze in her seat, lifeless as one of Johnny's stuffed animals, while she thought about what I'd set in motion. She didn't cry. She didn't yell or hit me. For a second I wondered if what I'd done had broken another invisible part inside her; the last one that held her together.

"Drive," she said, and I did. The rest of the way to school I swallowed the "I'm sorry" stuck in my throat and hoped the news would just drop it. I was nauseous that I might've ruined our shot at making it to Christmas alive by playing white knight.

At school my car idled in the parking lot. Neither of us was ready to walk inside or knew what to say. Jaycee looked like if I opened her door she would pour out onto the pavement. Taking her picture wasn't going to bring her back, so I did the only thing I could to remind her who she really was.

"Have you listened to this?" I asked as I put on Against Me's "Black Me Out." She nodded as she smooshed her face against the window. "I want you to sing it for me."

"I can't sing now," she said. "I probably won't sing again."

"Okay, then let this be the last time. Sing for me and I promise not to ask anymore."

"Forget it," she said, but when I started the track over it found its way into all those hollow places inside her. At first she only hummed along, but after a minute she was shouting the chorus, angry. Her hands beat against my dashboard like sledgehammers. Kenny's playlist had cut us up and sewn us back together. That punk rage covered us like armor. And I knew that even if we lost everything it didn't matter. Being lost was the same as being free.

***

Jenna's mom started our English class with this voice like she'd left a memorial service. That was the first sign that something major was going down. "Kids, this week our school is going to be a little strange," she said. I tried to zone out while she struggled to prepare us for what was about to hit without giving away what it was. I counted the days left until Christmas break on my fingers while she talked. "I want you to know that the faculty is behind you. I wish you the best and want to encourage you to be the best versions of yourself." She left it at that, and told us that we should use our time wisely because, "You never know how long you have."

"High school takes forever, and that's long enough," I said. If Paige had come to class, if she'd wedged herself in the bean bag across from me sulking, she would've laughed at that. It's funny what you miss about a person once they're gone, even when you only like them half the time.

Heather raised her hand, but Jenna's mom took out a book and pretended not to notice her panting for attention. It was nice to see her ignored for once. Maybe it would help her be an actual person. Heartbreaks, even little ones, are the only things that make you grow up.

"What book did you get?" I pointed to the backpack in Jaycee's lap. "I'm not doing your homework for you."

"Like I'd want you to," she said, then fished it out and carefully unwrapped it before holding it up for me to see. Her book had two punks on the cover and was called *Just Kids*. "What am I supposed to do with this?"

"Hold on," I said.

I took my book out from my backpack, and walked up to Jenna's mom who played deaf until I dropped it on her desk.

"Yes, Bryce?" she asked, without her usual spirit guide voice.

"How much of our lives do you want us to include?" Jenna's mom was reading a book called *Rip It Up and Start Again*. "Like, is it supposed to be an analysis or something?"

"Why don't you write what's in your heart without worrying about what I or anyone else wants. I probably won't even read those reports."

"Then why should I bother to write it?"

"Bryce, what you take from a book is for yourself." She rocked in her chair and gave me this weird smirk. "What was your group's motto for your semester project?"

"None of this matters."

"Those were your words. If you believe them, live by them. There are enough phony rebels in the world."

I walked to the loveseat where Tyler and Hanna had finally gotten the nerve to join us. They were texting like hyperactive kids on double-shots of espresso. Neither of them were able to last five seconds without checking the door to our classroom. When I crashed between them I heard the story for the first time. Each of them had a different version, so nothing was official and that made it worse.

This is how Tyler told it. He said his parents had pressured him about the news story and all, and were terrified that he might be involved since they had a reputation to protect. He played dumb and swore he'd find the real story for them so they didn't need to sweat. He guaranteed the news had their facts twisted since kids at our school were focused on making their dreams come true and all.

This is how Hanna told it. She said her mom asked her if it was one of the girls on the gymnastics team, if the team was in trouble. She said her mom couldn't stand the thought that the team wouldn't be able to compete over some drunk girl. Hanna promised the school would never cancel gymnastics over one stupid girl who probably couldn't even make the team.

I got on my phone to see if putting the word out had solved Jaycee's situation, but instead of shutting everyone up it only made them more brutal than before. Kids tweeted that Jaycee was fake for playing victim, that scholarship kids like her were ruining the school, and that she should do us all a favor and kill herself.

"Do you still have your mom's phone?" I asked Jaycee as she flipped through her book.

"Yeah, but the battery is dead. Why?"

"No reason," I said, and stuffed mine back into my pocket.

"What were you looking at?"

"Forget it," I said, as Jenna's mom asked me to step out with her. "You don't want to know."

When we walked out of the classroom this woman with too much makeup on passed by us with this skinny cameraman in tow. That turned Jenna's mom white as a snowman.

"Bryce." She scanned the hall to make sure no one was listening. "I've made a lot of mistakes this semester. People do that when they're sad and lonely, but I need you to be honest with me." She gripped her book between her hands like a strongman ready to tear a phonebook in half.

"No problem," I said. "We're crime partners." I reached out to touch her arm, to prove I was down with her, but she stepped back.

"Don't ever say that again. I'm your teacher. Forget about everything else." I dropped my arm to my side, and shrugged. "First, did you send your group project to anyone else?"

"I left a copy for the principal, but that's it."

"That's good. The last thing we need is for the local news to get their hands on that too. And you didn't tell any of your friends about your helping me out either?"

"I'd never do that. Sharing is caring, but I keep me shit undercover."

"That's a relief." She eased her death grip off her book. "What do you know about this news story? If they are shooting on location it has to be serious."

"I have no idea," I said, "and even if I do, I don't."

"But I thought we were friends?"

"I guess I forgot that," I said. "You're just my teacher." Then I went back inside.

***

Jaycee sat on the loveseat next to Hanna who was showing her something on her phone. When she saw me she jerked it away, and dropped onto a beanbag chair. It would've been easy to hate Hanna if I wasn't so sure she couldn't help being a total rumor addict.

Whatever she showed Jaycee had bleached the color off her. When she saw me she forced herself against the love-seat like if she tried hard enough she could bury herself into its cushions.

"Great plan," she said.

"It was the only move I could think of," I said. "I'm sorry."

"Don't ever apologize to me again. The only reason you do that is because you keep making things worse." She chewed on her bottom lip, and let out a little yelp when she bit through it by accident.

"I talked to my mom this morning. She said you can stay with us as long as you want. Maybe she always dreamed of having a daughter or something."

"She said that?" Jaycee pinched her lip to stop the bleeding. "Honest?"

"If things don't work out with your mom I swear you can crash with us." It wasn't right to lie, but I figured that if I could sneak her in one night then I could do it every night. My parents hardly noticed me, so what was one more kid to forget?

Class had almost ended when the school secretary came in and asked me to follow her, in a panic. There was no way to argue.

***

Principal Keys waited for me in the hall with this grim expression that reminded me of my mom's face when my dad disappeared for weeks.

"How are you feeling today, Bryce?"

"Good. I got some sleep for once. You?"

"You like this place, right?" he asked. "What I mean is you want this place to keep its reputation so you don't have to transfer. You're applying to college soon, correct?"

"I haven't really thought about college. Things have been kind of hectic lately you know?"

He grabbed my arms, not angry, but like he wanted me to focus. "I need to ask you some questions, and you have to be honest."

"No problem," I said as he caught himself and let me go.

"But the right kind of honest," he whispered, "the kind that prevents any unwanted attention."

"I got you," I said, even though I didn't, and together we walked to his office.

"Take a seat," he said once we were inside. From behind his desk he frowned, and shook his head as if I had somehow ruined his life's work, which I kind of had.

"Bryce, I chose you because your work had a point of view. It had a vision, but sometimes those with a vision are terrible at considering the larger picture."

"Is this about my video for your social media thing?"

"No. I had to cancel that given the breaking news this morning. I am sure you've heard it." I shrugged and turned away from him. My body felt freeze-dried. "Is that a yes or a no?"

"I've heard a bunch of dumb rumors," I said. "Kids love to make up stories."

"Remember when we talked about stories, Bryce? They work both ways. I have been taking calls all morning from reporters who want me to explain how I'm managing this cyberbullying scandal, but the trouble is I have no idea what they are referring to. You have to work with me on this. Tell me what you know."

Anxious jolts flared electric inside me. I pictured myself on camera in the country club while the girl from the picture got drunk and manhandled in the pool. I saw myself struggling to dress Jaycee on security camera tape from the gas station, footage of me dragging her into the elevator of her apartment building after she got caught.

This is how I told it, run together and senseless. I'd stood up for her, cleaned her up, and took her home. I was the only kid who tried to stop all the hating and sharing when she went virus. I did the right thing. Principal Keys' face turned the cover of skim milk as I went on about what the kids were saying online, about how Jaycee's mom had kicked her out, how she didn't even know who she was anymore. I didn't stop dropping details until I was stutter-mumbling so bad there was no use in trying to speak. See, you're not who you think you are. You're just who you are in pictures, in the version kids share. That's what makes high school so bad. Once you're in a story, once it's official, you're branded until you get out.

For what felt like a long time he sat without saying a word, and I wished I'd had the sense to play dumb. Maybe I was just tired of carrying everything around myself, and hoped that for once an adult had this clear idea of what to do next.

"Can I leave now?" I asked when I could.

"Bryce," Principal Keys said in this patient way that left me uneasy, "I'm sorry about what happened to your friend. I am worried though that you didn't bring this to me first." I started to explain that Jaycee had been on blast so heavy that the last thing I wanted to do was jump in, but he cut me off. "So you didn't tell anyone else?"

"Everyone already heard, but most of it is a total lie."

"Do you know who told the news?" And for the first time I got what he was searching for all along. He didn't care about Jaycee, or me, or anyone else. He only cared about the school's rep.

"No," I said. "No one does."

He stood, and walked to put his hand on me. Not because he wanted me to feel better, but because that's the thing you do when you're supposed to act like you care. "I am sorry that I'm not able to promote your work anymore," he said, before walking me toward the door.

"What happens now?" I asked, as he opened it.

"That's what I have to decide," he said, "but there is one more thing. If I am going to make this right I have to trust you. I can use a smart young man like yourself when the news cameras come looking for sound bites, but only if I'm positive that you are my man. You have to make that decision for yourself."

"What do you want?"

"I want you to unlock your phone and give it to me," he said. "Then I'll see that I can trust you."

I reached into my front pocket and grabbed hold of the cold plastic square inside it, but couldn't bring myself to pull it out. Principal Keys waited for me to make my move, but after a minute passed he sighed and took a step back. "Is that your choice?"

"I can't," I said. "It's not for you." Sometimes the best caring was not sharing.

"That is disappointing." He nudged me outside. "But not every student is meant for our school. I'm sure you'll find your way, and I'll do my best to make sure you get that chance." He moved to shut the door.

"What do you mean?"

"You will know soon enough, but regardless of what happens never forget that you are an artist," he said. "If the world still needs those then nothing can stop you from being who you were meant to be." Then he closed the door before I got an honest answer.

\*\*\*

I had to wait until lunchtime to locate Jaycee. She was eating alone at a table way in the back when I rolled up on her, and for a minute she acted like I wasn't even there.

"You can't see me," she said. "I've decided to be invisible so don't bother talking."

"I've got my phone charger in my backpack if you want to call your mom. She's probably worried about you."

"Guess what I found in my backpack?" Jaycee put her hand into her backpack and came up with two more Christmas cards. When she tossed them on the table a couple of girls sitting on the other side of the room saw them and giggled like mad. "Did you hear how I begged those bullies to do me?" she stuttered. "I mean, how could I resist?"

"I was there so I don't care what those kids say." I pushed the cards into her backpack to shut up those idiot girls who didn't get that it could happen to them.

"Nobody pays attention to the truth so who cares? Hanna showed me what everyone's posting. They think I'm the problem. That the school would be better off if I was dead. Why do they blame me?"

"Because they're assholes," I said, "and I'm tired of dealing with this place. I'm probably going to get expelled."

"Where did you hear that? Because of me?" This sound came out of her like a busted speaker, fuzzy and trembling.

"It's got nothing to do with you. It's on me."

"You just have to be the tragic hero, don't you?" She shoved her tray away.

"Stop it. I'm talking about what went down with Principal Keys. He thinks I screwed him over, got the school's reputation in trouble or something."

"Did he say that? Who told on you?"

"I pretty much ratted on myself. I'm not good at talking when I can't decide what's right to say. It all went wrong."

"I guess you were the one begging to get screwed," Jaycee smirked, and I agreed.

"Right? Look, go see your mom after school. You've got to smooth things with her. If it goes bad all you have to do is call. If he kicks me out then I'll find a way to post up in the closest desk to yours in wherever we land."

"And what if I want to run away?"

"I heard Florida is boss. It's like Spring Break never ends down there."

"That sounds like a dream," Jaycee said as the bell ring. "I miss the sun."

"Me too. I've got to get to class. You know, I see you every time I close my eyes."

***

The boxes from my dad's office were stacked up outside my front door when I got home. In the entryway there were containers that had his name written on them. I did my best not to notice them.

My mom sat in front of the television with her coffee mug and watched the news. I went over to get the latest on The Dream Academy, but once she saw me she shut it off and scooted my way all depressed.

"I missed you," she said as if I'd vanished and reappeared out of nowhere. She smoothed my hair out of my eyes, and I let her. It felt good to be back.

"Miss you too. I've had a lot to deal with lately."

"I know, but we need to talk." She got up to make sure Johnny was in his room, then said, "Your father has to go away for a while."

I thought of all the samples I'd lifted from his shipments and wondered if their turning up missing equaled "Federal" for him, but held tight. "Are you getting a divorce?" I hoped that was it since divorce was way better than prison.

"No. He needs me."

"Is he in jail?"

"No, he's not in jail," she said, and took a drink of coffee. I could smell that she'd spiked it, but everyone needs a way to get by when bad times come. "He's in rehab, Bryce."

"Oh shit," I said it before I caught myself.

"Oh shit is right," she said, then finished her mug in one drink. "I don't even know if he'll have a job when he gets out, given what he does." I didn't ask how long he'd be gone since he'd locked himself in his office for the past two years, and no rehab lasted that long. "I need more coffee," she said, and switched the TV back on. A reporter stood out front of The Dream Academy with a microphone, and talked about how Principal Keys was set to give a statement. "Isn't that shocking? The students at your school are supposed to be the best of the best, and then this happens. It's just horrible."

"What did the news say about the girl?"

"Only that she was a minor." My mom choked down another giant gulp, and shook her head. "I can't imagine the fires that man has to put out now."

"Who? Our Principal?"

"Of course." My mom sprawled back onto the couch. "He has to shoulder such a burden, leading you kids."

"But what's going to happen to the kids who tortured that girl?"

"And he's not bad looking either," she sighed. "Bryce, if your father doesn't get to go back to work, if it's against their policy, then you may have to go to a public school next year."

"Maybe I will, or maybe I'll run away."

"Don't joke. It's not funny."

"It's not funny," I said, as I turned what Principal Keys had laid on me over in my head, "but I'll figure things out for myself either way." I walked upstairs as she went to the kitchen to refill her mug. We didn't say goodbye. We never did.

# Chapter 15
# Kids on Fire

THE SUN PUSHED every cloud from the sky and melted the clumps of snow into streams that ran down the cracks in the sidewalk until they made tiny rivers that streaked across the parking lot. It was like the world had spun backward, turned winter into fall. I searched for that dried leaf smell in the air while I waited for Jaycee to step off the bus with this feeling inside me like we'd been given a second chance, like no matter how ugly things got we'd be okay.

When she walked over to me I inched her chin up so she could see what I did, but it was like we were looking at the same sky with completely different eyes.

"My mom took me back," she said before I had the chance to ask. "She said she was sorry, and like she was just terrified I'd end up in jail like my dad."

"You're too pretty for jail," I said. "You'd never last."

"Thanks, I guess." She crinkled her nose up at me and we headed toward the front doors, but before we got to them Tyler and Hanna bum-rushed us. They talked fast at the same time, but nothing they said made sense.

"It's on! It's on!" Tyler yelled, pointing inside. "Man, there are cameramen everywhere!"

"I heard that we're going to be on TV!" Hanna squealed as she bounced up and down. "I heard there are like five news crews here so it's got to be official!"

I tried to get them to chill out and start from the beginning, but it was no use. In a flash we all crashed through the door together.

The second we were inside we were ushered to our homeroom by Jenna's mom, who seemed crazy worried for some reason. It was hard to make out what was going on until the crowd of us could spread out, and as we passed the lunchroom it looked like the school was set up for a Model UN competition. Principal Keys sat at a table behind a row of microphones across from this wall of cameras and lights. Heather and her achiever kid crew flanked him on either side.

"Is this about me?" Jaycee asked, but I just held her tight as Jenna's mom hurried us along.

***

We settled into our spots while Jenna's mom closed the door. None of us said anything, we just waited for the new weirdness to drop. Jaycee squeezed my hand so tight my knuckles popped, as Jenna's mom let out a long sigh.

"God it's early, but you've probably already heard some pretty crazy stories about what's going on out there. I wish I had answers for you, but I've just been told to make sure you all listen up." Her head turned toward the clock on the wall as her face twisted like she would've given anything to stop the minutes from changing. "It's almost time now."

"Time for what?" I asked.

"Principal Keys is making a statement about all our current trouble," she said without taking her eyes off the clock. "You have to be patient and listen."

Jaycee buried her face behind me so she didn't have to see the other kids hate facing her, but I stared them down for her because hate gets hate. The intercom crackled to life and ended our standoff as Principal Keys started to talk.

"I want to thank the members of the press who came to discuss these troubling rumors. Since I'm still looking into whether they're true or not I can't comment on what we've found. I can only state that The Dream Academy is committed to challenging our students to be model citizens and that our values of friendship and purpose are entirely at odds with these claims. I can promise you, however, that any students who took part in this behavior, if proven true, will be dealt with appropriately. We remain committed to building bright futures for all of our gifted students. At this time I've arranged a panel of our best students to answer your questions about our school and what we do here. Thank you." A microphone whined then cut out as a dozen jumbled questions ran together in the background. Jenna's mom twisted a pencil in her fists, and stayed focused on the speaker above.

"Do you think they can do that?" Hanna whispered. "Like track us down?"

"Maybe," Tyler said, "but there's no way they're going to put money into trolling every kid's posts. It'd only make the story bigger."

"So is he just going to let it go?" Jaycee asked.

"No." I said. "He's got to make a show first. Play big, and kick some kids out. Maybe get rid of some teachers too. Who knows? They want the story to die fast, right, so next semester nobody will remember it." I thought of Paige and Jenna, already gone or on their way to a fresh start, and wished I was too. Even public school sounded like a dream.

"The ones who get caught will remember it," Jaycee said as she wiped her nose dry on my sleeve.

"Yeah," I said. "They always do."

The intercom stayed on long enough for us to hear Heather talking about how amazing the school was, that she'd never heard or saw anything, before it switched to announce that all the teachers had to go to the auditorium for an emergency meeting.

"That's my cue," Jenna's mom said. "Try not to worry. We'll find our way through this together."

"What are we supposed to do?" Tyler asked.

"Stay put," she said, "and try not to worry. Every ending is a beginning."

***

The teachers were in their meeting for hours, and the school turned into a mental hospital with no guards quick, once the news trucks pull out. Some kids screamed in the halls about how they were going to murder whoever ratted out the school. Others ran to the bathroom and flushed their phones to hide the evidence until the toilets backed up to flood the hallway. Jaycee was shaking, begging me to take her home, but I just held her steady since there was no way I'd be able to get her out alive. I'd seen kids go animal before, but not like that. Sooner or later they were bound to track her down so they could make every shitty thing they'd done her fault.

Tyler posted by the door to scope the halls while Hanna did her best to chill Jaycee out by asking her how she'd survive a zombie apocalypse since that was the vibe.

"I wouldn't," she said; not like a joke, but like she was okay with that.

Tyler bolted back to the loveseat as the psycho scene outside flipped off as fast as it'd started. We sat pressed into each other motionless, and for the first time since everything had blown up it felt like we were a crew again.

Jenna's mom came back to us with her pixie cheer washed away. Instead she talked like an actual grown-up and told us that classes were canceled for the rest of the week so that the school could sort out what to do next. She also made it crystal that we weren't supposed to talk to anyone about what had happened, or else Principal Keys would have our ass.

"What about our finals?" I asked. "Do we get a pass on them?"

"Business as usual next week as far as I know," she said. "Not that I've learned much that I can share with you."

"So we only have to make it through to Christmas?" Tyler asked.

"Can you do that?" she asked, "and really, no more questions."

"I hope so," Tyler said.

"I hope so too." She let the others leave so they could talk to their parents or clear their heads, but asked me to hang around. I gave Jaycee my car keys and told her to lock the doors until I made it back to her.

I got ready for Jenna's mom to interrogate me when she went to close the door, but something inside her shifted once it closed.

"Bryce," she said. "We need to talk." I never got why adults had to say that when we were already talking.

"What's up?"

"I think it might be time for me to find a fresh purpose in life. I can feel it in my heart. Does that make sense to you?"

"Are they firing you?" I asked. "Is that what they said?"

"No, but this year has made me realize that I'm not made for classrooms. It's time I live my life the way I was meant to."

"You can be an artist again," I said, sorry that she had to confess that kind of lost on a kid like me.

"That's true," she said. "The world needs artists."

"I hope so. Jaycee's an artist. I can be one too. Maybe I'm not made for classrooms either. At least not until I get back to good."

Jenna's mom put her hands on me and gave me this slow mom smile. "You've always been good. Will you do something for me?"

"If I can." My stockpile was gone. I had nothing to share.

"I want you and your friends to come to the party house tonight to celebrate my new beginning," she said. "It could use some bad behavior again. It's not made for a depressed middle-aged wino."

"Jenna won't come," I said. "I'll hit up the others, but I can't promise anything."

"Jenna has to figure out who she wants to be." She rocked back on her desk and gave me this strange face like she was proud of me for no reason. "The others have to come though. Put the word out. I'll be there with open arms." She switched back to cheery, and it was nice to see her that way. For a minute I considered telling my mom I was partying with a real ex-wife. She might've liked that. She could use a laugh.

\*\*\*

Jaycee waited in my car with her face in the book Jenna's mom had gifted her. Maybe she didn't want to take a chance on being seen, or was desperate to live someone else's life for a while.

"How's your book?" I asked.

"Like real life," she said. "It's raw and sad. No one gets what they want, you know?"

"Real life doesn't have to be sad. Besides, high school isn't real life. Look, there's a party tomorrow night. It's at the party house, but this one's going to be different. I want you to come with me."

"I don't ever want to see that place again," she said, and turned the page even though she'd stopped reading.

I flipped her blueberry ponytail to get her attention. "Let's pretend this semester was one long nightmare," I said, "and if we rub our eyes hard enough we'll wake up." I stopped, closed my eyes, and rubbed my eyes like I'd been hit with pepper spray. That made her giggle.

"Did it work?" she asked.

"No. You're still here, and the baddest kid ever."

"I'm pretty vicious." She laughed.

"Worse than that." I made my fist into an imaginary grenade, then pretended to pull the pin. "You're a bomb!"

We made explosion sounds that sent spit clouds into the air as I drove off, neither of us knowing if we'd ever come back. But it didn't matter. We had the *Now*. We were bulletproof.

\*\*\*

Jaycee and I were the last ones to show up at the party house. By the time we got there my friends were doing their best not to picture everything that could go wrong when we went back to school. The party house wasn't meant for stressing. It was meant for kids who needed to forget the things they couldn't stop or change.

Tyler sat on the porch with a bottle of vodka and a two-liter of orange soda next to Hanna. I was surprised she was okay with his getting deep again, but figured she decided it wasn't worth fighting about now that we all had real troubles to deal with. Jaycee asked her what her plan was, and she swore she was set to follow Tyler wherever he went if her parents let her.

Tyler handed me the bottle, but I passed it back. He choked down a huge drink, then told us he was definitely going to The Christopher School if he got bounced.

"Are you sure you don't want to go to a public school with the other busboys?" I joked, but that only made him hit the bottle again to ignore me.

***

Paige was inside on the couch. I'd texted her thinking she wouldn't come, and half-hoping she'd show so that we could get back to being whatever we were without love and what-ifs. She'd dyed her hair pink and sneered when she caught sight of me wrapped up on Jaycee, but it was so fake thug that I had to fight back bawling at her laid back in a brand-new Sex Pistols shirt.

"Did she get that at the mall?" Jaycee whispered. "She's *so* punk."

"Just wait. By New Year's she'll be more punk rock than you. One thing about Paige, when she goes, she goes all the way."

"Whatever," Jaycee said with a wink. "Wait here." Then she raced up the stairs.

Left by myself, the house seemed too big for only the four of us. For a second I missed Jenna, not the girl she'd turned into living some Cherokee Hills fantasy, but that angry girl who made us cry over all her steaming. On the kitchen table her mom had set up this dinky little Christmas tree, and I wondered if she was struggling with what used to be. I watched her stand behind the bar and hum a carol to herself. Maybe she was glad to have us bad kids crashing like old times, or maybe she was only remembering when the days weren't so short and dark. Either way I figured it was best not to bother her while she tried to get merry.

Whatever Jaycee was into was taking forever so I sat by Paige to take her in. "What's this? Are you going back to goth?"

"Does this look goth to you?" she asked.

"Emo?"

"Now, you're just being a dick," she said. "It's my own style. I call it neo-punk." She stuck out her combat boots with their Hello Kitty laces, then modeled all the work she'd put into cutting up her hippie skirt.

"Maybe you should be a fashion designer," I said. "You've had more looks than anyone I've ever met."

"I should do that!" she said, and gave up on her phony rage act. "I'd never thought of that before but it makes total sense. I think I'd really dig that."

"See, that's what you're meant to do. Dressing up is your thing," I said. "Hey, and really, no matter where you go I'll always be your friend. I mean it."

"Only a friend?" she asked, as Jaycee snuck up behind me and covered my eyes. "Yes," I said, and fought this itchy urge to sneeze.

"Oh my God?! For real?" Paige squealed as I heard Jaycee giggling behind me.

"Keep your eyes closed until I count to three," Jaycee said as she took her hands away. I held my eyes shut and listened to her count. When she shouted "Three!" I opened them and froze. She'd went way past all the way, and shaved her head bald.

"Total reboot," Jaycee said, palming her bare head. "Don't I look money?"

"You're gorgeous," I said as she fell onto my lap we both broke down. I rubbed the smooth skin on her skull and kissed her to taste the wildness in her that made anything possible.

Paige lifted herself up, touched Jaycee's shoulder, and whispered in her ear before walking off.

"What did she say?" I asked.

"Two words," Jaycee smirked. "You won."

\*\*\*

When the moon got high we made our way outside to check on Hanna and Tyler, but only found the bottle tipped over beside the drained two-liter. I worried that Tyler had raced off, staggered again, but before long saw him dragging two old metal shelves around the side of the house. I didn't yell to find out what he had in mind since it had to be trouble. Jaycee and I left him to his project and went upstairs to watch the moon shine down on us alone.

"Don't worry about Carol," Jaycee said. "She's out back getting ready for the big finish. We're safe."

"What big finish?"

"Do you remember the first time we hooked up here?" she asked as she pulled off her homemade rock shirt. "It wasn't about disappearing. You loved me. You just didn't have the nerve to admit it. I could tell every word you sputtered after we were done was a total lie." She pressed against me, then we wrestled out of our clothes. I prayed that if the story of what we did made it out of that room it'd play true romance. Kids should be able to change their stories, be better than they were before.

"Nothing happened before this second okay?"

"Deal. All we got is now," she said, then trailed kisses down my neck.

Neither of us had come to the party house to remember the terrible shit we'd lived through. I moved on her and she moved on me, both of us feeling free and young without a single thought beyond that night, and that night would last forever.

After we'd finished she laid beside me on the floor and played with my phone. She said I didn't have to keep playing those punk songs if I didn't want to since the semester was almost over, but I said it was too late, that they'd already left teeth marks on my brain. We were naked, spent, ridiculous, and alive. She thumbed the last track on the playlist, and between us The Mullets screeched out "Sign My Yearbook."

"I have to show you this," I said and pulled my List of Fantastic Promises out of my jeans' pocket with a pen. "I brought it for you."

"Why?" she asked as she took them.

"Because I need you to do me a favor. See number one? Draw a line through it. You're the reason I survived this year."

"You're dumb," she said, then blacked it out.

1. ~~Find out what makes me happy~~.
2. Save the party virgins when I can.
3. Make Paige love me again.
4. Figure out things with Jaycee.
5. ~~Listen to music that's not on the radio~~.
6. Lay low in school.
7. Don't get caught up in other kids' drama.
8. ~~Spend more time with my family~~.
9. ~~Learn to make movies~~.
10. No more dosing.

"So you know what makes you happy now?"

"Yes. I made movies this semester for real, but you're the reason I'm happy."

"Why is that?" Maybe she couldn't see it, or maybe she just needed to hear one good thing about herself again.

"Because you care. You always did, even when you didn't have a reason to, when there was nothing in it for you but hurt." I said. "Because you're real."

"Real like this?" She flopped onto her belly to fish the Christmas cards out of her bag. When I took them, she rolled onto her side to watch the moon heading our way. "After that announcement today do you think those kids will erase what they posted, what they saved?"

"No doubt. See, most kids are terrified to admit how messed up they are. They'd die to stop anyone from finding out."

"Anyone can see how messed up I am now." She brushed her hands over her mannequin head in the blue moonlight, then got dressed.

"We're all messed up," I said, "but you've got the nerve to show it. That's what makes you beautiful."

***

It was late when we gathered by the empty swimming pool out back to see what Tyler had been building while the rest of us were busy boozing each other apart or loving each other back together. It must've taken him hours to make a pile that huge, but when he'd finished it was amazing. Somehow he'd managed to heave that ratty couch, the wobbly chairs, and shelves together until they made this pyramid of junk. We stood together across from where it sat on that dirt lot while Tyler danced and shook a gas can over his sculpture of suburban trash.

"Are you cool with this?" I asked Jenna's mom, but she was too blitzed and giddy to hear me. Snow fell slowly. I hoped that my mom would feel that kind of joy again soon.

Tyler threw the gas can on top of the pile then darted back inside the house.

"I'm dizzy," Paige said. "He's moving too fast."

"You need another drink," Hanna said as she passed Paige her Solo cup. I was glad to see her back to her bitchy self.

Tyler came back with a new bottle and handed it to me with a lighter. "Do the honors, man."

"That's doesn't look at all safe." Jenna's mom slurred through this cheesy grin.

"It's *not* at all safe," I said, then made my way past the empty pool to the mountain of trash. When I was close enough I threw Jaycee's evil Christmas cards on the pile, then paced back until I could see the moon heading our way and all that black endless behind it going on timeless and forever. Tyler gave a war cry while the others started to scream for me to light it up. I stuffed my List of Fantastic Promises into the bottle and sparked it. It caught easy and in no time the flames burned through every promise on my survival guide before dipping down into the bottle as I launched it. My aim was true. The bottle crashed into that jagged pyramid of trash and exploded in one huge white flash. I raced back to watch the big finish with the others who stood arm in arm, as the bonfire raged and left us gold in its light.

Before long the pile collapsed in the flames, and the others made their way inside to recover or start again. Jaycee and I huddled together on the edge of the pool, alone. For a long time neither of us said anything. We just let our feet swing free like we were little kids again.

"They look like broken toys," Jaycee said, pointing to where the metal shelves glowed hot and bent like stick figures.

"Yeah," I said, "but they won't melt. Some things never do no matter how much heat they catch."

"You think?"

I leaned in to smell the ash on her skin. "I'm positive." I took her hands in mine. "I've seen it."

"Maybe you only dreamed it."

"No," I said. "My eyes were open and you were there. You're the truest thing I've ever had."

\*\*\*

People who didn't know better called us Dream Kids, but we were misfits. We were bad kids, but we were survivors. I held Jaycee close and we watched the flames burn our history away. The future was ours.

# Acknowledgements

I would like to thank Roz Foster for her editorial guidance and support in developing this work. I would also like to thank Jessica Bell, Amie McCracken, and the entire Vine Leaves Press staff for their careful attention and belief in this book. And finally I want to thank the Ohio Arts Counsel for their generous support which made this book possible.

# Vine Leaves Press

Enjoyed this book?
Go to *vineleavespress.com* to find more.